IN THE SHADOW OF DEATH ALLEY

A NOVEL OF EMMETT DALTON

Rebecca Rockwell

Outskirts Press, Inc.
Denver, Colorado

In the Shadow of Death Alley
A Novel of Emmett Dalton
All Rights Reserved.
Copyright © 2011 Rebecca Rockwell
v3.0

Cover Photo © 2011 JupiterImages Corporation. All rights reserved - used with permission.

Outskirts Press, Inc.
http://www.outskirtspress.com

ISBN: 978-1-4327-8098-2

Outskirts Press and the "OP" logo are trademarks belonging to Outskirts Press, Inc.

PRINTED IN THE UNITED STATES OF AMERICA

For Emmett, because of who he turned out to be

And

For my Grandparents, Clyde and Virginia

ACKNOWLEDGEMENTS

First and foremost, a *huge* and heartfelt thank you must be given to Kith Presland, without whose comprehensive website on Em (www.kayempea.net), much-appreciated assistance with my research and much-enjoyed e-mail chats I could not have gotten this book written—or perhaps not mustered the enthusiasm to finish it so quickly! Thank you, Kith, for your assistance, support and encouragement, and I hope you enjoy my attempt at bringing Emmett to life.

Thanks also to my "editor," my sister, Leigh Ann Swarm, and to my dear friends Tiffany Garrison and Tricia Daniel, for being willing to read portions of the manuscript. As always, thanks to all the family (Daddy, Mom, and the rest) and friends (Gus, Tony, Cesar, Natalie, Luis, Julie, Kate, Kelsey, Catherine, Amy, Sally, Anja, Rickey, Sherry, Krista, Mckenzie, Brian, Bobby, Linda and everyone else at SBPH) who encouraged this endeavor, read excerpts, or just asked me how it was going.

Thanks, too, to "the boys:" R.M., B.L., G.F. and D.H. for the musical inspiration when I was looking for a subject to write about.

AUTHOR'S NOTE

Countless stories have been told over the years about the Dalton Gang; some true, some exaggerated, and some simply false.

This book is a work of fiction, based on accepted historical fact, but with a few adjustments made here and there to help the story flow better. Emmett Dalton himself would tell several versions of his life with the Dalton Gang following his pardon from prison; he clearly knew that the most engaging stories are often rooted in fact but get better in the telling when embellishments are added.

Emmett would prove to be the sole survivor of the Dalton Gang, and his voice is the most logical one to tell the story, not only because of his incredible perseverance, but also because the glimpses revealed of his personality in various articles, interviews and his own books give a more fascinating edge to an already fascinating story. In my research I found him to be a man of great depth and ultimately good character who, I believe, got in over his head at a young age and found it impossible to get out. I find it admirable that someone so deeply enmeshed in the criminal element of the "Wild West" would so firmly grasp the second chance given to him and rise above the acts of infamy he had taken part in, dying a well-respected and well-rounded member of society in 1937.

-Rebecca Rockwell, 2011

PROLOGUE

Coffeyville, Kansas
June 1908

JUST BEFORE TEN in the morning the train began to slow, and I sat up a little straighter in anticipation as the depot came into view through the windows. I'd been dozing uncomfortably in my seat, caught in limbo between wakefulness and slumber for longer than an hour. My bad arm was throbbing and it had kept me from succumbing fully to sleep. It did that often, but I'd grown used to it by now. The pain of it was a constant reminder, as if I needed one, of another day I'd spent in the town I was arriving in, fifteen years earlier.

The train lurched to a stop, letting out a shrill whistle and a cloud of steam. The conductor came into the car I was in and called, "Coffeyville."

I let out a breath I hadn't realized I'd been holding in and slowly stood from my seat. When the other passengers in the car with me had filed past, I edged out into the aisle and followed them as they chatted and laughed and exclaimed over the beautiful summer weather, heading for the depot platform.

Part of me dreaded getting off that train. That part of me made my feet shuffle slowly as I moved along, made me dawdle there in the aisle. But there was another part of me that spoke reason in my mind, and told me I had to do this. No matter what I'd said, both in public and in private, no matter what I'd done with myself since the last time I was here, I'd never really be able to move on with the new life I'd been granted if I didn't close this chapter of the old life I'd led before.

And so I stepped off that train car and looked around, afraid of what I'd see.

Surprise made me blink and I had to look up at the sign on the depot building to make sure I really was at my intended destination. Of course, I had known the town would have changed, but I had always thought I'd be able to recognize it easy when I came back.

I didn't. What I'd once taken for an insignificant little town seemed to have become a city in the last fifteen years, and I had to take it all in for a minute. But then I started to walk. Instinctively I knew which the direction the plaza was, and it was there I needed to go first.

The streets were bustling as folks went about their business, different from that quiet morning so long ago when we had ridden in from the west. For a while, the clattering of automobiles, the dull thuds of horse hooves and the unintelligible voices of the citizens I passed met my ears in a steady stream as I walked. But after while other sounds came to me, ghost-like and imaginary.

I heard the sound of gunfire splitting the air, heard the frightened whinnies of horses. I heard the cries of men as bullets tore into them. I walked a little faster then, getting dust on my new shoes, trying to outrun those imaginary sounds.

Then I started to feel things, smell things, taste things, as if I was reliving every moment of that long-ago day, something I hadn't done for years. I felt the weight of the bag of money in my hand as I'd pitched myself up onto my horse. I felt again the bullets smash into my arm and hip, tearing flesh and splintering bone. I smelled blood and gun smoke. I tasted grit on my lips, kicked up by the horses and the scrambling boots of dozens of men as they ran for guns or dove for cover; tasted blood in my mouth as I hit the ground, after the shotgun pellets ripped into me and knocked me from the saddle.

And when I stopped still in the street and closed my eyes for a minute, trying to shut all that out, I started to see things in my mind. I saw Grat and Bill Power's dead bodies in the dirt. And I saw Bob's eyes, glazed with pain, looking up into mine just before he died, an image I'd long tried to tell myself was behind me. That's when I began to wonder if I really *had* done the right thing by coming back here today. All the old ghosts, it seemed, were not going to let me be. They were not going to make this easy.

If I'd learned anything, though, from what I'd been through in the past fifteen years, it was that a man's got to look to himself to make his path in life, not follow others' leads. As hard as this was, I *had* to do it. I had to finally make peace with all that had happened here, and all in my life that had led up to it.

Standing there and collecting myself, I noticed a man and a woman standing frozen on the opposite end of the street. The man was staring at me, not unkindly, but there was a look of awe on his face, and I knew he recognized me. And I allowed myself a wry smile and thought that it was only fitting that folks would know me by sight, and not leave me in peace to confront all of the ghosts that waited for me here. After all, the last time I'd come here, I'd been recognized, too, and that had either been my damnation or my salvation—depending on how you looked at it.

More people were staring at me, now, and I heard my name murmured among them. I steeled myself. The name of Dalton is still famous in this town, even so many years later. For a minute I imagined the people were sizing me up, trying to see if I was heeled. Maybe they thought I'd come to finish what the gang started all those years ago.

I hadn't, of course. I had no gun under my coat, no horse waiting ready in an alley like before. I didn't care a lick about the money in the banks of Coffeyville now—in truth, I never really had. That was all Bob's doing, and nowadays I don't believe even he cared as much about the money as he did about the fame. In the end, he got his fame—but he paid for it with his life. Just like Grat and Bill Power and Dick Broadwell had, then later my brother Will, and my old friends Bitter Creek Newcomb, Charley Pierce and Bill Doolin. They were all gone now, leaving only me to repent for all we'd done together, only me to face the citizens of Coffeyville today.

I squared my shoulders and walked on. I'd faced a

lynch mob in this town before; surely now I could face a few curious gawkers. I wouldn't bother anyone while I was here; wouldn't give anyone a reason to doubt my often-published—and completely sincere—claims of wanting nothing more than to live out my days as a decent, law-abiding citizen. I'd made that promise to myself and to the world the day I'd been pardoned and set free after fourteen years in prison. If these people planned to take me down, I wouldn't try to stop them.

But to my great surprise, no one slandered me. No one shunned me. In fact, people I didn't know came up to shake my hand, to speak encouragingly to me. Strangers told me they'd heard my story, and that they were glad I'd been pardoned. I was humbled by this reaction, and more grateful than ever to have been given the chance to start over in life. Since I was sixteen, my brother Bob had been all I ever wanted to be. Today, for perhaps the first time in my life, I had the thought that maybe being Emmett Dalton wasn't so bad after all.

It was that thought that kept me going, moved me closer and closer to the plaza, the place where it all went down on that crisp October day. There were still people trailing after me, but I focused on my destination. And then, suddenly, there it was.

The bank buildings were still standing; unchanged from the last time I'd seen them. I remembered Isham's Hardware store next door to the First National, the bank Bob and I had been in. It was that hardware store that had supplied most of the townsfolk their guns that day. I turned and looked at the building that had housed the Condon Bank—Grat's downfall, as well as Bill's and Dick's. And when I turned a little more, I saw that the alley was still there, where we'd had to tie our horses, and where the others had met their ends—the alley where my life had changed forever in the span of a few seconds. Someone told me they call it 'Death Alley' now. I'd been living my life in its shadow ever since.

A wave of nausea hit me out of nowhere; in my mind's eye I could see myself at twenty-one—foolish, reckless and finally pushing my luck too far—diving out the back door of the First National, following Bob as the fight started. I could hear all those shots again. And I closed my eyes once more, fighting to overcome it all, once and for all.

"Mr. Dalton?"

A liquid, pleasant-sounding voice broke through my struggle and I opened my eyes. There was a young man standing hesitantly next to me, not much more than a boy, really, a look somewhere between curiosity and awe on his smooth, boyish face. I stared at him for a minute, still caught halfway between memory and reality, too full of emotion to say anything.

I didn't have to, for he spoke again, quickly, cajolingly. "Mr. Dalton, my name is Jim Whitney. I'm a writer for the *Coffeyville Journal*."

Here it comes, Em, I told myself, having heard some variation of this young man's impending speech before— many times, in fact, since I'd gotten out.

"I've heard your story, of course," he said smoothly, "but I'd like to write it the way *you* saw it. Would you be willing to give me a few minutes of your time?"

I looked him over again, noting his crisp, expensive suit,

and his shoes, obviously brand-new. He couldn't have been more than twenty-two or so, not much older than the age I was when I was last here. Not really old enough to remember the event he wanted to write about. I could see in his face how badly he wanted me to consent to his request for an interview and wondered if it would cost him his job if I refused. I wondered if he was really interested in my story—or just interested it *getting* it. I spoke quietly, when my voice came back to me.

"You want to know about the raid." It was not a question, and my voice sounded flat, even to me.

He shook his head almost violently and his voice was earnest, now. "Not just the raid. I want to write about *you,* how you ended up in the gang. I grew up hearing stores about you and your brothers. But now that I'm standing here with you, I can't picture you doing the things they've said you did." He paused and looked me square in the face. "The raid's been written about a hundred times, Mr. Dalton. Don't you think you should tell your side of it, all the way through?"

I shifted my weight from one foot to the other. "That'll take more than a few minutes of my time, Mr. Whitney," I said dryly. As I spoke I had to avert my eyes from that alley, and the staircase at its head that led up to the doctor's office where I'd been carried after the fight.

"I've got all the free time in the world, Mr. Dalton," he said cheerfully. "And so, I believe, do *you.*" He flashed me a bold, friendly grin.

I gave him a little smile in return, thinking this kid was gutsy for coming up to me like this, intent on coaxing the story out of me—the *whole* story, not just the one everyone wanted me to tell. I liked him—he reminded me a little of myself, back in better times. Back when the name of Dalton commanded something different than it did now.

I slid my eyes away from his for a minute, somehow finding what I remembered as the exact spot in the alley where Bob had died, and where I'd *almost* died, trying to pull him into my saddle. Bob couldn't tell the story, nor could Grat or Dick or any of the others. But I could. And maybe in the telling, I could find some sort of meaning in their deaths. I could pay tribute to the good parts of them—for they'd all, in my mind, had *some* good in them, somewhere. And so I turned back to young Mr. Whitney, who was making me feel suddenly much older than my thirty-five years, and said, "let's find a quiet place to sit down, and I'll tell you."

ONE

THEY SAY WHEN you're sentenced to hard time, part of the reason is so you can sit there, your freedom gone, and think, day in and day out, about why and how you ended up in such a place. It was certainly true for me. Every morning that I was in prison, the first thought I'd have after I'd opened my eyes was, *how did I end up here?* That one was always followed by, *why did I do what I did?* And I never was able to come up with the full answer to those questions, probably because doing so would mean placing some of the blame on Bob, and it's always been hard for me, even now, to find much fault in that brother of mine whom I had always looked on as a hero, plain and simple.

I suppose, looking back on it, that it all really started for me in January of 1889. I was seventeen then, and for over a year I'd been working for a cattle outfit on a ranch in Indian Territory owned by a man named Courtney.

I should, of course, have stayed there. I was younger than most of the other hands, but I'd worked hard and earned their respect. I had friends in the outfit and most of the neighboring ones by that time. But we were all restless men in those days, never content to leave things as they were. We were always looking for excitement around the next bend in the trail, always had a score to settle with one thing or another, and it was that restlessness that started all the trouble.

I had decided, that winter, to leave the ranch and meet up with Bob and another of my older brothers, Grat, who were both Deputy U.S. Marshals in the District of Kansas, and see what kind of work might be available to me there.

Trouble was what was available to me there, and a lot of it, but I didn't know that yet.

———◦◦◦———

It was cold, the morning I set out, and my breath and my horse's breath hung in white mist as I saddled up. I could hear the cattle lowing out in the pastures, and the other hands calling to one another as they made ready for another day's work. All were familiar sounds to be, but I wasn't sad to be leaving the life I'd grown used to. Seemed like I never could stay put in those days for any great length of time.

"Well, now, just where the hell are you going off to?"

The voice came out of nowhere, and it startled me so bad I nearly jumped against Blackjack. He snorted and threw his head up, pulling his reins taut against the hitching ring and getting light on his front feet. I moved out of his way quick and turned to see who was in the barn with me, my hand automatically going for the gun in my holster.

Bill Doolin, a fellow cowhand and a good friend of mine, was leaning against a post nearby and he held his hands up when he saw my hand on my hip. "Easy there, Em, don't shoot me, now." He was laughing, though, as he said it.

I let out my breath and let go of my gun, reaching a hand out to stroke Blackjack's neck, murmuring to him to calm him down. "Damn it, Bill, why'd you sneak up on me?" I asked, grabbing Blackjack's reins close under his bit.

"'Cause I couldn't resist it," he replied breezily, smiling at me. "I'm not sure if you know this, but when you get intent on somethin', Emmett, you don't pay too much attention to anything else, and that makes you easy to sneak up on. You oughta work on that." He jerked his chin at my horse. "You gonna answer my question?"

I went back to tacking up, tightening my saddle-cinch. "I'm going to visit Bob and Grat in Wichita," I said. "I settled up with Courtney this morning."

Bill pushed his hat back a little and leaned against the pillar again, scuffing the rowels of his spurs in the dust. "So you ain't coming back here, then?"

I shook my head. "Don't plan on it," I replied. I looked at him. "Why don't you come with me, Bill?" I asked impulsively. "You can't tell me you're not getting tired of this place, too. And you'd like Bob. I'm gonna try to get on with him as a guard. Maybe you can, too."

Bill grinned at me. He was a good thirteen years older than me but was one of the few that didn't treat me like a kid. He was a likeable fellow and fun to be around. I wouldn't miss the ranch, but I would, I realized, miss Bill and the other men I'd come to know.

"Thank you kindly for the invitation, Emmett, but I'm gonna stay on here for a bit," he said. "I'm afraid I just ain't

— 3 —

got the constitution for workin' with lawmen. Sometimes I think I'll be lucky if I stay on the right side of 'em, to tell the truth." He watched as I secured my saddlebags and tied on my bedroll. "You think you can persuade him to take you on, Em? What with you bein' so young, and untried?"

I didn't look at him. "I ain't really that young," I muttered. "I'll be eighteen soon. Bob's only two years older than me, and he's a Deputy Marshal. Besides, you all thought I was too young to work cattle, in the beginning, and I convinced you I had the sand, didn't I?"

Bill shook his head. "You convinced us just fine after awhile, Emmett, but bein' a lawman's a sight different than working cows. I ain't sayin' you ain't got the sand, 'cause you got a hell of a lot of pluck in you for bein' just seventeen, but you're still between hay and grass, when it comes down to it. I'm just warnin' you. Shooting a man ain't the same as hunting."

His voice was more serious than usual and I glanced at him, suddenly curious. "Have you ever shot anyone, Bill?" As I asked I tried to imagine it. Bill was a crack shot; I'd seen that for myself, but he always seemed so jolly to me that I couldn't picture him killing a person. That's how I thought, back in those first days. I didn't know any better then; didn't know that a smile and a joke could hide an appetite for killing, or for other things a man might do that he shouldn't.

He was quiet for a minute, then straightened up and crossed his arms over his chest. "I have, once or twice, and that's all I'm gonna say about it. I hope you don't ever have to."

"I guess we'll see," I said with a shrug, trying to be light about it. I untied Blackjack's reins and tossed one up over his neck, then took the other one in hand. "Will you tell Dick and Charlie and the rest of the boys I said good-bye?" I asked him, and he nodded. I walked over to him and stuck out a hand. "So long, then, Bill," I told him, and he shook my hand.

"You take care of yourself, now, Emmett," he said, jolly again. "And if the law don't work out, or you're ever out this way again, you look me and the others up. I imagine we'll be around these parts for awhile, seeing as how none of us got the ambition to do anything else." His voice was dry and I chuckled under my breath. I'd never seen Bill in a bad mood, and he always had a joke at the ready for any occasion. I put my foot in the stirrup and swung into the saddle, glad for my buffalo overcoat as I urged Blackjack out of the barn into the thin sunshine that couldn't seem to put any warmth into the air.

Bill lifted his hand in a wave as I set off, and just before I put my spurs to Blackjack's sides, I turned in the saddle and waved back.

As we loped out the front gate of the ranch and headed out, I felt a little tingle of excitement go through me at the prospect of seeing Bob again. We'd grown up real close, being only two years apart, and I'd always admired the ease with which he seemed to do everything he tried his hand at. He always looked out for me, and it seemed to me I'd never spent a dull moment in his company. Mother used to caution me about following Bob so blindly; she always thought Bob was too wild and too loose with his tongue and his temper. But I didn't see it that way and so I never listened to her.

To tell the truth, most of us Dalton boys got called wild

at one point or another, not just Bob. There were a few of my oldest brothers that didn't, like Ben and Frank, but the general thought in most folks' minds was that most of us were going to grow up to be bad business. I guess that came from Mother's side. Mother was a Younger; her nephews were Cole and Bob and Jim of James Gang fame, and people who knew *that* got it stuck in their minds that Adeline Younger Dalton's boys were going to go the way of their infamous cousins. I thought that was pretty unfair at the time, especially seeing as how Frank, Grat at Bob all went into the law for their living, and Will went into politics out in California.

I didn't like to think about Frank much; it made me miss him even more when I did, and there wasn't any help for that. He'd died in '87 in the line of duty as a U.S. Deputy Marshal at Fort Smith in Arkansas, and it was in his honor that Grat and Bob became deputies. They'd looked up to Frank, just as I looked up to Bob. We each looked up to the brothers before us, and in the end it would lead to our downfall, but none of us really seemed to see that until it was too late.

I rode for a good long while, stopping only when I needed to rest Blackjack or scrape together a meal out of my saddlebags. I was anxious, as always, to get to where I was going.

When I camped that night near Bird Creek, I hobbled Blackjack so he wouldn't wander and built a small fire, keeping my gun close and one eye open even as I rested. There were horse-thieves all over the place in Indian Territory, and Blackjack was just the kind of stud that would get stolen right out from under me if I wasn't careful. He was big and long-legged, out of Pa's best racing stock, and he could outrun just about any other horse I'd ever come across. I'd met more than one cowhand who'd tried to buy him off me, and once at a poker game one of the other players had tried to weasel me into betting him, but I'd refused, being an inexperienced poker-player then and knowing I'd likely lose him. Pa, and my brothers, had always taught me that there were two things a man needed most in these times—a good horse and a good gun.

As I lay there in my bedroll, listening to the crackle of the flames and the sound of Blackjack cropping the grass nearby, I started thinking about what Bill had said to me before I left. I looked down at my revolver where I had it in my hand, resting across my middle. I was a good shot; my brothers had taught me well, but I wasn't sure about shooting at a man, instead of an animal or a target. I'd never done that before, never had any call to. But I knew that if I could persuade Bob to hire me on, chances were good I'd have to someday. Secretly I wasn't sure I had the stomach for it, though I knew I could never admit that to anyone. I supposed I'd find out soon enough, if things worked out the way I hoped they would.

I got into Wichita around dusk, and snowflakes were drifting down thick, glittering silver as they passed into the light from the street lamps. The town was alive with noise; I heard laughter, shouts and piano music tinkling from the saloons. Folks walked the sidewalks in droves, and the muddied streets were thick with wagons and horses.

I'd been around nothing but cattle for the last year, and coming into a city like Wichita was a little overwhelming. I stopped at the first livery I found and paid the stable-hand, telling him to rub Blackjack down and water him, but to leave the rig on. The hand looked at me funny, like I was up to something, but I stayed firm. I'd had a saddle up and disappear at a livery in Vinita once, and I never forgot it. Since then I always had them keep the saddle on the horse, until I could come back and collect it myself.

The stable-hand, who looked about my age, took the money I handed him and watched as I stripped off my saddlebags, slinging them over my shoulder. "Don't know if you saw the sign, but there's a no-gun law in town," he said, eyeing my gun belt when my coat shifted. "You'll have to check your iron."

"I'm headed to the jailhouse, anyway," I said. "My brothers are Deputy Marshals."

"Which?" he asked, looking me over with new interest.

"Bob and Grat Dalton," I replied. "Which way's the Marshal's office?"

He moved to the door and pointed off deeper into town, and I headed that way, my boots crunching into the packed snow on the side of the street.

"Hold it right there, son," I heard a familiar, gravely voice say firmly from behind me. "If you got a gun on you, you'll need to hand it over before you go any further." I stopped, tensing up. When I turned around I saw my brother Grat standing on the gallery along the street.

When he saw it was me, he smiled—or as near to a smile as I'd ever seen Grat make. He never was the warm type—in fact, he'd always been the sort of brother that would beat you near to senseless just for looking at him wrong—but I'd learned to avoid the whuppings he enjoyed dishing out by either staying on his good side, which was narrow, or avoiding him when his temper flared.

"Well, now, look who came in with the cows," Grat said, sauntering off the sidewalk and coming toward me. He looked me up and down. "You sure shot up like a stalk since I last saw you," he drawled. He didn't look overjoyed to see me, but with Grat it was hard to tell what he was thinking at any given time, unless he was angry. None of us ever had any trouble reading him then.

"Hello, Grat," I said, giving him a half-smile. "I was just on my way to the jailhouse to find you. Bob around?"

"I expect he's around here somewhere or another," Grat said. He jerked his head in the direction the kid at the Livery had pointed and spat a stream of tobacco juice into the slush in the gutter. "Come on."

His greeting done, he started off, and I followed him. Our boots and our spurs rang out on the gallery as we walked, with me hanging a little behind. His steps were heavy and deliberate; mine were light and almost meek-sounding as I dogged his heels. I realized I was tensed up like a scared rabbit and tried to relax a little; Grat had always made me uneasy, for all that he was my own brother.

Grat was tall, like most of us boys were, but he had more muscle on him than the rest of us did and that gave him the appearance of being bigger than he really was. His gruff voice, his size and his unpleasant disposition made him in-timidating, and I could imagine him staring down a rustler or horse-thief easy. I'd often wondered just what made him the way he was, but I never tried to find out any too hard. He liked to fight, and from experience I knew he'd use any of us for that purpose without too much provocation, if we were handy, particularly if he'd hit the whiskey bottle first.

There was a kind of darkness inside Grat that was never too far beneath the surface, and it rattled me if I really thought about it too much. Brothers can be different from one another in so many ways, but at the end of the day, they're all cut from the same cloth. I never liked to think, even then, that I had anything in me close to what he did, never wanted people to look at me the way they did him.

And so we were silent as we walked, the two of us never really having had much to talk about when we were solely in each other's company. It was a relief to me when we finally reached the jail and Marshal's office and Grat led me inside.

There was a coal heater in one corner of the small room, and it and the lamps gave off a warmth that felt good to me after riding all that ways in the cold. The walls were hung with maps and reward notices of all sorts, and there was a desk near the heavy door that led to the cells. Seated at the desk, leaned back in his chair with his boots propped up, was Bob.

The lamplight cast a glow over his spurs and the bullets in his gun belt, and his watch chain and the badge on his vest. Even sitting there idle like that he had an energy about him that I imagined I could feel, like he was ready for anything and everything that might happen. I never in my life, before or since, met a man that had a presence like Bob's.

He didn't look up right away when we came in; he was reading something in a newspaper and was intent on whatever it was. Grat took off his overcoat and hat and hung them up on a nail just inside the door and said loudly, "look who I found pacin' the street, Bob."

Bob looked up then, and his blue eyes lit up with gladness at seeing me, his favorite brother. "Why, if it isn't Em!" He stood up quick and shook my hand, first hugging me, then pounding me on the back while Grat struck a match and lit a cigar, watching us.

"Hello, Bob!" I said, grinning at him. At that moment I was more glad than ever that I'd decided to quit Courtney's outfit, no matter how things turned out.

"What brings you out this way?" Bob asked, still smiling. "You get tired of working cows?"

I nodded. "I was hoping you could use another guard," I said, straight out. There was no sense beating around the bush.

Bob's smile grew and he threw a look at Grat, who shrugged a little, flicking ashes into the spittoon at his feet and pulling a flask of whiskey out of his coat pocket. Bob turned back to me and put a hand on my shoulder. "The pay ain't good, Em; I'll be straight with you about that. Hell, half the time Grat and I don't even get our wages when they're due, but if you can look past that, I reckon I've got a spot for you."

I grinned at him once more. Though it would matter a great deal to me later on, right then I didn't care about the pay. I was just glad to be with my brother again.

TWO

SINCE FRANK HAD been a Deputy Marshal and Bob and Grat had worked as guards and Deputies for a time before I joined them, I knew a little bit about how the system worked. Bob explained it to me better, though, while we were having a late supper with Grat that first night, in a café near the Marshal's office.

A lot of the camps and settlements in the Territory didn't have jails, so it was the job of the guard to keep any prisoners the deputy might arrest in line so the deputy could keep on with his work until they were jailed. Deputies and their posses could be sent all over the Territory after one suspect or another, so I might have to guard for several days at a time, maybe longer. The guards were paid by the Deputy they worked for, and the deputy in turn was paid by the Marshal.

This turned out to be a big problem for us; Bob hadn't been lying to me when he said he and Grat had a hard time collecting their wages. Marshal Walker never seemed to get around to paying them, and finally the three of us got fed up and left Kansas, heading for Fort Smith, where Frank had worked. The situation wasn't much better there, for Marshal

Yoe, our new employer, thought Bob and I were too young to do the job. We finally got hired on with Floyd Wilson, a deputy in the Oklahoma Territory. Grat was commissioned at Muskogee, and Bob and I went to Tulsa.

Even with all the trouble we had getting paid, I hadn't found myself regretting my choice to leave the cattle business. In my mind, I thrived in Bob's company, stopped being a boy and started into being a man. I was eighteen by that time, settling into my new vocation. Bob was a good teacher and a good Deputy, and everything might have been fine, if not for the Dalton restlessness in us and a seemingly insignificant encounter with two men and a band of Indians.

<hr />

"Look over there, Em."

Bob's voice startled me; we'd been trotting over the snowy prairie for over an hour, and it was so cold and we were so heavily bundled in our coats and mufflers and hats that we hadn't spoken much. It was hard to talk in that kind of weather, and when we were concentrating on watching out for deep snowdrifts the horses could trip up in, since we couldn't really be sure where the road was.

It was Christmas Day of '89, and the air was crisp and clear. We'd had a big snowstorm that week, but it had finally stopped coming down before Bob and I had set off on our ride, intending to head out of Pawhuska and back into Tulsa.

I looked over at him as he brought his horse up next to mine, and then I looked where he was pointing.

Aways off the road, or where the road should have been, I could see a wagon stopped. It was near an Indian camp and I could see Indians gathered around the wagon. I looked back at Bob and raised my eyebrows.

"Could be whiskey-peddlers," Bob remarked, then barked a command at his horse, which was reaching over to nip at Blackjack.

"Maybe," I answered. I pulled Blackjack in a little, waiting for Bob to decide what he wanted to do. It was illegal to sell liquor to the Indians, and Bob had the authority to arrest anyone he caught doing it.

Bob pulled his big mare up and stopped, and I stopped with him. I saw him push one side of his coat back aways, exposing his revolver. He stared at the wagon, just watching. From where I sat, it sure looked like they were whisky-peddlers. I tightened up on the reins; Blackjack was tossing his head and mouthing the bit, anxious to keep going.

"Stay here, Em. Wait for me." Bob put his spurs to his horse's sides and took off through the deep snow toward the wagon and the Indians. I did as he said, but I was alert, ready to ride to his aid if he needed it.

I watched as he approached the wagon, and I could see him lean down a little from the saddle as he spoke to the two white men who'd been driving it. They talked a minute, and then I saw Bob ride around the group of Indians, slowly, as if looking for something. He stopped again at the wagon and got off his horse, and I couldn't see what he was doing then. Blackjack started fussing again, pawing at the snow and chomping at his bit, and I had to turn my attention away from Bob for a minute. When I looked up again, Bob was coming toward me at a lope.

"Well?" I asked.

Bob shrugged. "They ain't doing anything I need to arrest them for," he said quickly. "Come on, let's go."

I stared at him. "But were they selling—"

"Don't worry about it, Em," Bob ordered, cutting me off, and taking off at a trot again. Puzzled, I followed him. I waited for him to say more, but he didn't, and I didn't press him.

We got into Tulsa tired and hungry, and we went for a meal at the hotel we had rooms at. The desk clerk handed Bob a letter as we came in, and it was from our mother. Bob scanned it and told me the news of the family. After we ate we went out to walk the streets and keep the peace, and I forgot all about that wagon and those Indians.

———— ◦《◦》◦ ————

"Emmett Dalton!"

The voice that said my name was a deep one, scolding and firm, and I felt like I was being called out. I turned around from where I'd been looking over some notices sent in from Fort Smith on prisoners to transport, and my hand went for my Colt, seemingly like it had a mind of its own.

Lafe Shadley was standing in the doorway of the office, his own hand on his gun belt. Behind him were two members of his posse, and they had Winchesters, held up like they were planning on aiming them at me. Then they did, and I drew my gun, my thoughts racing so fast I couldn't sort them out.

I stared at Lafe. He was a Deputy Marshal, and a man Bob and I had worked with many times. I didn't like him, nor did Bob, and I knew he didn't like us much, either, but seeing him ready to point a gun at me threw me for a loop. "What in the hell is going on here, Shadley?" I demanded. I didn't lower my gun; I was dammed if I'd let anyone point a rifle at me without any cause.

"Drop that Colt, son," Lafe ordered, drawing his own revolver.

"I will, Shadley, when you tell your boys there to lay down those rifles," I said coolly. My voice sounded strange, even to me—cold and steely. Inside, I was shaking, and I was afraid my gun hand would start to shake, too, but my aim stayed steady. "I asked you what the hell you're doing, and I want an answer."

"You're under arrest, Emmett," Shadley said. "You and your brother Bob. We've already got him. You'd better come along quietly, now."

"For what?" I demanded, so stunned I couldn't think straight.

"The Indian Territory Marshal's wired in a writ for you and Bob for liquor-peddling. Seems some Indians and two traders came forward to say Bob gave out whiskey to Indians near Bird Creek in December, and accepted a bribe from the traders to look the other way. You were with him. Now put that iron down before I do it for you. Don't be a fool and get yourself shot, boy."

My mind went back to that time on the prairie last year, but before I could think any further, Lafe cocked back the hammer on his gun and took a step toward me. A rage I'd never felt before seemed to boil up inside of me, but reason stepped in and pushed it down. I could get off a couple of shots, maybe, before Shadley could, but I was outnumbered. Slowly I put my gun down on the desk, and as soon as I did, Lafe grabbed my wrists and slapped shackles on me.

I felt like I was in the middle of some nightmare right then, and it got worse when they led me around to the lot at the back of the office. Bob was in the saddle of his horse, its reins in the hand of another mounted posse-member. Bob's hands were bound behind his back. His eyes met mine and flared like blue flames were in them; I could tell he was madder than a hornet but there wasn't anything he could do. His badge was gone from his vest.

"Let Emmett go, Shadley," he growled at Lafe. "He wasn't even close to that wagon!" They pushed me toward Blackjack and practically lifted me into the saddle, since I couldn't mount up properly with my hands behind my back like that. Shadley took all the bullets out of my gun and put it in his saddlebag, not even looking at Bob.

"Shut up, Dalton," he said. "Save your excuses for the courtroom. I don't give a damn about them. I'm taking you two back to Wichita, and I won't have you talking my ear off on the way."

I looked over at Bob, who looked like a thundercloud had landed on his face. I'd never seen him so mad; his eyes looked right through mine, as if he didn't see me. I didn't say anything, but a chill went through me and I knew right then and there that my brother was not going to go down for this, no matter what happened.

The two men with the Winchesters mounted their nags,

and Lafe did the same. Another horse came cantering around to join the bunch, and in its saddle was Burrell Cox, another Deputy out of Tulsa whom Bob and I knew well. He gave me a sympathetic look, like he didn't agree with the situation, but he said nothing, and neither did I. Shadley slapped his horse's rump with his reins, and the group of us went off, heading out of Pawhuska toward Wichita.

Riding a ponied horse with your hands tied behind your back ain't easy. It throws a man's balance off, and all the little jolts in the horse's gait seem to come up through the saddle and toss you around like a child's toy. I was exhausted and every bone in my body was hurting by the time we camped.

They didn't unchain us, even to eat. Cox brought our hands around in front of us and shackled them that way, so we could at least pick up bits of food or raise our canteens to our mouths. All that time Bob stayed silent, and I could sense his mood growing blacker and blacker. That aura he always had about him seemed to grow enormous and dangerous to me, till I thought surely the others must be able to feel it. But Shadley and his men ignored us, like we were dogs, not worth acknowledging.

I was still trying to wrap my mind around what was happening to us. I thought back to the day we'd come across that wagon and that Indian camp. I wasn't even sure what had gone on that day. I hadn't seen Bob take any bribe or drink any whiskey; he hadn't even told me for sure that the men were peddling it. I'd been on the road, waiting for him like he'd said. Yet here I was, chained like one of the common rustlers I was paid to guard. I knew as well as Bob did that if we were found guilty we could be thrown in the penitentiary;

I'd seen enough similar trials in the courts at Fort Smith.

When we got into Wichita, they took us to the jailhouse and hauled us inside. Marshal Walker was sitting behind the desk, and he rose and shook Shadley's hand. "Thank you for bringing them in promptly, Lafe," he said, tossing the remnants of his cigarette into the spittoon. He looked at me, then at Bob. "I'm very disappointed in you both," he said, as if we were two misbehaved children, talking fancy, like he was some upper-class lawman, when we knew he hadn't had any more education than the two of us.

Bob shot a glare at him that could've frozen hell. "You son of a bitch, Walker," he hissed, something deadly in his tone. "You ain't got a right to stand there and act so Goddamned holy. You never even paid me or Grat for the arrests we made for you, and now you're trying to pin whiskey-peddling on me and Emmett? If you've got anything on us, I'd like to see it."

Walker's gaze turned cold and he dropped his fancy-Dan act. "You talk too Goddamned much, Dalton," he replied. "I've got witnesses, is what I've got, and you'll shut your mouth until you're in front of the judge." He looked at Shadley. "Put them in a cell and shut the door so's I don't have to listen to their griping all night."

As Shadley grabbed Bob by the shoulders and one of the possemen took ahold of me, I heard myself speak. "Please, Marshal Walker, at least let us wire Grat, so he'll know what happened."

Walker let out a humorless laugh. "I'll wire him, but your brother ain't gonna be able to help you any," he said. "I guess you didn't know he lost his commission. Marshal Yoe discharged him because he buffaloed a man near senseless with the butt of his six-gun. So it looks like the bunch of you Daltons are in some hot water, don't it?" He signaled the posseman and Shadley, and they hustled us into the back room and fairly tossed us into a cell. Then the cell door shut with a clatter, and they went away into the office, laughing under their breath like the two of us were a great big joke and banging the door behind them.

I went and sat on one of the cots, the clang of the iron door still ringing in my ears. I felt numb and strange, still not quite able to process what happened.

Bob jumped up and started pacing the cell, anger making his cheeks flush red. I could see him working his jaw back and forth and could almost hear him gritting his teeth.

"This is a load of horse shit, Em," he said, speaking to me for the first time since before we were arrested. "I didn't take any bribe on that road, and anyone that says I did, or says you were anywhere near it, is a Goddamned liar."

"What about Grat?" I said. "Do you think it's true he lost his commission?"

"Probably so," Bob said with a smirk. "You know as well as I do, how Grat is."

I didn't say anything else. I wanted to ask him what we were going to do, how we were going to get ourselves out of this mess, but I was afraid of what he'd say, so I kept quiet. I kept quiet a lot in those first days when things were changing for us forever, but all it ever seemed to do was to get me into more trouble.

THREE

THEY KEPT US in that stinking cell for five days, and then on the 26th they hauled us out for our hearing. Grat had come into town by then and he was in the courtroom, his eyes glittering like pale blue hunks of ice. As I was led past him I could see him working his big hands around in his lap, picking at his fingernails; that was a nervous habit he'd had since he was young and it was the only outward sign of his mood. I saw him meet Bob's eyes, and then we were made to sit in the box near the judge.

The hearing was quick; I was so keyed up that I didn't remember half of what was said. Then, suddenly, I heard the judge say my name.

"Emmett Dalton, the court has been unable to substantiate any claims that you participated in the activities you've been charged with. Therefore, I order that you be released." He banged his gavel, and after a few awkward moments, I got up and moved to sit with Grat, who silently moved over on the bench to make room for me. I couldn't even be happy that I was free, I was so worried for Bob. Bob stayed in the box and the judge spoke again.

"Robert Dalton, the court has found sufficient eyewitnesses in this matter to warrant a trial. I'll set your bail at one thousand dollars. Have you the means?"

"He's got it," a voice called from the back of the courtroom, and Grat and I both turned to see who had spoken.

Cyrus Reardon and Alf Houts, two citizens who had always been friendly with us when we worked out of Wichita, were standing up in front of their bench. "We'll stand that money, Your Honor."

I saw Bob's posture change as relief went through him. He knew neither Grat nor I had the money for his bail, and there wasn't anyone in the family I could think of right off who might be able to spare it. I watched as the judge looked at Bob again, disapproval clear on his face. His long gray whiskers wagged when he spoke, reminding me of a goat. "I'll set your court date for September first," he said sternly. "You are to appear here and answer for your actions at eight o'clock that morning, and in the meantime you are to obey the law to the letter. Do I make myself clear, Mr. Dalton?"

Bob knitted his long fingers together in his lap in an almost serene manner and looked the judge in the eye, and a more innocent expression I'd never seen on anyone's face before. "Perfectly, Your Honor."

The judge banged his gavel again, and everyone got up and began to file out of the courtroom. I saw Marshal Walker and Lafe Shadley shoot glares of disapproval in Bob's direction, but they were out the door and gone before anyone could say anything.

Bob didn't come over to me and Grat right away; instead he went up to Cyrus and Alf to thank them for posting his bail. I couldn't hear what they were saying. Then they left, and Bob joined us. "Come on, let's get the hell out of here," he said, and we followed him.

"Where are we going, Bob?" I asked, glancing over at Grat.

"To collect our horses and our gear. I ain't staying in this damn place tonight. I can't think in this hole." He was walking very fast, ahead of us.

Grat and I followed him and we tacked up fast after getting back our guns and saddlebags from the Marshal's office. Walker wasn't there, nor was Shadley, and I was glad of that—Bob was in a temper and because of it I knew he wouldn't give any kind of thought to what he was doing. He was liable to shoot Walker or Shadley or both for what we'd been put through, right there in broad daylight.

We rode out of Wichita and by nightfall we'd stopped near an old, lonely cemetery to camp. Bob hadn't said much; he was real quiet, like he was thinking something over. Grat never talked much, anyway, and tonight was no exception. He did, however, admit to losing his commission, and I wondered what the hell we were going to do now. Bob and I had pay coming from our last time out with Deputy Wilson, but it wouldn't be much and we'd need more to defend Bob at his trial come September. Mother and Pa didn't have the money, either.

I sat there by our little fire, listening to the crackle of the flames and the sound of the horses cropping the grass where we'd hobbled them. An owl called, lonely in the dark of the cemetery. The headstones, most of them broken or tipped over, looked ghostly in the moonlight. Bob and Grat stayed silent. Grat was stretched out, leaning against his saddle and knocking back swigs from a whiskey bottle he'd pulled from his saddlebag. Bob was sitting aways off, dragging the blade of his knife around in the dirt like he was drawing something. His back was to me and his shoulders were slumped a little like he had a weight on them, but I knew he was still alert, on edge. No one could ever sneak up on Bob.

Since we weren't doing any talking, I started thinking. I thought again about Bill Doolin and what he'd said to me the day I left the ranch, about shooting at a man being different than hunting. That day in Pawhuska I hadn't had to shoot Shadley or his posse, but I'd been ready to, and though I'd been scared, my hand hadn't shook, and I knew I would've fired, if I'd had to. I thought about how the gun had felt in my hand right then, and how my mind had sort of stopped working for a few seconds, and how all I'd felt inside was rage. Thinking about it made me feel sick, so I started trying to think about something else.

I flopped down on my back, my hands behind my head, and stared up into the night sky. The snow had all melted earlier in the month and spring was showing all over the place, but it was still cold, and I stretched my boots out a little closer to the fire. I started to think about Frank, and for once, I let myself. I remembered him with his big strong hands, and his kind gray eyes that were the same shade as mine. Frank had been strong and firm with ruffians, and good to everyone else. He'd been respected by his peers at Fort Smith and liked by the citizens. In my way of thinking, he'd represented the law to me.

But now, after I'd been labeled and jailed for something

I didn't do, I found myself thinking different. What good was the law, in the end, if a man could get jailed and tried for something he hadn't done? Why should I, or Bob or Grat, go back to work for the very thing that had painted us black?

"What do you wanna do, Bob?"

Grat's rusty voice startled me, brought me out of all them serious thoughts I was having. I sat up partways and watched as he downed another sizeable portion from the bottle.

Bob stopped playing with his knife and got up, coming over to crouch down by the fire and hold out his hands to it. "First, I want you to quit hogging all that whiskey." Grat handed him the bottle without a word, and Bob took a big swig of it, then handed it over to me. I took it but didn't drink right off; I wanted to see what Bob would say.

"How it's gonna be," Bob said with finality, "is we're gonna head up to Newton tomorrow, and we're gonna have us some damn fun for a change. Then I'm gonna figure this thing out."

Grat gave a kind of grunt in reply. "What the hell's in Newton?"

Bob gave Grat a wicked grin. "All sorts of things, my brother. Anything a man could want." Grat gave a snort of laughter in return and for a second it was like the two of them were sharing a message in some secret lingo I didn't understand.

Anger seemed to boil up in me, out of nowhere. Grat thought I was still a kid, that was plain to me. But I'd never felt that yet from Bob—until right then. Grat stopped his chuckling and looked at me.

"If you ain't gonna drink any of that, little Em, then hand

it over," he said.

"Who says I ain't gonna drink it?" I shot back, and tipped back the bottle. The liquor burned my throat, but I didn't cough, like I had the very first time I'd drank whiskey, with Bill Doolin and Dick Broadwell in the bunkhouse at the ranch.

Bob was watching me; I could see the firelight dancing in his eyes. One corner of his mouth was up, but it wasn't the kind of smile that made me mad. It was the smile he usually gave me, the one that made me think he was proud I was his brother. "Easy, now, Em. You don't need to drink the whole bottle in one tug."

Grat was watching me, too, and he must've been feeling the whiskey by now, 'cause his eyes were all heavy-lidded, like he was liable to fall asleep at any second. I drank again, not because I wanted to get liquored up, but because I knew if Grat got any drunker he'd start to get ornery and take to scrapping with one of us.

After my third swig my head started to feel woozy and my tongue felt thick. Bob came around to me and took the bottle, quickly draining it of the last few tugs. Grat didn't say anything about it—he was out by then, snoring good. Bob rolled his eyes at me, and I laughed, some of my worrying gone from the liquor. I figured neither Bob nor I was going to get any sleep with that racket, but the thought didn't make me sore.

Bob laughed, too, that deep laugh he had that made everyone else around him set to laughing when it rolled out of him. The bitter blackness that had been on him since we were arrested was suddenly gone from his face and his eyes danced in their old devil-may-care way. "Aww, hell, who cares about the Goddamned court in Wichita? We're out, ain't we? And now we'll have some time on our hands to *really* do something with ourselves."

He set the empty bottle on top of one of the nearest tombstones, then drew his gun and popped off one single shot, his draw like lightning and his aim sure, despite the liquor. The bottle exploded into fragments that glittered as the firelight caught them. Grat just rolled over at the noise and pulled part of his saddle blanket over his head.

I guess it was the whiskey, or maybe it was the fact that I was still pretty naïve yet. But I didn't have any idea yet what Bob had in store for us.

FOUR

I'D NEVER BEEN to Newton before but I'd heard of it; there'd been a big gunfight there back in '71 and eight men had died. It had been a big cowtown back in the seventies but was now just famous for its nightlife, since it wasn't a shipping point for any of the big herds anymore. When we rode in late in the afternoon I realized quick that Bob knew it well. We put the horses up at a livery near the edge of town—their rigs left on—and then went straight to a saloon Bob liked called the Gold Room.

I was good at cards; so was Bob, but it was Grat who got the real talent for games in our family. He liked to brag about a lot of things—his skill at tracking, his shooting, and the like, and we didn't pay him much mind when he did it, but in card-playing he'd earned the right to brag. He wasn't a cheater and he wasn't a sharp, he was just good at the game and at remembering everything that went down at the table. I'd watched him play poker once in Baxter Springs and he'd come away from the table with near eighty dollars—and that after he'd only put up a dollar to ante. Grat was a lot sharper than some people liked to give him credit for, and that worked in his favor at the poker table. And if anyone ever disagreed with the outcome of a game, they never got any further than complaining. Grat would only have to give them that stare of his that'd make a man's knees knock together under the table, and that would be that.

The Gold Room was a lot fancier than most of the watering-holes I'd been in before; the bar was made of wood so polished you could see your face in it, and there was gilt-patterned paper on the walls. The bartender called out a hello to Bob as we came in.

It was late afternoon and there weren't too many men in there yet, just two saloon girls and three cowboys over at the table in the corner. The saloon girls, a blond and a redhead, set to batting their eyelashes right away at Bob and giggling, like they knew him well, but Bob paid them no mind. Instead, he went right over to the cowboys' table, with Grat and I following close behind.

"Why, if it ain't Marshal Dalton!" one of them called jovially.

"*Both* Marshal Daltons, Charley," the one sitting next to him added with a grin that reminded me of a fox. He was long and lean and cut a dashing figure, with a sweeping auburn moustache and lively brown eyes. The man who'd spoken first was smaller, almost scrawny, with curly black hair peeking out from under his hat and beady little black eyes. He was smiling, too, and walking a poker chip back and forth over his knuckles like it was some kind of nervous habit.

Bob was smiling back at them, widely, like the three of them were sharing some inside joke. "I'm afraid it's just plain Bob and Grat, now, boys. We ain't in the law business anymore."

The one with the copper hair frowned and his moustache drooped a little like the jowls of a hound dog. "Since when?"

"Since a week ago," Bob said breezily, like it didn't matter none. He hooked an arm around my neck. "Boys, this is Emmett. He got tired of punching cows and ended up out here with his two no-good brothers. Em, this is Bitter Creek Newcomb and Charley Pierce." he gestured to the man with the copper hair, then the dark one in turn. Then he pointed to the third man. "And then this is—"

I blinked. "Dick Broadwell!" I exclaimed in surprise, before Bob could finish his sentence. It'd only been a little over a year since I'd seen him last, but he'd shaved his heavy beard and slicked back his light brown hair and so I hadn't recognized him right off.

"Why, Em!" he said to me, shaking my hand enthusiastically. "Ain't you a sight for sore eyes!"

Bob and Grat were looking at me, and I chuckled. "Dick here worked at Courtney's outfit with me for a time," I explained. I looked back at him. "What are you doing out this way, Dick? And did you bring Doolin with you?"

Dick shook his head. "I got tired of cows, just like you. And Bill's around, but I ain't seen him lately. He's always off doing Lord knows what—I can't keep up with him for more'n a week or two."

Bitter Creek gestured to the empty chairs. "Pull yourselves up a chair, Daltons. Our game was gettin' stale, anyway."

Charley's eyebrow shot up and he looked at Grat as we

sat down. "You playing, Gratton? 'Cause if you are, I'm gonna just watch."

Grat rolled his eyes at the use of his full name and took the deck of cards, shuffling it so fast it became a blur between his palms. "Hell yes, I'm playing, and if you ever call me that again, Pierce, I'll make you eat a bullet out of my gun. You follow me?"

"Sure, sure. Take it easy, you old cross-patch," Charley said, laughing, his hands up. "With a fifty-dollar handle like that, you oughta get yourself a nickname, like Bitter Creek, here."

Grat rolled his eyes again and began rapidly dealing the cards, skipping over Charley. "Grat'll do just fine."

I must have had a confused look on my face, because Charley looked at me and chucked. "We call him "Bitter Creek" 'cause he don't ever sing about anything else," he said to me.

"Ain't you ever heard that song, Emmett? 'I'm a wild wolf from Bitter Creek?'" Dick asked me. He didn't wait for an answer. "When George here is soaked, he don't ever shut up with that song until he passes out—or someone buffaloes him over the head with a pistol butt. I ain't gonna call it singing, 'cause he can't carry a tune in a bucket."

"I believe you're just jealous," Bitter Creek said to Dick in a good-natured way, "of my fine musical talents."

I smiled and took up my hand after flipping in my ante. I liked Bitter Creek and Charley; they seemed to have the devil-may-care take on life that I always envied but could never quite allow myself, then or later, to adopt. It was that narrow outlook they all had that would make things go so wrong, in the end.

We played a few games and naturally, Grat won them all. Bitter Creek was good but even he couldn't beat Grat, who, on the rare occasion that he didn't have the cards, could bluff like no one I'd ever seen. I stopped playing after his third win and stood up, moving behind the table to lean against the back wall, watching the door, and keeping one eye on the table. Grat and Bob and I had a habit of one of us guarding any game we were in, just in case things got fishy. I liked all the men we were playing with, but aside from Dick I didn't know them any too well yet—and even Dick was really only an acquaintance.

Turned out I didn't need to be suspicious; not a one of them tried anything. They didn't get sore when Grat took all their money, either; they just laughed and acted like it didn't matter. They talked with us a lot; asking questions about what had happened up in Wichita, and Bob told them straight out, so I figured he must've trusted them somewhat. Then Grat started in on corn whiskey after we'd been there two hours and everyone backed their chairs up a little from the table. By that time I was tired and I caught Bob's eye.

He nodded a little and tossed his hand down onto the table. "I fold."

"Me too," Dick added.

Bitter Creek toyed with one end of his moustache and ran the tip of his tongue over his teeth while he looked at his cards like he was trying to stare a hole through them. Then he cocked one eyebrow at Grat, his eyes dancing like Bob's did when he was in a good humor. "I suppose I'm plumb off my nut, but I'll call." He gave Grat his fox-grin.

Grat cocked an eyebrow back, deadpan, and put his cards on the table. He had a straight flush. I shook my head in amazement.

"I'll be Goddamned," I heard Dick breathe. "How's he *do* that?"

"We ain't figured that out yet, Dick," Bob chuckled, crossing his arms over his chest and leaning back in his chair.

Bitter Creek's moustache drooped again as he frowned, then he shrugged and laughed. "Aww, hell, I said I was off my nut, didn't I?" He put his hand on the table, and it was only a pair of jacks.

Grat gave him a smug look and scooped the pot into his saddlebags, which he'd brought in with him.

Bitter Creek gave him a little bow and spoke in a theatrical voice. "Mister Dalton, I am down to the blanket, so that was my last hand. It was a pleasure playing you. Remind me never to do it again." Bob, Dick, Charley and I laughed, and even Grat chuckled a little.

I have to admit that about that time I'd gotten to thinking how carefree we all were right then, with no jobs to worry us, no one to answer to but ourselves. For the first time since Shadley'd pulled that gun on me and slapped those shackles on my wrists, I felt like maybe the dark cloud of that whole mess wouldn't stay over my head forever.

They were lighting the lamps above the tables now and more men had come in for drinks. Someone started up a Faro game in the other corner. The two saloon girls slunk over to our table and zeroed in on Bob and Grat, and pretty soon they'd gotten the two of them to head upstairs. Grat took the bottle of corn whiskey with him, but he left his saddlebags with me. I guess he wasn't that drunk yet if he had the presence of mind to keep his poker winnings out of easy reach of the whore, who'd been eyeing the pot as it grew.

I heard Bob laughing out loud as he disappeared up there, his arm around the redhead's tightly-corseted waist. They left me down in the saloon to fend for myself, which suited me fine. Though I couldn't call myself a saint, I'd never had much taste for cheap saloon floozies; secretly I'd envisioned myself courting a quality young woman someday, the way Mother had brought me up to, but I'd never said anything to Bob or Grat about it, knowing they'd only laugh.

Bitter Creek and Charley and Dick and I went outside to the gallery, and Newcomb and Pierce headed off toward the red-light district after calling goodbye, but Dick and I leaned on the hitching rail and talked about ranching and some of the other men we'd known in our cattle days. After an hour more I paid for a room at the boarding house next door to the Gold Room, and was out like a light as soon as I'd hit the mattress, Grat's saddlebags under my bed.

FIVE

WE WENT BACK to Tulsa in mid June to pick up the pay owed to us from Wilson, and about halfway into July, when we were getting ready to move on, Mother's telegram came.

It was bad news; I could tell that right off. I could see it in the way Bob's face paled, the way all the light went out of his eyes; they looked glazed and empty as he read. Grat saw it too and his brow furrowed. "What'd Mother say, Bob, that's got you lookin' like someone walked over your grave?" He reached for the telegram and took it out of Bob's hands.

"Pa's dead," Bob said, straight out. He didn't try to soften the blow none, and I felt myself take a step back, like someone had just taken a swing at me. I looked at Grat, and I was thrown by what I saw in his face. Grat, who never showed much emotion save anger, had an expression in his eyes of utter grief, and his fingers curled into the paper, crushing it. Grat had been close to Pa; they'd spent a lot of time together in California a few years back when Pa had taken some of his racehorses out there, back before Frank died. Seeing Grat like that seemed to snap Bob out of his state, because he reached over and put a hand on Grat's shoulder, squeezing his fingers in as if to brace him against his sorrow. Grat was a lot older than both of us but it was Bob, as usual, who was acting the part.

"What happened?" I managed to get out. I pictured Pa in my mind as I'd last seen him—sitting proud and tall in the saddle of one of his racing studs. I couldn't ever remember him being sick a day before, except when he'd had too much to drink.

"Mother says it was cholera," Grat said, and his voice sounded slower and gruffer than normal, like he was too broke up to get his words out good.

"She wants us to come home for the...the funeral and see to the estate," Bob told me, and I saw his jaw clench under the fuzz of dirty blond beard he'd let start to grow over his face.

My throat felt funny, like I had a necktie on too tight. I reached for the telegram. "Lemme see that, Grat," I said, and he let go of it. I had to smooth it out some to be able to read it, and when I was done I crumpled it into a ball in my fist.

We set off for home, camping out along the way. Grat got drunker than I'd ever seen him that night, but neither Bob nor I tried to stop him; we knew he was just trying to drink away his grief. He didn't try to start a scrap with either of us; instead he just threw the bottle hard against a tree trunk when it was empty, watching it shatter. The horses all threw their heads up and shied away from the noise when he did it. Then he laid down in his bedroll, turned away from us. When he was sure Grat was out, Bob went over and eased the gun from Grat's hip holster, putting it away with his own gear.

The sun was higher up in the sky than we wanted it to be by the time we got riding, but Grat's head was pounding and his eyes were red from the whiskey, and he felt too sick to get up on his horse. Bob didn't fuss at him, just took his time watering the horses at the creek, giving him some more time to sober up. When we finally set out Grat was weaving a little in the saddle and I was sure he'd be pitched right out of it, but he managed to stay on. He held off on the whiskey the next few nights.

Pa and Mother had taken a claim near Kingfisher in Oklahoma Territory, but they hadn't moved out there yet. They were still up near Coffeyville, where most of us kids had grown up. It was getting dark when we rode up to the house, and Mother had the lamps burning on the window-sills. As we rode up to the stable to put up the horses, the lean-to door opened and the youngest of our sisters and our little brother came out to meet us, their faces bore a mix of happiness that we were home and sorrow because Pa was dead.

Sam came right up to me, and I was stunned by how much he'd grown since I'd left home. He was pushing twelve and already almost up to my shoulder. Leona and Nannie hung back and pulled their shawls tight around their shoulders, almost like they were shy of us. They'd turned into young ladies, with their hair pinned up and their skirts all the way down to their shoe-tops.

We all went into the house in a big group, and Mother turned from the stove, wiped her hands on her apron, and came over to hug us. Her dark hair had more silver in it then I remembered and she looked small in her mourning dress.

"My boys are home," she said, tears in her eyes. "I'm so glad you're here." Her arms lingered around me the longest and I hugged her back, hard, like I'd used to do when I was little. Mother and I had always been close, and I hadn't realized how much I'd missed her until right then. We always understood each other. I looked like her, had her dark hair and gray eyes. The other boys had all got Pa's blond hair.

She pulled back and looked me over, biting her lip and trying to hold the tears back. "Em, you've gone and become a man since you left," she said as she looked up at me, her voice real soft. I gave her a crooked smile and cleared my throat, scuffing the rowel of one of my spurs against the floor. Mother saw my embarrassment and smiled, a sad smile through her tears. She put a hand on my arm, then moved to speak quietly with Bob and Grat.

My brother Ben, the oldest of all of us, came out from the parlor to greet us. He was even more sober than usual and he looked like an undertaker in his black mourning suit and bushy side-whiskers. He had filed on a claim not far from Mother's in Kingfisher and I was glad he'd be going out there with her; I knew she'd still go, even with Pa gone.

Pa had never been able to stay put in any one place for too long, and Mother'd gotten used to being without him over the years. It was her, mostly, who raised us up, since he was always gone doing one thing or another; racing his horses or dealing his cattle. I knew he'd loved us all but it wasn't in him to show it any too much, so Mother had always done that for both of them. It was her we'd all come home for, more than Pa.

My sister Lelia had come, too, and sister Eva and her

husband John, so the house was so crowded it was hard to think straight. As Mother was getting supper with the girls' help, I turned for the first time toward the parlor.

Pa's coffin was set in there; the hearse would come for it for the funeral tomorrow morning. I hesitated, then went in, almost tiptoeing. My spurs and footfalls sounded loud on the floor and it seemed disrespectful, somehow.

There was just one lamp burning, in the corner, and it gave off a flickering, feeble light that was almost eerie. The coffin was plain pine and it had already been nailed shut. It looked too small to hold Pa; he'd been six-foot-two and had always seemed like a giant to me. I stared at it for a long while. Then I figured I should maybe say something, but my throat got stuck and I had to swallow, hard.

I'd never been too close to him; none of us had, excepting Grat, for we hadn't really known him all that well. But he was my Pa, and for all his faults, I'd loved him. He'd tried, and I knew that in his way of thinking, he'd done the best he could by us.

So I stood there and stared at that pine box, and finally I said, in a near whisper, "I ain't got the words, Pa." I turned and went back into the front room, where everyone else was.

Bob saw me come in, and his face was sober. His eyes were still, they weren't dancing like usual. He motioned me over to where he and Grat were sitting at the table, and said, in a low voice, "let's go out and have a look at the stock."

Grat heaved a funny sort of sigh and ran a hand over his stubble-covered chin. "It's dark out, Bob," he pointed out, unnecessarily. "We ain't gonna be able to see 'em all. Not in the pasture."

"We'll take the lantern and give her a try, anyway," Bob replied, and he gave Grat a hard look. It was clear he wanted to talk to me and Grat alone and was using the horses as an excuse. Grat knew it, too, but he didn't want to go. I saw him dart a quick look toward the parlor, then turn his face away.

"Come *on*, Grat," Bob hissed firmly. Lelia heard him and gave us a look, but she didn't say anything, just took a deep breath and kept setting out plates on the big table. I kept looking at her and thinking how citified she looked, with her blond hair pinned up in one of them fancy curlicued knots and her little gold earbobs. Eva, too, looked more done up than I remembered her, in her rustling black taffeta mourning dress. It was strange, I thought, how brothers and sisters could like to lose track of each other, after just a few years away. I felt out of place in my clothes that were coated with dust and grime from the trail, and my gun belt around my waist.

Bob ignored the girls' looks. He got up and headed for the door, and with another sigh, Grat got up and followed him, taking the lantern with him. I went with them, murmuring to tell Mother where we were going. She nodded and tucked a stray piece of hair behind her ear, barely turning her attention from the stove. I shut the door quietly behind me, even though there were so many voices in the house I could've banged it and no one would've noticed.

We went out around the house to the big pasture Pa'd fenced off. His best stallion, Prince Albert, was in the small corral and he nickered when we came past, trotting up to thrust his head over the gate. The lanternlight shone over his black coat and finely-shaped head. He was Blackjack's sire, and one of the finest-looking studs I'd ever seen. We wouldn't sell him, not for a mint. I figured Bob would take him as his saddle horse from how on.

I could see the fuzzy, indistinct shapes of the mares far out in the pasture. Pa only had four left, and only one other stallion—a big, sturdy bay with a wide blaze. Grat would take him. The mares we would sell; Mother had already told us she wanted us to take them. Any profit we could get would be that much more toward defending Bob at his trial, if we could hang onto it that long. Bob hadn't mentioned it once since we'd left Wichita, and I knew he wouldn't say anything to Mother.

Bob put his foot up on the lowest rail of the fence and folded his arms on the top one, and Grat followed suit after hanging the lantern on a nail driven into the gate frame. I got up on the fence and sat on the top rail with my legs dangling into the pasture, like I'd used to do when I was a boy. Grat let out a sharp whistle, and some of the mares came over to poke their muzzles at us, hoping for food.

"When we leave here we'll take these horses and find a buyer," Bob said, twirling a long piece of grass in between his thumb and forefinger, then holding it out to one of the mares, who plucked it out of his hand with her nimble lips. One of the others came over and nipped at my boot; I shooed her away with a swing of my leg. Grat took the head of a third in his hands and rubbed her muzzle almost tenderly. I watched him and thought to myself that if Grat would be just half as nice to folks as he was being to that horse, he might get a little further in life, but of course I didn't say it aloud.

"Where do you want to take them?" I asked.

"Toward Nowata. There's a man there named Mitchell I want to see. We can stay over at their place."

Grat threw him a sharp look and let go of the horse. She shied away from the sudden movement of his hands. "You wanna see Mitchell, or do you wanna see his daughter?"

Bob shrugged his shoulders. "If I see one, I see the other, don't I?" He wasn't looking at Grat.

I *did* look at Grat, questioningly. One corner of his mouth went up and he looked like he was holding back a laugh. "This feller's got a pretty little daughter that's sixteen. Bob's sweet on her."

"I ain't 'sweet on her,' Grat," Bob growled.

"She's more than just another poontang to you, though, ain't she?" Grat asked crudely, and he laughed in a patronizing way. I cringed at his language; not even the cowboys I'd known had talked so low as that.

Bob's face was turning purple in the lanternlight and his eyes went cold. "Shut the hell up, Grat." His voice sounded low, like an animal. The hair on the back of my neck rose. Bob was serious when he talked like that.

"*Make me*," Grat responded, still laughing. "Good Lord, you're gettin' awful riled up over that little girl you ain't sweet on!"

Bob lunged for Grat and I dove off the fence and out of the way, springing to one side of them. "Bob, Grat, knock it off, damn it!" I yelled. If they got started with one another, one or both of them were going to end up with black eyes for Pa's funeral. "Stop!"

Bob's fists were pounding into Grat and Grat was fighting back, good and mad now. They struggled with each other. Grat's big body hit the fence and shook it, spooking the mares, who wheeled away into the darkness, their hooves thudding over the grass.

I thought about pulling my gun and firing a shot into the air to break them up, but before I could do it I heard a scream. I whipped around and saw Eva standing near the corner of the house, her hand to her mouth in horror as she saw Bob and Grat grappling with one another. Her cry surprised them so much that they broke apart, breathing hard, their eyes wild and their hair mussed. Bob had a tear on his shirtsleeve.

"What is *wrong* with you?" Eva cried angrily, her normally sweet, reserved manner completely gone. "Pa's lying in the parlor in a coffin and you're out here *fighting*?" As she spoke, Lelia, John and Ben came hurrying up behind her, then Mother and the young ones.

Bob's face went red with embarrassment and I flinched. Bob *hated* to be embarrassed. Grat shot him a black look, straightening his vest and brushing dirt from the fence off his britches.

Eva let out her breath angrily and stormed back inside, like it wasn't worth waiting for an answer from them. Lelia and the girls followed. John lingered a minute, then followed, hurrying to calm Eva down. Ben looked at the three of us and shook his head like we were all a bunch of unruly children. That made me mad, because I'd had no part in it, but there was no sense telling him that. He went back inside. Sam hung in the shadow made by the house, but I could see his face and his eyes were enormous as he stared at Bob and Grat.

"Simon Dalton!" Mother called sharply to him, "you get yourself back inside now, you hear me?"

"Yes'm," he muttered, and ran off. Then it was only Mother left out there with us, and she came up to us.

"What's gotten into the two of you?" she asked Bob and Grat, and they clenched their jaws and hung their heads so they wouldn't have to look her in the eye. Mother was the only one could've made them cower like that. She barely came up to our shoulders but she could still get any of us with a look.

When they didn't answer she looked at me for an explanation. "They're just on edge, Mother," I soothed. "We all are, ain't we?"

"*'Aren't,'*" Mother corrected me in that same sharp tone. "You've been around cowboys too long, Emmett. You've forgotten how to speak properly."

She turned back to Grat and Bob and put her hands on her hips. "I don't know what started this, but you will *not* do it again. You've upset your sisters and it's disrespectful to your Pa. You're old enough to know better. If you're going to act like children, then that's how you'll be treated. Get inside and wash up, and when we sit down to supper it'll be as civilized folks, not trail ruffians. Understand?"

"Yes, ma'am," they muttered in chorus, and I had the sudden urge to laugh at the sight of my two older brothers, former U.S. Deputy Marshals, being dressed down by our mother. They trudged into the house, stiffly avoiding each other, leaving Mother and I standing by the corral.

She sighed. "I declare, those boys will drive me to distraction." She looked at me. "What was that all about?"

I shrugged uncomfortably. "You know Grat, Mother. He doesn't need an excuse."

She touched my arm. "Let's go inside. Supper's ready. Eva was coming out to get you."

We went inside and sat down to supper. Mother did most of the talking; she seemed determined to not bring up Grat and Bob's fight again. Instead she told us all how Will had sent a telegram saying how he couldn't come for the funeral because of his political obligations, but he wanted all of us to know he was with us in spirit. Littleton, another of our brothers, was in the same position, unable to travel from his ranch in Fresno. He wouldn't have come even if he could have, I knew; Lit had been hateful toward Pa ever since I could remember, and didn't think much of most of us.

We ate and listened to her, but no one made much conversation, just passed the food around silently, everyone still upset about the brawl outside. It wasn't exactly how I expected my first supper in two years with the family to be.

Later, as I was going off to bed, I noticed Grat slip into the parlor with Pa's coffin. He shut the door and didn't come out.

SIX

PA WAS BURIED at ten the next morning, in the cemetery near Coffeyville. It was windy and we all stood around the grave with our heads bowed through the whole service, not just the prayers. I spoke the words along with the others, but I found I'd forgotten some of the Psalms, which bothered me; I'd never forgotten any Bible passages before. I'd never been real big into religion but I'd been raised up with it; we'd always gone to Sunday School, and Mother had made us recite and taught us verses herself whenever we lived in places where there wasn't a church. I clasped my hands in front of me as they lowered Pa's coffin down, just studying on how I couldn't remember those Bible verses. Eva cried into John's shoulder, and Lelia dabbed at her eyes with a handkerchief and kept Nannie and Leona against her skirts. Sam sniffled. Mother didn't cry at all; she wasn't the type. Whatever grieving she'd done for Pa, it was done in private.

When the gravediggers started filling in the grave, they all turned away and went back to the wagon and the buggy, and Grat and Bob and I put our hats back on and untied our horses from the picket fence around the graveyard. Bob was riding Prince Albert, and Grat had the bay, Baron.

They still weren't speaking to one another. By some miracle neither one of them had a black eye, but Bob's jaw was bruised and one ear was a little swollen, and Grat had a big scratch on his neck that he'd hidden with the collar of his shirt and his necktie. His knuckles were banged up pretty good, too, from where he'd hit them on the fence, trying to swing at Bob.

Instead of coming with me, they trotted off together out into the brush, surprising me. They didn't call to me to join them, and I let them go, sensing they were likely planning to share a bottle of whiskey and bury the hatchet. Mother didn't say anything about them being gone, so she must've figured they needed to talk it out, too.

They didn't come back until the next morning, and they were both hung over pretty good, but they were speaking again. I didn't ask them where they'd been, neither did Mother. We spent a little more time with the family, but by noon Bob was ready to go. He and Grat went to the barn to saddle up, while I said my goodbyes.

Mother kept her hands on my shoulders after she'd pulled back from our hug, and she took a deep breath. Her eyes came up then and met mine, searching them. "Emmett, you keep yourself safe now, you hear me? Keep yourself out of trouble. Trouble seems to follow your brothers, and I don't want you to get mixed up in it."

I smiled at her. "Everything will be fine, Mother. You don't need to worry about us." I leaned down and kissed her cheek.

By then Grat and Bob had returned and they said their

own goodbyes to Mother, apologizing to her for the grief they'd caused and assuring her, just like I'd done, that the three of us would be fine and do our best to stay out of trouble. I had no way of knowing right then that while my promise had been sincere, Bob's was about as far away from sincere as you could get.

⸺⸻◆⸻⸺

"See that light?"

I stood up in my stirrups a little, squinting out into the darkness. It wasn't that late at night but there was no moon nor stars out; they were hidden over by thick clouds. For over two hours we'd rode into that emptiness, at a walk since we couldn't see to steer our mounts well.

I wasn't sure what time it was; we'd been riding all day and hadn't stopped to camp. I'd been following Bob by the sound of Prince Albert's hooves on the trail, and Grat did likewise with Blackjack. I was ponying two mares, and Grat had the other two, and the whole situation didn't agree with me a bit. Not only was it too dark to see where we were going, but the studs kept getting all riled around the mares and the mares were nipping at them and each other. We had to pony them, though; If we drove them, as we'd been doing for the last few days, we'd lose them in the dark.

"I can't see a damn thing, Bob," I replied. Blackjack kicked out behind him, real sudden, with one hoof, and I heard a mare squeal. I cursed loudly and checked him, hard. I wasn't sure how much longer we could keep on in this fashion.

"Over there," Bob said. I figured he was pointing, but there wasn't much point in it; I could barely make out Prince Albert's one white sock as he walked ahead of me, let alone Bob in the saddle. I rolled my eyes, about to chew him out, when I saw what he must've been pointing at.

I could make out a soft glow from what must've been a window, about a half-mile ahead. As we got closer I saw the dark blob of a house, and a big stable set back against a hill.

"That's the Mitchell place," Bob said. "You boys hold here a minute; I'll go get Mitchell to let us turn the mares out." Without waiting for our answer he cantered off—bravely, I thought. The terrain was full of prairie dog holes, and if Prince Albert put a hoof in one, he'd be done for and so would Bob. Grat and I stopped like he wanted us to, both of us muttering cuss words at the mares and at our studs.

"How does Bob know these folks?" I asked Grat, in between dressing down the horses.

I heard him shift in his saddle; the leather creaked. "We met them a few times before you came out from Courtney's," he replied. "Mitchell has a pretty big spread of horses—good ones. He's got a bay stallion Bob's been after him to sell, but Mitchell won't do it." I heard him spit tobacco juice off somewhere.

I heard a sharp, two-note whistle I recognized as Bob's; he'd used to whistle like that when we were little if I was in the house and he wanted me to come outside. I turned in the direction I thought Grat was and said, "come on."

We picked our way down toward the house, easy-like 'cause it was set down in a little low area. The mares snorted and shied at every little turn, and I hoped to God above that Mitchell had said we could pasture them. Bob had hinted he knew of a buyer for them, and I hoped it was Mitchell he'd been talking about. If I had to pony them any longer I wasn't sure what I'd end up doing.

"Does Bob want to sell these mares to Mitchell?" I asked Grat as we moved slowly forward.

"More than likely," was all Grat said.

We finally got to where Bob was and he led us, on foot, to a small pasture. Once we'd turned the mares loose, we took the studs to the barn, then trudged up to the house, leaving our Winchesters on our saddles but keeping our gun belts on. I was so saddle-sore I felt like my legs didn't remember how to walk straight, and my arm was aching from pony-ing the stubborn mares. I was hungry and tired besides, and the whole of it made me cross, a state I normally didn't find myself in.

Bob let us into a big, warm room lit by many lamps, with a cookstove in one corner and a table in the middle of it. A plain, middle-aged woman was in it, wearing a calico dress and apron. She had circles under her eyes and she looked frazzled as she stirred things on the stove, probably because she'd just been told there'd be three extra mouths to feed. Bob spoke kindly to her, though, and she smiled at him and Grat, then at me when Bob introduced us.

"This is Missus Mitchell," Bob said. "She makes the best suppers in the Cherokee Nation."

Mrs. Mitchell rolled her eyes to the ceiling but she was smiling a little as she did it. "It won't do you any good to flatter me, Bob Dalton," she said. "Now sit up to the table. You boys have been riding a long ways, from the sound of it."

We pulled chairs up to the table, and made a little conversation with her. The door to the lean-to opened and Mr. Mitchell came in to join us. He was stern-looking fellow with gray hair starting to mix in with his black, and his skin was weathered, the way most ranchers' were. He introduced himself to me, then turned to Bob.

"Where'd you come by those mares?" he asked. "I took my lantern to them when I fed them. Nice-looking animals."

"They're from our Pa's estate," Bob said, taking a big swallow of the coffee Mitchell's wife had set before him, then cupping his hands around it. "Pa only had them and the studs left."

Mitchell raised an eyebrow. "You looking to sell them?"

"We surely are. We ain't got any need of them, and we can't travel with them well, not with the studs we're riding."

Mitchell nodded slowly. "Well, you'll have to let me think on it. I already got a lot of breeding mares."

Before Bob could answer, another door opened, this one from a bedroom, and a young woman came in, shyly, pulling a shawl around her shoulders. She had hair the color of wheat, her eyes were a lovely blue, and she reminded me a little of a china doll Nannie used to have. She was a lovely, fresh-looking young thing in her sprigged calico dress, but she wasn't a little girl—there was a womanly nature to her and she had a woman's curves. I could tell right off this was the daughter Bob and Grat had been fighting about. She hung back a little, seeing all of us there, then came to the table, sitting across from Bob, whom she greeted kindly.

"This lovely little lady is the Mitchell's daughter, Ella,"

Bob told me. His voice was almost theatrically polite, but as he spoke he looked around me and gave Grat a look that warned him to keep quiet—or else.

"Miss Mitchell," I said politely. I thanked Mrs. Mitchell as she set plates down before all of us, but I was watching Bob out of the corner of my eye. I'd seen Bob look at women all kinds of ways before, but never the way he was looking at Ella Mitchell. I studied on it for a minute and then realized with a start that Bob knew this girl well, and cared for her—*really* cared for her.

That threw me so much I almost forgot how hungry I was. Bob loved women, and they seemed to love him; I couldn't remember a time when we'd gone into a saloon or game house and not seen bunches of them flocking right to him. But those were always saloon girls and whores, not quality folks. I'd always thought Bob was too wild to ever find one girl he could be sweet on, and that was part of the reason I'd never told him my hope to eventually do just that. Seeing him mooning over this rancher's daughter was almost like looking at a stranger, not my brother.

Ella was shy, and she didn't talk much at the table. She just ate in little dainty bites and glanced up at Bob through lowered lashes. Her Pa talked with us about farming and horse-breeding for a bit, but after awhile I started to notice that in between sentences he was watching Bob closely—and watching his daughter. And his manner became suddenly cooler. Grat appeared not to notice—though he never did notice much when it came to anything that required intuition of any sort.

Bob didn't seem to notice, either, which surprised me.

Bob was the sharpest man I ever met, observant as hell. But he was so busy drinking in his fill of pretty little Ella that he missed her daddy's darkening looks.

When we'd finished eating Mitchell looked at the three of us. "We'll put you up for the night, of course; I won't refuse a man shelter. But we don't got a whole lot of extra room..."

"We don't want to put you out, Mr. Mitchell," I said quickly, speaking up. "If it's all the same to you, we can make ourselves comfortable in the stable. We've got our bedrolls." Bob and Grat both looked at me, but I pretended not to notice.

Mitchell looked relieved, and his gaze softened some when he looked at me. "I reckon that'll be fine, Emmett."

Ella got up to help her Ma with the kitchen work while Bob and Grat smoked cigars with Mitchell and I sat with them. I'd never been much for tobacco, either smoking it or chewing it; Grat could make just about any habit unattractive, and so I never took it up, not even when I worked cows. After awhile we said our thank yous and goodnights and headed outside to the stable, our arms full of extra blankets Mrs. Mitchell had lent us. Just before we went, though, I saw Bob meet Ella's eyes with his, and he gave her a long look. She looked back at him for a minute, then gave a little nod and looked away, her cheeks going pink. I touched Bob on the arm and motioned him outside, sensing trouble if we stayed any longer.

Neither Grat nor I mentioned Ella to Bob as we arranged ourselves on top of the fresh, sweet-smelling hay in the corner of the barn, our rifles and guns at hand. I didn't want to upset Bob, and I knew Grat was thinking of their scuffle at

Ma's and wasn't keen on starting it up again. We were so tired we said very little at all to each other, and I was asleep almost as soon as I pulled the blanket over myself.

I awoke suddenly a long time later, disoriented and stiff. Grat was awake, too, up and fumbling with a match to light the lantern we'd hung on a nail nearby.

"Grat?" I whispered hoarsely, my head feeling like it was filled with cobwebs. I hadn't got near enough sleep. "What's the matter?"

Grat got the lantern lit and looked back at me over his shoulder. The lanternlight threw harsh shadows over his face. "Ain't you noticed?" he jerked his thumb toward the far wall of the stable. "Bob's gone."

I looked, and sure enough, Bob's bedroll was empty and his blankets tossed aside. His guns were right where he'd left them, except the one he wore in his hip holster at all times, even when sleeping.

"Where'd he run off to?" I murmured, looking back at Grat.

"I don't know. I woke up when I heard the stable door open, but it's been a little while and I ain't sure where he went."

I threw back my blankets and headed for the door, my Winchester in my hands. I heard voices as I eased it open, and across the stable-yard I could see Mitchell standing on the back porch of the house, a lantern in one hand, a rifle tucked up under his other arm, its barrel pointed downwards. Ella stood to one side of him, her head hung, her shoulders hunched forward. I thought she might be crying. Bob was below them on the bottom step, his back to me, and I could tell from his posture, even in the dim light, that he was very, very angry.

"... And then you take advantage of my hospitality by convincing my daughter to sneak of the house to meet you in the middle of the night?" Mitchell was saying to Bob, his voice hard.

"Papa, it's not his fault!" Ella cried out. I saw her clutch at his arm, but he threw her off.

"You get yourself back in that house, girl, you hear me? You're not to come out here again until these boys are gone, understand?" He took her arm just above her elbow and roughly shoved her toward the house. She went, stumbling over her skirts. When the door had shut, Mitchell turned to Bob again.

"I should shoot you right here, Dalton, but I'm not going to. You and your brothers take your mares and be on your way. I don't ever want to see your faces around this place again! That girl's going to be married into a good family and I'll not have her chances ruined by the likes of you."

To my surprise, Bob said nothing. Not a word came out of him. Instead he just turned and came back to the barn. I ducked away from the door just in time; he threw it open like to rip off its hinges. He had that black, bitter look in his eyes again, the one I remembered all too well from when we got arrested. "Rattle your hocks and tack up, now, boys," he ordered us, his voice cold. "I expect I've just worn out our welcome."

I busied myself with Blackjack, getting his saddle on quick and pulling his headstall up over his ears so fast the bit rattled against his teeth. Bob in this mood wasn't to be trifled with, nor disobeyed, and I didn't try to pry into what happened. Grat didn't either. Both of us knew without anything being said that Bob would want some kind of revenge for the dressing-down he'd been given; Mitchell had embarrassed him, and no one embarrassed our brother without paying for it later, and paying heavily. Bob always had to have the last word. I finished my cinching quick and prayed Bob would leave it alone, just this once.

Grat got tacked up quick, too, and in a few minutes we were out of the stable, ready to mount up. Bob swung up onto Prince Albert and spurred him so hard he reared up a little. Grat and I followed, and the three of us took off at a gallop toward the mares' pasture. There was a lamp burning inside the house and I was sure I saw Mitchell at the window, watching us.

We got the mares out quick; I had my rope on my saddle still and I caught them that way, leading them over to Grat so's he could get the halters and lead lines on them. Then Grat took his mares off his saddle, and I took mine, and we started out, moving faster than I wanted. I tried not to think of the rough ground and all them prairie dog holes. The mares snorted and plunged on their leads behind me. Some of my worry left a little bit as we made our way further from the house. Maybe Bob really would leave it be this time.

Suddenly Bob veered Prince hard to the right, cutting off the trail and back onto Mitchell's land. Our horses followed, nearly pitching both of us out of our saddles.

"Bob, what the hell are you *doing*?" Grat bellowed, cussing good as he tried to keep his balance.

"Getting us into a new business venture," Bob threw

back over his shoulder, carelessly giving Prince his head.

We were moving too fast to talk any more, and so Grat and I just followed, gritting our teeth, shoving our heels way down in the stirrups and praying our horses would keep their footing. We rode on along what I figured was the edge of Mitchell's property until we came to another pasture, this one wire-fenced and filled with horses. Most of Mitchell's stock, I imagined. The first faint tendrils of sunlight were starting to creep up in the sky and I could see about twenty or thirty head, horses of all colors, both mares and geldings. Bob got off the Prince and threw his reins to Grat, who took them, his brow furrowed so deep his eyebrows knitted together. He looked at me, then back at Bob.

Bob rummaged in his saddlebag and pulled out a pair of wire-cutters, the kind cowboys carried sometimes for cutting and repairing fences. He crouched down by the gate and cut the fence-wires clean through, at one end of the section and then the other, leaving a wide opening right by the gate. I was too surprised to say anything, but Grat spoke up.

"Bob, I asked you what in the hell you were—"

"I told you, Grat," Bob said calmly. "We said we were gonna sell horses, didn't we? Well, I've decided we're gonna sell these."

"But...they ain't ours," I heard myself say, like a dimwit.

Bob raised his head and gave me a level look, his eyes strange-looking, like all the color had been taken out of them. "I know that, Em. That's why we're stealin' them. Now, you got a rope on that saddle. Get in there and help me drive 'em out while Grat stands watch and hangs on to those mares." He went over and took back the Prince, mounting up and pausing to see whether I would obey him or not.

I held Blackjack firm, and for the first time in my life, I stood up to my brother, even though my heart was pounding like to come right out of my chest. "Bob, they hang horse-thieves. It's too risky. I ain't doin' it."

Bob edged Prince closer to Blackjack, turning him so his saddle was right up against mine. And he gave me a look I couldn't even begin to describe, one that made me cringe inside, made me feel like I was less than the dirt under his boots. "Why not, Emmett? You *scared*? I wouldn't have taken my own little brother for a yellow-belly."

I forgot the way I felt a second before; now all I felt was hot rage. No man likes to be called a coward, and I was no different. But to have my own brother, and a brother I looked up to so much at that, call me one…

Something changed in me right then; I could almost feel it like a physical thing. I forgot Mother's teachings, the morals she'd pushed on me, that I'd always tried to go by. I forgot everything, I think, except my burning desire to prove Bob wrong and redeem myself in his eyes. I turned my face away from him and put my spurs to Blackjack's sides, so hard he jumped forward with a little squeal. We plunged into the middle of that herd, scattering them, and I set to rounding them up, quick and clean, just like they were a herd of cows I was penning for slaughter.

Bob was in there with me now and even though he'd never worked cows or horses other than our Pa's, he remembered what to do. We had all of them pouring out of the opening in the corral, like blood coming out of a wound, in no time. Grat hung back at the gate, keeping an eye out while holding back Baron, who was tossing his head up and half-rearing as the herd plunged past. When the last horse went out the fence, we took off after them, running them hard, not looking back until we were well off Mitchell's property.

Bob didn't say anything more to me while we rode, but he looked over at me once just as the sun was coming up, and that horrible look was gone from his eyes. He looked like my brother again, and he looked like he was proud of me. My stomach turned a little bit but I pushed it down. I'd gotten myself into this by my own hand, and I couldn't get out of it now.

SEVEN

WE DROVE MITCHELL'S horses out of the Nation, along with some others we'd come by on a neighboring ranch owned by a Cherokee named Rogers. Bob knew him from the other times he and Grat had been up this way and didn't seem to think twice about stealing his horses. I'd said nothing this time, just rounded them up like Bob told me to do, and we pushed on. I'd felt numb, that first time out. Bob didn't press me to talk. For days we'd driven our new herd, heading for Baxter Springs in Kansas, where we sold them easy to a rancher named Scott. We cleared seven hundred dollars, money that would go toward Bob's defense in Wichita. It wouldn't be enough. So we stole another bunch. Bob somehow always knew where to find the best stock.

During the day, driving and herding, I could keep my mind off it some. I switched myself off somehow, just concentrating on moving the animals where I wanted them. The nights I stood watch over them I did the same thing. It was the other nights, the nights when Grat or Bob took the watches and I was at my leisure, that I had trouble.

Even though I'd never been much for the habit, I started

drinking Grat's whiskey regular-like on those nights, trying to get some of the guilt to leave me. Once or twice I drank so much I blacked out. I figured out pretty soon that the whiskey wouldn't make all those feelings I had go away, but I didn't know how else to push them down.

Finally one night, Bob left Grat to watch over the horses and came to find me. He plucked the whiskey bottle out of my hand and started drinking it himself; I figured out he was doing it just so I wouldn't. After a few minutes he put the bottle away and started talking to me, low and serious-like. He told me he knew now he could count on me to stand with him, that he knew I wasn't a coward. He told me he'd never thought I was, but he'd had to say it or I wouldn't have stayed with them. He said he'd gotten to where he wanted me with him from now on, and couldn't have stood it if I'd left. He talked about how close we'd always been, and how brothers should stand together no matter what. Then he put his hand on my shoulder and told me he never wanted to see me drinking Grat's whiskey like that again.

"A man who drinks just to forget something ain't a good kind of man, Em," he'd said. "You've always been the best of us. You've always had the most heart of us, and you've got a good head on your shoulders. I don't want to see you lose all that just to forget stealing some nags off of some son of a bitch's ranch. It don't matter none, Emmett. It ain't worth fussin' over, and it ain't worth gettin' loaded over, either."

I hadn't said much during all of this; I couldn't seem to make my tongue work good and my head ached. So I just looked at him there in the firelight. He kept his hand on my shoulder for a good while, bracing me, and then he took the whiskey bottle with him and left me alone.

I still didn't feel any too good about what we were doing, but I didn't see any way out of it just then. And no matter what he'd done, I still saw more hero in Bob than villain. I couldn't help it. I couldn't forget the way he'd always looked out for me and the things he'd taught me—things Pa should've but didn't get around to—just 'cause he'd decided to steal some horses to beat a bad rap in Wichita.

I'd laid back and stared up at the stars, thinking on the life I'd had before this, before Pawhuska. They all seemed so dull now, those times before Shadley and his posse had come for us. At least now I had a little excitement in life, the thing I'd always seemed to crave. And it *had* been easy...

It was a weak excuse, I knew, but it was all I could come up with. And given what I'd started taking part in, I knew that excitement was about all I was liable to get out of life anymore—if I even got to live much of a life. We were already looking over our shoulders, and we knew that if we were caught it meant the gallows, though Bob was too cocky to ever say it, and he wouldn't let us, either.

At that moment I'd hated the gift I'd always had for seeing the larger scope of things. All it was doing was making me miserable.

Well, Em, I'd thought to myself, *if you're gonna be a horse-thief, you should just get as much excitement out of it as you can. The only other choice is a noose around your neck.*

With that less-than-comforting thought, I'd rolled myself up in my bedroll. My last thought before sleep claimed me was how odd it was that I'd gone from lawman to longrider in a mere year and a half, and all at only nineteen.

EIGHT

THERE CAME A night not too long after that when I came to the realization that Bob had no intention of appearing in the courtroom at Wichita, and likely never had.

He told me that straight out after we'd eaten supper and were sitting around the fire, with Grat out watching the herd. I'd asked him how we were gonna find a buyer in time to make it back for the hearing.

"Why, Em, I'm not going back to Wichita, 'cept if it were to spit on Walker's boots...or maybe put a piece of lead in him," he'd said, like he was surprised I would've thought so. He was loading his guns, and I watched the firelight chasing itself over the nickel as his long fingers shoved bullets into the chambers. I heard the horses moving around behind us, grazing or swishing their tails at mosquitoes.

"But..."

He looked at me, pausing in his loading, holding a bullet between his thumb and middle finger, rolling it back and forth. "If it were you, Em, would *you* go back? After that bullshit charge, and the way Walker treated us?"

I took a deep breath and looked into the fire for a minute,

then back at him. "I guess I'd want my name cleared," I said.

Bob let out a snort of sarcastic laughter. "Keep dreaming, Em. They wouldn't clear my name any sooner than they'd let me put a tin star back on. Walker and Shadley've got it in for me, and you know damn well they'd love to lock me up and throw away the key." There was a bitter edge to his voice that I hated hearing. I wanted the old Bob back, the Bob who was fun and carefree, not this vengeful stranger.

Then what're we doing all this for? I wanted to shout at him, but of course I didn't.

———————

Bob had decided we'd take our second bunch of horses into Baxter Springs to sell them. I wasn't sure about the wisdom of this, seeing as how that was where we'd sold the first bunch, but when Bob planned something, he planned it to the letter; butting heads with him about it did no good. He always had an answer for every 'what-if' Grat or I proposed. And he gave those answers quick and firm, so as not to allow any further arguing about it. Grat and I, and later the others who rode with us, learned right quick that you either followed Bob's plans or you packed your gear and went the other way—for good. So I gave in and kept the rest of my bellyaching to myself.

We were in too deep to bail out, and we *were* close to Baxter Springs, after all. I wanted to be rid of that herd as soon as possible. With the money from the sale we'd have a good cushion in our pockets, and maybe then we could get shed of this way we'd started spending our time.

Bob made us stop in the area where the tree line thinned out, just before we got close to the town. We could see it about a mile off in the distance, and Bob decided Grat would ride on ahead and scout things out, just in case. If all was clear, we'd head into town with the herd.

Grat took off at a lope through the tall grasses, the mid-morning sunshine glinting off the bullets in his gun belt. It would be the last time Bob or I saw him for three months.

Bob and I waited, then waited a little longer...and then waited some more. When Bob took his watch out of his vest and saw that an hour had passed, he looked grimly at me. "What in the hell is taking him so Goddamned long?"

I squinted off toward town, my hand up to my face to ward off the sun. It was getting hot. I'd taken off my coat and tied it behind my cantle, and I'd rolled my shirtsleeves up to my elbows. Sweat was starting to bead up under the edge of my hat and on the back of my neck. I untied my canteen and took a long drink of water before I answered him.

"Maybe he got into a poker game," I suggested, but I didn't sound very convincing, even to myself. Grat could be careless at times but he wouldn't have gone astray of a task Bob told him to do, not when we were waiting on him like this.

Bob paced the tree line, growing antsy now. Finally he went back over to Prince Albert and put his foot in the stirrup. "All right, that's it. I ain't waitin' anymore. Help me get 'em going, Emmett." He nudged Prince and started to circle around to the herd's right.

"Bob, what if something's happened to Grat?" I asked

from atop Blackjack's saddle.

"We need to get these horses sold," Bob said firmly. "We'll find Grat when we get there. Let's go."

I set my jaw and tugged the brim of my hat lower down on my brow, then reined Blackjack to the left. I kicked him into a trot and let out a series of sharp whistles, slapping my rope coils against my thigh. The nags started forward into the meadow.

We drove them along, slowly, toward town. Then on the outskirts, Bob called to me to hold up.

He trotted over to me, wiping his wrist across his brow to stop the sweat from going into his eyes. The stock started grazing, swishing their tails and stamping their feet at the flies that buzzed up around them.

"One of us should ride in, just to see," Bob said. "I've got a funny feeling. Something don't set right with me."

I took my hat off and pushed my fingers through my damp hair, then put it back on. "I'll go," I said.

Bob looked troubled, but he nodded. "All right. I'll hold the nags here and wait for you. Just watch yourself, Em. If it's clear, we'll get 'em in there and pen them at the livery, then go look for Grat."

I gave him a nod, then clicked my tongue at Blackjack. I didn't make him run; his coat was starting to shine with sweat in the heat and his head was a little lower than I wanted it. I could tell he was getting tired, so I let him trot easy. Plus I knew that if I came into town at a run, I'd arouse suspicion. I kept hoping I'd see Grat coming back toward me, but I didn't.

At the edge of the main street, I rode Blackjack up to a

hitching rail and dismounted, intending to take a walk up and down the street and see if I could spot Grat anywhere—and get a look at any law that might be around. Before I could go a step, though, I caught the words of two men walking up the gallery from behind me.

"You hear about them nags Scott bought?" one of them said. "Turns out they were stolen. Injun feller named Rogers is in town hunting them, and he's as mad as a rattlesnake. There's talk it was the Dalton boys. Word's gone out from Fort Smith to watch out for them; they been stealing horses right and left, from the sounds of it."

I froze, moving in close to Blackjack's side, lowering my head and pretending to be busy with my cinch. I was glad for my wide hat brim as I held my breath, listening, glad they were walking slow.

"It *was* the Daltons," the other man replied. "Word is they've got another bunch somewheres nearby right now. Scott and the deputies've got a posse going, and they got one of them a little bit ago. Arrested him right here in town. They're gonna take him to the calaboose at Fort Smith soon as they find the other two boys and that second herd."

My heart nearly stopped at that. Grat had been arrested, and they were looking for me and Bob. I bit down on the inside of my cheek, forcing myself to wait until the two men were past and into a general store on the next block. Then I casually untied Blackjack, mounted up and trotted back the way I'd come, keeping my head down and tugging my hat down to better hide my face. Once I figured I was out of sight enough, I kicked Blackjack into a hard gallop, heading for Bob as fast as I could go.

His posture went as tense as a panther on the hunt when I flew over to him, reining in Blackjack so hard he nearly sat back on his haunches. "What is it, Em?" he demanded. "What's the matter?"

My heart was pounding and I was as out of breath as if I myself had been running instead of Blackjack. "They got Grat, Bob, and they're onto us. I heard a couple men talking. There's a posse out after us. Rogers and Scott are in it."

Bob's eyes narrowed. Before he could answer me I caught sight of two men on horseback coming toward us, and there was no mistaking Clem Rogers in the saddle of one of them. I saw his long black hair, braided in a pigtail down his back. The other man looked like Scott.

"Bob!" I hissed, jerking my head at the riders. "It's Rogers and Scott!" Blackjack danced under me, mouthing his bit and throwing his head up.

"We gotta go *now*," Bob said in a hard voice, gathering up his reins.

"What about the nags?" I asked, still staring at those two men coming toward us. They were close enough for me to see the gun belts around their waists and the stocks of rifles in their saddles.

"Leave them! *Come on*, Em, we gotta *go*!" Bob's voice was all excited. He spurred the Prince into a gallop and wheeled away, rocketing off through the tall grass. I kicked Blackjack hard and went after him, flattened out over the horse's neck.

Blackjack's mane flew back, whipping at my face and stinging my eyes till water started coming out of them. The breath came grunting out of him as he opened his stride, showing well his breeding. Once I looked back under my arm and saw not only Rogers and Scott chasing us, but about thirty or forty more, at the least. They all had guns, and they looked to me like they were catching up to us. I didn't look back again.

Bob did, though, at one point, and then he reined Prince over toward a small trail that led off the main road, plunging off into taller grass. I followed him, kicking Blackjack and digging my spurs into him—he was getting tired and I hated to push him so hard, but if we lost any speed we'd be caught up to.

There was a fence coming up, and I could see crop fields ahead. Bob gave the Prince a big kick and put him over the wire, wobbling a little in the saddle when they landed but staying on. I jumped it too, more neatly since I had time to prepare.

We kept on our way, jumping fences about every quarter mile. Finally the horses grew so tired they wouldn't jump them anymore, so Bob got off and started cutting wires. The posse had dropped back a ways; I couldn't see them any longer, but I knew they hadn't given up. We had to keep going.

We cut our way through fence after fence until I lost track of how many we'd gone through, though in my estimation we'd had to have gone a couple of miles. When we got to the last field I felt my heart like to fall down into my boots; it was full of men threshing wheat.

Bob didn't hesitate, he just barreled on through, and the men scattered out of our way and yelled out what they thought of us. We didn't pay them any mind though, until a man on horseback came plunging out of the wheat toward us.

We reined in, hard.

Bob and I both recognized him at once. It was Scott, and he was by himself, somehow having rode around to cut us off. "Get off your horses and disarm yourselves, Daltons," he ordered, but his voice sounded wobbly, like he was scared. "You boys are done. There's a posse of fifty or sixty men on your tail."

Some of the threshers picked up pitchforks, coming toward us. Bob suddenly pulled out one of his pistols and shot into the ground, as a warning. The threshers backed off, but Scott didn't run.

Bob lifted his arm and pointed the gun right at Scott. "Get out of our way, Scott, or I'll send you to hell, right here. I ain't kidding." His voice was like cold steel and he cocked the hammer back. Behind us I could hear the sound of many horses coming, faint but getting louder.

Scott's face went white and he turned his horse's tail to us, going off at a gallop. Bob put his pistol back into his holster and turned to me. "Come on!"

We kicked our lathered horses and took off, but we weren't out of the woods yet. Blackjack and Prince were tiring so that they couldn't even keep up a gallop; they kept dropping back into a canter, no matter how hard we spurred them or how often we slapped at them with our reins. I knew we'd have to somehow get ahold of fresh horses or we'd be done for. We plunged into a cornfield, the stalks whipping back at our faces as we plowed through the rows. I couldn't hear the posse anymore.

After awhile we had to slow down to let the horses breathe. Sweat was pouring off me and my heart was going like a rabbit's. I couldn't think straight and fear of being caught was eating at me. But Bob was strangely calm now. He turned in his saddle and called, "look there, Em."

The field had thinned out and on the road coming up I could see a man riding a big chestnut and ponying a tall dapple-gray mare. I knew what Bob wanted to do and my heart sank a little; I would have to leave Blackjack behind. But there was no help for it.

"Hey there," Bob called to the man, and he pulled in his mount up, looking over at us. He had a suspicious look on his face at the sight of our horses both covered in white lather, their heads hanging almost to the ground. We dismounted and so did the man.

"Seems we're in need of some fresh mounts," Bob said, his tone pleasant but underlined with iron. "What'dya say to a trade?"

The man, who looked even younger than me, shook his head. "Those studs of yours look like they're gonna drop any second," he said scornfully. "And it'd serve you right, too. If you didn't ride 'em so hard they'd serve you some better."

Bob smiled, but it was a humorless smile and his eyes looked like ice. "All right, I asked you nicely. Now we're gonna do things my way." He pulled his gun so fast it seemed to just appear in his hand, and in an instant he had the barrel under the boy's chin.

He wasn't heeled, and I doubted he would have even gone for his gun if he had been. Bob was too fast, and the kid was too scared. He froze, putting up his hands and showing us his palms. "Take them! I don't want no trouble!"

Bob took up the chestnut's reins and put himself up into

the saddle. I went for the gray mare, taking up her lead line. I led her over to Blackjack and transferred my tack as fast as I could, while Bob kept his gun on the boy till I was through. As quick as I'd been, all this had taken time and I knew the posse would have made up a lot of the ground it had lost.

I mounted up and we took off. I forced myself not to look back at Blackjack. I'd grown attached to that horse but there wasn't anything to do about it.

The mare kept my mind off it. She was wild, ornery and skittish, and she kept refusing my commands, bucking or getting light on her front feet when I put my spurs to her. We'd only gone a few yards when she up and threw me off.

I landed on soft ground, and as I picked myself up I saw Bob halt the chestnut. I caught the mare, cussing good under my breath, then got up on her again, for good this time—I was damned if I'd let her pitch me off again.

I dug in my spurs and got her good on the rump with the reins, and she got going. We were coming up on a creek bed and I braced myself, figuring she wouldn't want to cross it. On the other side I could see a little thicket of trees, with trails going off to either side of it.

"When we get across, let's split up," Bob called to me. "They'll only go after one of us and we'll have a better chance that way." He and the chestnut plunged into the water.

I gave the mare another slap with the reins and threw my spurs into her, the first time in my life I'd been so rough on a horse. She went in, then jumped the last part, almost losing her footing as she landed on the far bank. The posse was coming behind us now; I could hear horses running and men shouting to one another. I thought I even heard shots, too, but my mind was running wild and I might've imagined it.

I veered the mare to the left, and Bob went to the right. Both of us picked up speed and gave the horses their heads. I heard the posse coming still and knew they'd followed me instead of Bob. I lost sight of him but concentrated on getting as much stride out of that mare as possible.

The trail joined together again after about a mile, and Bob was already ahead of me. The posse'd fallen back aways but I knew we couldn't let our guard down—they wanted us bad, it seemed, and wouldn't give up easily.

That damned mare started her ruckus again, kicking at Bob's horse and trying to get the bit in her teeth. When I checked her she threw her head from side to side, and I thought my arms were going to tear right off my shoulders.

"I gotta get shed of this Goddamned nag," I growled to Bob. "She's gonna slow us down!"

Bob nodded. "Next horse we see, we'll switch," he promised.

We came to a road crossing our little trail, and a team and haywagon was going along it. The horses pulling the wagon were bays, small and compact, but quick-looking. Morgans, I thought. I went right up to the wagon and hailed the man driving it. This time I was the one who pulled the gun, my patience gone, desperate to be done with this whole affair. "Seems I have need of a better horse than this," I told him flatly. "I don't want to hurt anyone, I just want to trade nags."

He set the brake on the wagon and got down without saying a word. He quickly unhitched the team and got one of the Morgans out of its collar, unfastening the hames and stripping off the tailpiece, then unsnapping the traces from the whiffletrees. I got off the mare and handed her over to him without a word, still keeping my gun on him.

I took the Morgan under its bit, intending on saddling it up, but we could suddenly hear the sound of horses coming again, and close. I shot Bob a grim look and he shook his head at me. "We gotta go, *now.*"

I grabbed ahold of the Morgan's mane and jumped on, clamping on good with my legs. I'd used to ride bareback all the time when I was young but I hadn't done it in awhile. I took the long driving reins in my left hand, folding them over so's the horse wouldn't trip on them, then wove the fingers of my free hand into the horse's thick mane and took off after Bob, praying I could stay on. My coat, saddlebags and my rifle were all still on my old saddle, but I didn't dare go back for any of them.

We galloped along, pushing the horses hard. I managed to stay on but after a good half-hour I felt my lower body going numb. I called to Bob. "I gotta have a saddle or I ain't gonna make it!"

Bob checked his horse and dropped into a walk. "We gotta breathe them, anyway."

I gritted my teeth against the pain coming into my legs. "How long do you think we're gonna have to keep this up?" I asked, my dark mood making me speak my mind, instead of holding back like usual.

Bob glanced over at me. "They seem pretty determined," he replied, looking back over his shoulder.

I shifted on the horse's sweaty back and didn't answer him.

Pretty soon we came across a small section of poor-looking

crops, with a shack set next to it. There was a man out front, poor white farmer by the looks of it, getting ready to get up on a crowbait horse that looked like a dime's worth of dog meat. I could see the poor nag's ribs and it looked older than dirt, but the saddle on its back looked decent. I shot a look at Bob and he nodded.

We rode up to the man, and this time neither of us pulled our guns. Bob asked him if he'd want to sell us his saddle, seeing as how we'd come along way with me riding bareback and I was getting tired of riding that way. I wondered why Bob had said that, though; my money was still in my saddlebags on the gray mare and whatever Bob had we were going to have to hang onto as long as possible, since it was clear we were wanted by the law now.

The man wasn't any too bright, which I was thankful for. If he'd been any smarter he would've wondered why we were riding around so heavily armed with only one saddle. He scratched his head and looked at the rig, then told Bob we could have it for twelve dollars.

I slid of the Morgan and almost fell over; my legs felt as weak as newborn kittens. But I stayed upright and quickly untacked the old nag, throwing the saddle onto my mount and cinching up.

Bob talked with the cracker while I worked, and I heard him tell the man that we didn't have the money on us now, but he could come by our farm this evening to pick up payment for the saddle. I shook my head to myself and sprung up onto the Morgan. At Bob's signal we took off.

"Wait, you never told me where your place is," the man called after us.

"Don't you worry none about that, old timer," Bob shouted over his shoulder. "There's a big bunch of fellows coming along the way that'll pay you for it. They're paying our expenses on this trip." He gave the horse his head, and I did the same, and we were off at full speed before the man could reply.

NINE

WE LOST THE posse somewhere after we crossed the Kansas line, and by nightfall Bob felt it was safe for us to stop and rest. We camped along the Neosho River for several nights, then pushed on through Indian Territory, heading for Texas. From there, Bob said, we would make our way on to New Mexico, through Arizona, and ultimately California, where we planned on taking refuge with our brother Will at his ranch. He was renting a big spread on the Estrella River; Bob figured we could hole up there while we thought on what to do next.

Leaving Grat to the jail at Fort Smith was giving me pause, not because he and I were particularly close, but because he was our brother and it didn't seem right for us to go off and leave him. Bob didn't want to, either, but we both knew there was no way we could help him any. If we rode into Fort Smith, we'd like as not get ourselves shot or lynched at worse, and at best we'd end up in jail with him.

We rode hard, and we changed horses several times, trading along the way, always willingly now since we weren't pressed by a posse and didn't have to use our guns to convince anybody quick. I ended up with a big black stud again that rode a lot like Blackjack, but I didn't name him, nor get attached to him. I knew we'd likely change horses a lot from here on out.

Bob let his beard grow, and that and the hard, hunted look in his blue eyes made him look older than his twenty-one years. I let the stubble come up on my face, too; I figured they probably had descriptions of us going around. We did a lot of hunting and went without a lot of provisions since we didn't want to go into towns too often.

I suppose it was just because we only had each other to count on during that time, but Bob and I grew closer than ever. We often talked of Grat and wondered how he was holding up in jail, and about Bitter Creek Newcomb, Charley Pierce, and Dick Broadwell, wondering if they were still hanging around Newton. I wondered what had become of Bill Doolin. We talked about Mother and wondered how she and the little ones were, and how things were going on the new claim. We weren't sure if we'd ever see any of them again. I wondered if Bob ever thought about Ella Mitchell, but I didn't ask him.

One night after we'd ridden into Texas, we were sitting by our little fire, and Bob remarked, "I was surprised when you pulled a gun on that fellow with the team, that day we were being chased."

I shrugged and looked away from him, uncomfortable. "I was about out of patience just then," I said, "and that seemed like the quickest way to get what I wanted."

Bob didn't say anything, just looked at me for a long minute. A slow, kind of knowing smile spread across his face, like he was satisfied about something. When I asked him about it he just said, "now I know you got the sand I always thought you had."

———))((((———

We were riding near Santa Rosa in New Mexico one morning when my stud threw a shoe. Bob told me to head for town; we'd have to find a blacksmith. We were in need of provisions besides, and we both thought some whiskey sounded good about then. I was also hoping for a decent meal for once; I was so tired of eating game.

We were cautious as ever, but after we took a look around Bob seemed satisfied with things. We found a blacksmith and had my horse reshod, and Bob's too since we had a long way to go yet before we got to California. Bob looked over the money we had and figured after the horseshoes, livery expenses, provisions and a good meal for both of us, we'd be pretty low. I looked at him and pushed my hat back to wipe sweat from my brow. "What'd you say to a poker game, then?"

Bob nodded. "If we can both win a little bit, we should have enough to get by on."

We put the horses up at the livery, leaving them under saddle as usual. The man running the livery didn't seem to think our request was odd, in fact I saw two or three other horses there that had saddles on in the stalls.

We stopped in at a dry goods place and picked up fresh shirts, then bought more bullets and provisions for the trail.

Then we paid for a room at a hotel. Bob gave the clerk a false name, just in case. We were both caked with trail dust and a bath and a shave sounded like heaven to both of us. Going into a poker game straight off so many days on the trail might get folks to wondering where we were going, and where we'd come from.

After we'd washed up and shaved and put on our new clothes, we headed downstairs for a meal, then went out to find a game, taking our saddlebags with us, just in case. I was feeling much better about life in general by that time.

We'd seen a saloon Bob liked the looks of, a fairly quiet place on the corner near the livery. We went in and found a game with only three other players, an kindly older man and two young laborers, locals by the looks of it. They dealt us in after some exchanging of pleasantries, and shared some of their whiskey with us. Now, I'd never been a hard-drinking man by any means, not even after all I'd done back when we'd first starting stealing horses, but that night the liquor tasted damn good to me. Bob too, from the looks of it. I was glad we hadn't gotten our own bottle or else we might've let it go to our heads.

Bob and I both had a fair talent for cards, and we both had some success, but I wished Grat had been with us. We would've walked out of there rich if he had been; none of the men we were playing with were very skilled, and they didn't know when to quit. They just kept betting until they were down to the blanket. Bob and I both made sure to lose a couple of hands, though; I wanted us to be able to walk out of there with our backs turned.

Long about six o'clock, the old man bowed out, wishing

us luck on all our endeavors and taking what little money he had left with him. One of the laborers left soon after, leaving two empty places at our table. The saloon wasn't very crowded by then; only one other game was in progress on the other side of the room, and it was four old-timers with long gray beards hanging down from their chins. I didn't see any saloon girls about, which I could tell disappointed Bob, who was in the mood for one.

Everything would have been fine if we'd just left then, too, but Bob wanted to stay for a bit. Two men about Grat's age, just shy of thirty, came in and asked if they could join our game, and Bob and the other laborer agreed.

I collected my winnings and went outside to get some air, and when I came back in I leaned against the wall, picking up the old Dalton habit of watching the game for any trouble. Bob won two more hands.

By the third, though, the new players had started winning, and they kept on, every hand. They were acting fishy, too; jumpy and overly friendly. I spoke up, sharp, when I saw one of them deal from the bottom of the deck during a discard. Bob looked at me a minute, then back at the newcomers, narrowing his eyes a little. The laborer we'd been playing with all along, a fellow named Smith, got a nervous look on his face when he saw Bob's narrowed eyes.

"Now, we ain't gonna have any cheatin' in this next hand, I hope," Bob said, staring them both down as he dealt. "I don't care much for chiselers. I'd imagine that goes for Mr. Smith here, too."

Smith nodded vigorously. The other two stared back at them, innocent as babes. "We ain't chiselin'," one of them said indignantly.

Santa Rosa had a no-gun law, so our revolvers were inside our saddlebags and Bob's Winchester was still on his saddle, but he had the gun he kept hidden in his boot. I shifted my grip on my saddlebags so I could get to my gun easy if I needed it, and watched that game like a hawk.

The newcomers were either brave or stupid, because one of them pulled an ace out of his coat sleeve during the discard, when he thought Bob was distracted. I saw it, though. Before I could do anything, Bob suddenly had his gun in hand, the hammer cocked back, pointed right at the man's heart. He'd seen it, too. I got my Colt out, too, knowing I'd likely have need of it.

Everything happened fast then. Smith pushed his chair back and got out of the way. The bartender went for something under the counter, likely a shotgun, but I stopped him, ordering him to throw up his hands. I heard that same cold tone come out of me that I'd used on the fellow with the haywagon. He did as I ordered. The old men in the corner all put their hands up, too, evidently scared stiff.

Bob stood up and tossed his chair to one side, ordering the cheaters to put their hands to the ceiling. They did, and they looked scared, their faces white, sweat popping out on their brows. I figured maybe they were new to cheating at cards.

Bob swept the pot and all the money on the table into his saddlebags, then threw them over one shoulder, the gun still aimed. Then he started backing toward the door. "I ought to shoot the both of you Goddamned chiselers," Bob said to them, low and cold, "but I'll just settle for taking your money." He waited in the doorway until I was next to him, then fired a few shots into the ceiling to distract them while we got away. The old men dove for the floor, and the two cheaters ducked under the table.

"*Go*, Em!" Bob bellowed, shoving me toward the livery. Smoke was pouring from the barrel of his Colt and his eyes were wild in the light of the lanterns hung above the gallery. I ran for the livery, hearing him follow.

We went into the stable and grabbed for our horses; the owner ducked out of our way quick when he saw our guns. I thanked the Lord above we'd left the rigs on; the last thing I wanted to do was ride away bareback again. I mounted up, Bob did the same, and we high-tailed it out of there, quick as you please.

Bob was laughing as we drew abreast of each other. "Well, we took more outta Santa Rosa than we brought in," he shouted to me. "C'mon, Em, let's get the hell out of here."

TEN

GRAT HAD OFTEN talked about how beautiful it was in California, and he hadn't been exaggerating. The day Bob and I rode up to Will's spread near the Estrella River in the San Joaquin Valley, I had already decided that I'd never seen a more lovely place and that if God allowed me to live that long, I would someday settle down in California, when all of this craziness was past.

Will and his wife Jane lived in a long, low ranch house set back among lovely old oak trees, and I could see fields of wheat spreading golden behind. We found the place easy after asking a few folks we'd met along the way; Bob wasn't worried about the law now that we were all the way across the country. He said no one way out in Estrella cared about a bunch of stolen horses in Kansas.

Will had two small children, Charles, whom they called Chub, and Gracie. I'd heard from Ma that Gracie was crippled; she'd taken a fall as a baby and had never been able to walk properly since. When we rode up a little boy and a little girl were playing in the grass near the porch, and they looked up at us with big eyes as we dismounted. We figured they were Will's children; we'd never met them yet.

Bob leaned down to them. "Are you Chub and Gracie Dalton?" he asked them kindly, and they nodded.

"Well, I'm your Uncle Bob, and that there's your Uncle Emmett. You wanna tell your mama we've come to see y'all?"

Chub jumped up, a big smile on his face. He had Will's eyes and his mischievous expression. I figured he was about five. "I'll tell her, Uncle Bob!" He ran pell-mell into the house, banging the screen door behind him.

Bob smiled at Gracie again and then came over to me, where I was tying the horses to the porch rail. "Good Lord, but it's beautiful here, ain't it?" he asked me in a quiet voice. "Grat wasn't blowin' smoke." I nodded, taking in all of the oak trees, the green fields, and the sky that seemed bluer than the skies in Indian Territory or Oklahoma.

The screen door creaked, and we turned to see a young woman wearing a pale pink cotton dress come out, wiping her hands on an apron. She had brown hair run through with streaks of gold and she was pretty in the face, with big brown eyes. There was a thin gold ring on her left hand.

"You must be Bob and Emmett," she said warmly, extending a hand to us. "I'm Jane, your sister-in-law."

We shook her hand in turn, a little embarrassed at our disheveled state. She didn't seem to mind. Bob clasped his hands in front of him. "We're sorry to just show up like this, but..."

"Don't say another word, Bob, you hear?" she said with a smile. "Our home is always open to any of Will's kinfolk, and for *any* reason."

I felt relief flood me. I'd known Will would welcome us, no matter what, but I hadn't been sure what Jane would say, not having met her. Something about her made me think she wouldn't turn us out even if we told her what we'd done. After all, Will had a wild streak a mile long, so she must've been somewhat used to it.

"Why don't you put your horses up? We've got a big corral in the back you can turn them loose in, and there's plenty of hay. Then come on inside and we'll get you some dinner. I bet you're half-starved."

Bob and I thanked her and did as she said. We hadn't known a whole lot of hospitality recently, having been on the run like we were, so Jane's kindness meant all the more to us. I heaved a big sigh as we headed back toward the house, and Bob shot a look at me.

"You all right, Em?"

I glanced at him. "I'm just glad to stop running for a time."

We went into the house and came into a big front room with a big table, two rocking chairs near the front window, a camel-backed sofa and a coal heater. Jane was in a smaller room off it that was obviously the kitchen; I could hear her rattling pans on the cookstove. There was a big framed etching of a hunting scene on one wall, and a rifle was hung over the door, under a horseshoe.

"Take a seat and make yourselves comfortable," Jane called. "There's water in the washstand if you need it."

Bob and I went over to the bench by the door and poured off some of the water from the pitcher into the bowl. We took turns washing our hands and dusty faces. Then we sat down at the table as Jane brought us out plates of beef stew and biscuits.

"Go on ahead and eat up, now," she said. "Don't wait for us." She went to the door and called in Chub and Gracie, and they came up the steps, Chub helping his sister like a little gentleman. The sight made me smile.

When Jane and the children were seated and eating with us, I complemented her on her good cooking and asked after Will.

"He'll be home soon, I expect. He's attending to business in town."

When we were done eating, Jane showed us to a spare room at the back of the house, with two single bedsteads set into either corner of the far wall and a washstand under the window. There was a kerosene lamp on a little table between the beds, and a narrow chifforobe was in the corner near the door. "It's small, I know," she apologized, "but comfortable, I hope."

I smiled at her, grateful once again for her kindness. "It looks like heaven to us, Jane, after so long on the trail," I said, and it was the truth.

Bob thanked her, too, and when she'd left us to get settled, he looked at me. A kind of tightness smoothed out of his face and he lost that hunted look he'd worn in his eyes since Baxter Springs. They started to dance again with his old merriment and I could literally feel the relief go through me. Maybe now, we could relax. Maybe now, our trouble was behind us. We could find work here, and come by our money honestly from now on. I felt so cheerful just then I started whistling as I took off my gun belt for the first time in weeks and slung it over the bedpost.

We heard a child's squeal of excitement come from the front room, and the screen door banged. I heard loud boots on the floor, and Will's booming voice as he greeted the children. Jane spoke in soft tones to him, and then I heard him exclaim, "Bob and Emmett? Well, where the hell are they?"

We went through the narrow hallway and came out into the front room, and Will was there, his big, cheerful personality filling the space like a tangible thing. He gave us a big grin when he saw us. "We-ell now, looky what the cat's dragged in!"

We grinned back at him and he shook our hands and hugged us. He'd come along after Grat and before Bob, and he'd left home young, so I hadn't seen him in years, but he still had that same easygoing, fun-loving air about him I remembered so well. "My God, look at you, Emmett!" he exclaimed. "You've gone and grown up like a sturdy oak! And handsome, at that! The ladies are all over you, I'll wager."

I rolled my eyes, embarrassed, but still smiling even as my cheeks flamed. Will turned his attention to Bob then, much to my relief. "And here's the younger Marshal Dalton. Still the same dandy devil!"

I waited for Bob to tell him we weren't in the law enforcement business anymore, but he didn't. Then I looked at the children and figured he probably didn't want to say anything in front of them, just in case.

Though he would eventually grow infamous, known to history as Bill Dalton, Will was then a hard-working, affable man who'd made a name for himself in politics and worked at farming besides. In meeting folks on our way in we'd come to find that Will was generally well-liked and considered a good neighbor, though he'd held firm to that Dalton wild streak—he had a bit of a devil in him. He loved to joke and tease, and he was smart as a whip, a crack shot, and often even cockier than Bob, if such a thing were possible. He wouldn't condemn us for what we'd done, like some of our other brothers would, but he'd help us get our feet under us. My good mood grew.

Jane took the children in for their naps and then went to get an early start on supper while Will went to put his horse up. I went with him and watched as he untacked his big buckskin in its stall.

"You've come a long way in a short time, haven't you, Em?" he asked me, without looking up from his uncinching.

"All the way from Kansas," I said uneasily, and then, all of the sudden I heard myself saying words I hadn't had any intention of speaking. "We had to get out of Indian Territory, Will. We ain't in law enforcement anymore."

He glanced at me. "What're you running from?"

"The law."

"I figured that, Em. What'd you do?"

I took a deep breath. "Stole a few bunches of horses."

He looked up at me again, clearly stunned. It took him a minute to find his voice. "Well, now, I have to say I'm thrown, Em. I wouldn't put it past Bob to get mixed up in that business, since he don't give a damn about anything, but *you...*"

"We had to do it, Will! Or at least, I thought we did at the time," I said in a rush. "They pegged us for something we didn't do in Pawhuska, threw us both in the calaboose. They let me off but they charged Bob. We needed money for his defense…or so I thought at the time. It all just sorta happened. Bob got sore at this horse-rancher we were staying with and…" I let my voice trail off. What was the use of explaining?

Will looked at me, a long, steady look that was uncharacteristically sober. "So Bob got you mixed up in it, didn't he? And now you're up to your neck."

I winced at his choice of words and nodded wordlessly.

Will shook his head, letting out a sigh. "Just you?"

I shook my head. "No. Grat too. They got him in Baxter Springs, when we were going in to sell the second herd. He's locked up at Fort Smith. There was nothing we could do for him, Will. They would've shot us if we'd gone after him. As it was, we barely got out of Kansas. They had a posse on us for miles." I felt my throat clench up funny, almost like I wanted to cry. Hearing myself admit it all just made me more ashamed than I'd already been. My cheerful mood of earlier disappeared.

"So you came here to hole up," Will said, taking his horse's head in his hands and rubbing its muzzle absently.

"To get straight, Will. I don't want to do this anymore. I never wanted to do it in the first place. I want to make an honest living, like I was doing before." My voice was earnest.

Will looked at me, his face still sober. His eyes weren't twinkling. "How'd Bob get you to do it?" His voice was quiet.

I clenched my jaw. "Called me a coward," I admitted, not looking at him now.

Will sighed again. "'Course he did," he muttered, almost to himself. He kept stroking the horse's nose for a minute, like he was thinking on something, then looked at me. "Well,

Em, I ain't gonna judge you by what you did, 'cause you're still young yet, and I know how close you've always been to Bob. And I ain't a saint, either, when it comes down to it, so I got no right to come down on you much. I've got more work on this place than I've got time, so I'm glad to have the help, and I'm glad to see you, at any rate."

"Thank you, Will," I said quietly.

He came out of the stall and latched it, then walked with me back to the house. "So what do you think of Jane?" he asked shooting a sly grin at me.

"She's a sweet thing, Will. Seems to have a real big heart. Pretty, too."

He nodded, still smiling. "I reckon she's just about the best thing ever happened to me, so far, she and the young'uns," he said. He shot me a look. "We're gonna have to find you a little girl."

I chuckled under my breath. "You got one in mind?"

"None in particular," he said, "but they got socials all the time around here. Dances and the like. We'll find you one before too long." He gave me a brotherly slap on the back.

We were laughing as we came into the house. Will went to talk with Jane in the little kitchen, and I went toward the bedroom to see what Bob was doing.

He was sitting on the bed, cleaning his guns. There was a pile of bullets on the blanket beside him. He looked up at me. "You tell him?" he asked me, bluntly.

I nodded. "I told him everything, pretty much," I admitted.

Bob gave a short nod in reply, almost to himself, and kept polishing his Colt. "He gonna let us stay?"

I nodded again. "He says he's got a lot of farm work we can help with," I told him.

Bob nodded again. He stayed quiet all night, even through supper, and we both slept hard as soon as we put our heads to the pillows and drew the quilts over us. I didn't even dream.

ELEVEN

IF THERE WAS one thing my brother Will liked, it was guns. He had more of them than anyone I'd ever known, and he was good with them—he could drill a dime at ten yards and hit a moving target in the dark just by sound. When he took us around the ranch that second day, he pointed out an old oak tree shot full of bullet holes and told us he liked to keep up his target practice while he plowed by hanging buckskin off the tree and hitting it when he went past. He also had a Winchester he'd rigged up to shoot when the safety was on—why he'd ever have the need of such a gun I couldn't figure, but he was proud of it.

Bob and I would go out and practice with him after supper, laying on our backs in the barn and aiming for the holes in the shingles. I'd always been good with my Colts and my rifle but after a few weeks with Will, I became even better. Bob, who was the best shot of all of us, couldn't get much better than he already was—I pittied any poor fool who ever dared to cause Bob to draw his gun. Will and I practiced, but neither of us could ever draw quite as fast as Bob, who could shoot like a trick gunhand in a sideshow.

We relaxed a lot after the first few weeks, once it became clear that no one was out after us, but we still wore our guns all the time. Will didn't mind, and neither did Jane; she didn't ever comment on them. I guess she was used to Will and figured his brothers were the same way.

The months passed slowly. We spent our days plowing, doing other tasks around the ranch and practicing our shooting, and at night after supper Will would get out his guitar while Jane did the supper dishes and the children played on the rug set in front of the sofa, clapping their hands at the music. Will was one of the best guitar-players I'd ever heard and it was pleasant to be around a family again. Other nights we'd leave Jane and the children and go play poker together.

Sometimes we'd go to socials at the schoolhouse, as Will was always up for a good time, and Jane loved to dance. Our brother Littleton had a ranch in Fresno and a saloon in the valley, and sometimes he'd come, too, but he'd never gotten along too well with any of us and so he usually avoided our group. Bob started collecting admirers as usual—but not at the socials. He preferred the local saloons and their ware. I enjoyed myself at the socials, though, and danced with several pretty girls, but I didn't find one to take a fancy to, until one Saturday evening in early January.

———— ⊲⊙⊳ ————

"Emmett!"

I turned from where I'd been talking to Will and saw Jane hailing me from the opposite side of the room. I started over to her, moving slowly through the mass of people. There was a big turnout tonight and a lot of the guests were loitering outside since it was warm inside the schoolhouse.

"Em, I want you to meet Miss Laura Stevens. She's new here; her Pa just rented a place near my brother's."

I turned and saw a slender young woman of perhaps seventeen or so, in a dress of fine white cotton that reminded me of a christening gown. She had thick dark hair that looked as soft as silk; only half of it was pinned into a big knot at the back of her head, while the rest of it fell in soft waves down to her waist. Her eyes were as green as the leaves of the oaks around the ranch, and her face was so beautiful to me I couldn't even find words to describe it. She was smiling shyly at me and her eyes were shining in the lamplight. My chest felt like I had a weight placed on it and I couldn't seem to make my mouth work. Jane touched my arm. *"Em..."*

I started and opened my mouth. "How do you do, Miss Stevens." My voice sounded strange to my own ears, higher and squeakier than usual. I tried not to wince.

She didn't seem to notice. She just put her soft little hand in mind and smiled at me. "A pleasure, Mr. Dalton."

I shook my head. "Call me Emmett."

She smiled even bigger at me. "All right, if you'll call me Laura. I hate formality."

I figure it must've been then that Jane left us alone together, but I wouldn't notice until later. I felt like I'd been running a mile. "Care to dance, Laura?" I asked her. I didn't remember saying the words, but I heard them come out of my mouth.

She nodded, and that lovely hair swayed. "I'd love to."

One of the locals had brought a fiddle and they started up a waltz. Thankfully, I knew how to waltz, and to my great surprise I managed not to step on her toes. She was a graceful dancer, and she had a way about her that put me at ease. As I whirled her around the floor, she looked up at me and laughed, real soft, under her breath.

"What?" I smiled down at her.

She shook her head a little, following my lead easily. "You don't do this often, do you, Emmett?"

"Do what?"

"Go to socials. Dance with girls." There was a tease in her voice.

"What makes you say that?"

"Because you're not trying to smooth-talk me any. Most of the young men I meet at these things make a career out of seeing how far they can get with me. You're not trying it."

I shrugged, feeling a smile come out over my face. "Maybe I ain't that type of man."

"No, you ain't. I can tell that already. And I'm glad you asked me to dance."

"I'm glad you agreed to it." I caught sight of Will standing against the wall with Bob as we came past, and both of them were grinning at me so wide I could see every tooth in their heads. Bob looked like a hunting cat besides, and I felt my ears redden. I looked back down at Laura, determined not to let them get to me, though I knew I'd have a lot to answer to later on.

When the dance ended we applauded the fiddler, and we went outside for some air, since Laura didn't have a fan with her. I was glad to escape my brothers, and glad too that she'd let me come with her. Her neighbor, a Mrs. Lawson, was chaperoning her but she didn't bat an eyelash when she saw us leave together.

We went a little ways away from the other folks outside, and she told me about coming to California from Texas. Her Pa was looking to raise wheat, like most of the ranchers were in this area. In Texas he'd raised cattle.

"Where'd you come out from?" she asked me. "I've heard talk you and your brother Bob haven't been here too long."

I looked at her quick, feeling myself stiffen. What did she mean, *talk?* Was someone onto us? Had word come out this far, of what we'd done?

"Folks talk about us?" I asked finally. My voice sounded weak. I covered it with a quick, uncomfortable laugh.

"All the time. You Daltons are wild." She said it plain like that, like she was stating a fact. "Everyone knows who you are just by the guns you got on you." She gestured to the bulge under my coat and I gaped at her. She didn't seem scared or upset; instead she just looked at me like she was waiting for something. "You didn't answer my question, Emmett." I could see her eyes dancing in the moonlight. Her little gold earrings were swinging against her slender neck.

"Oklahoma," I answered finally, deciding not to mention Kansas, just in case. "And we ain't *that* wild."

She laughed at me, but it was a friendly, almost affectionate laugh. "They say all you boys do all day is shoot at things, even while you're plowing. My Pa says you all must go through a whole box of bullets in a day!"

"Not a whole box," I said indignantly. "Maybe half of one."

She laughed, and I laughed too, feeling better. We had a reputation, all right, but at least it didn't seem like the kind I was worried about, and Laura didn't seem to be bothered none by it. I was relieved by that, because after only half an hour in this young woman's company, I'd already decided that she was the girl I'd always wanted to find for myself. We went back inside and shared a few more dances, and by the time it was time to leave, she'd agreed to let me escort her to the next social.

Bob and I had taken our horses to the social, and Will and Jane had gone in the buggy, so by the time I got done talking to Laura, trying to stretch out the time we had together that first night, I was the last to get home. After I put my horse up in the stable and came inside, I found Will and Bob sitting in the front room, smoking cigars with a lamp turned low and apparently waiting to pounce on me. Jane must've gone to bed; the back of the house was dark.

"Well, if it ain't our little Don Juan," Will said loudly, saying the Spanish name like a gringo. I saw the flash of his grin in the feeble light and rolled my eyes to the ceiling.

"Pretty little girl you found yourself, Em," Bob chimed in, blowing smoke toward the ceiling. "What's her name?"

"Laura," I muttered, taking my gun out of my shoulder holster, then shrugging out of my coat. I knew Bob knew it already; Will would have told him.

"Oh-ho, on a first name basis, are we?" he teased.

I'd known this was coming but I wasn't in the mood for it; I hated it when any of my brothers treated me like a child, especially Bob, after all we'd gone through together. "Shut up, Bob. I ain't in the mood."

Both of them went still, like they were too surprised to speak. Will stopped smiling. I didn't stick around to see any more. I headed for the bedroom Bob and I shared.

After a few minutes the door opened and Bob came in. I was undoing my necktie at the shaving mirror and I caught his eye through it. His face was sober and he looked almost ashamed. I'd never seen him look like that before.

"I'm sorry, Em. We were just teasing you. It's all in good fun."

I started undoing the buttons on my vest. "I don't much like being teased, Bob."

"Sure, Em. We won't do it again."

I was surprised by how sincere he sounded. It chirked me up some; Bob's taking the trouble to apologize like that meant he held even more respect for me than I'd thought. He sat down and reached for the bootjack. "She seems like a sweet little girl, though," he said carefully.

I nodded. "Seems so." I turned toward him. "I didn't mean to get so sore at you, Bob. It's just that she ain't one of your saloon floozies. It ain't like that at all."

He nodded. "She reminds me a little of Ella Mitchell," he said quietly.

We didn't talk anymore; he was too lost in thought, and I was too surprised.

TWELVE

THE FOLLOWING WEEK, just two days before the next social was scheduled, I was coming in from plowing when I caught sight of a big roan horse coming up the road at a trot. I paused in the shade of an oak with one hand on my gun, waiting to see who it was, and to my shock, its rider was none other than Grat.

"Grat!" I exclaimed, a strange feeling somewhere between gladness and apprehension going through me at the sight of him.

He reined in and dismounted abruptly, meeting my eyes with his as he did so. He looked older than I remembered him, even though it had only been three months.

"Em," he grunted.

"Where...where'd you come from?" I asked stupidly, still stunned to see him.

"Fresno," he replied, not mincing words, as usual. "I headed for Lit's. Just got there yesterday, late. When he told me you and Bob were here, I got on my horse."

"Grat!" Bob called, coming around from the barn. He looked just as surprised as I felt. "What the hell happened to you?"

Grat looked at him. "They arrested me for horse-theft in Baxter Springs, that day we took the herd up there. Locked me up at Fort Smith. Then the grand jury cleared me." He looked at me again, then back at Bob. "They've got it in for you back there," he said. "There are warrants out for both of you. I heard all about that chase you led that posse on. There's a bunch of noise going on about you boys getting shot if you set foot in Indian Territory again."

Bob made a snorting sound. "The hell we will," he said angrily. "I guess we could go back there, if we wanted to. No son of a bitch is gonna get the bulge on me, not while I'm breathing." He stalked off toward the house.

I looked at Grat. "We ain't planning on going back there, so far's I know," I told him.

We started walking toward the house. I didn't say anything else. I'd grown accustomed to not having Grat around, and now that he was back that darkness in him that had always unnerved me was almost suffocating. It was clear he was full of rage for being jailed like he'd been, and I sensed a new capacity for violence in him that made me want to cringe.

Finally I felt I had to speak, so I said, "Bob and I've been working on the farm here. Staying out of trouble."

Grat glanced at me. "That won't last long," he said with finality.

"Why not?" I asked, irritated.

"Because you know Bob," was all he said. He swept past me into the house.

Finally the day came when the next social was to be held, and I felt the anticipation of seeing Laura Stevens again. Will let me take the buggy, and I went out to the Stevens place to get her.

Her Pa and Ma were nice, but they were a little cool toward me; I knew it was because I was a Dalton. Her Ma looked like she wanted to forbid Laura from going with me, but she didn't. I used my best manners with them and I'd left my gun in the buggy, just in case, but it didn't seem to help any. Laura didn't seem worried. She laughed when I mentioned something to her. "Once they get to know you, they'll be all right," she said, and I smiled. It sounded like she'd already settled on me courting her, which suited me fine.

Grat didn't come to the social, nor did Bob. They'd gone out drinking together. Will and Jane were there, though, and I introduced Laura to Will. He behaved himself and smooth-talked her, and when we were going off to waltz he winked at me. I was in such a good mood that I winked back.

All the bumbling nervousness I'd once felt around her was gone, and we talked and laughed easy with each other, both in between dances and during them. Afterward we went outside and walked along the creek bed arm-in-arm, and when she let me kiss her, I was almost glad about everything that had happened back in Indian Territory, for if it hadn't, I wouldn't have come to California, and I wouldn't have met her.

———————⊷⦅◍⦆⊶———————

On February 4th I was awakened from a sound sleep by Bob coming into the bedroom and lighting a lamp.

I was tired; I'd been up late the night before playing poker with Will and two other men, and after a full day at the plow I'd gone to bed early. Jane was off visiting her brother and his family for the evening, and Will and Bob had gone to a saloon. Grat had gone back to Fresno a few days earlier to help Lit with his land.

I rolled over and shielded my eyes against the light. Bob was leaning over the lamp, and its light illuminated the dark circles he'd had under his eyes the last few days. He'd been hitting the poker tables and the whorehouses hard lately, and I knew he was getting bored with our routine here.

"Bob?" I questioned.

"Em. Time to get up, now," he said, a strange note in his voice. He extinguished the match with a flick of his wrist and tossed it into the chamber pot under his bed.

"What the hell time is it?" I asked grouchily, sitting up.

Bob took his watch out of his vest and opened its case. "Almost midnight," he said, shutting it with a snap. "Will and I need to talk to you."

I shook myself awake, staring at him. "Now?"

"Yes, now," he replied. "It's gotta be now before anyone else comes back to the house. Get dressed and meet us in the front room," he said shortly, then left.

I stared at the door for a second, completely lost as to what Bob could possibly be talking about, then I put on my britches and shirt, pulling my galluses up over my shoulders and sliding my feet into my boots. I left my vest off.

I rubbed the heel of my hand over my eyes as I trudged out into the front room. "What's this all about?" I yawned and massaged a crick in my neck.

"Sit down, Em," Bob said briskly. He looked at Will for a minute, then back at me. "This farming venture has been a peach and all, but I'm personally sick of it—no offense," he said to Will, who didn't say anything back. Will, I noticed, had an odd expression on his face and his eyes were glinting in a different way than usual. I could tell he'd been drinking.

Bob turned back to me. "I think it's time we had a little fun, Em. Plus, it seems like we could do with a little more cash."

I felt a strange nervous flutter in my stomach. "What for?"

Again, Bob glanced at Will. "I'm not sure how much longer we'll stick around this place, Em. Could be we'll go back home pretty soon."

I jumped up, wide awake now. "Are you *crazy*, Bob? We can't go back there! You heard Grat, they've got warrants out on us!"

"Settle down, Emmett, and don't talk so loud," Bob ordered. "I ain't gonna be told where I can and can't go in this world, you understand? If I want to go back to Indian Territory, then I will. I don't give a damn about those warrants." His jaw was set and his eyeballs looked red; I could tell he'd been drinking pretty good, even more than Will. He had that old dead look in his eyes, too, the one I remembered from every time we got into trouble. The flutter in my stomach got worse.

"So what are you saying, Bob?" I asked miserably." You want to go after horses again, is that it?"

Again, my brothers shared a glance. Then Bob shook his head. "No, we ain't gonna go after nags. Just one, this time."

I sat back down and looked at him, my brow furrowing. "I ain't following you."

"The Iron Horse is what he means, Em," Will said, very calmly.

My mouth fell open and for several seconds I couldn't get my voice to work. Then I finally spoke. "You want to hold up a *train?*" My stomach turned over good this time, like I was gonna puke. I'd been hardened over the last year, all right, but nothing could've prepared me for this. I looked helplessly at Will, unable to say anything else.

Will suddenly crouched down by my chair, looking at me all serious-like. Then he started talking. "Emmett, you know how the Goddamned railroads work. They force honest farmers off land at their will. Their land-grabbing is like a Goddamned plague. The way I see it, any haul we get in a hold-up ain't any more than's due after all those bastards have done."

I was surprised at the bitterness in his voice. I'd known Will hated the Southern Pacific; most farmers did, but I never would have thought he'd approve of a plan to hold one up. And he'd said 'we.' Did that mean he wanted to take part in it? What about his political career? What about his family? And what if we all got caught, after all that effort to get away from the law back home?

Both of them were staring at me, hard. I'd never known

until now that Will got that same cold, dead expression in his eyes like Bob did, when he got angry. As usual, I was the only one to see the larger picture. They'd already made up their minds.

"Bob," I said finally, my tone cautious, "holding up a train's a sight different from stealing some nags. Have you thought about that?"

He made a snorting noise. "'Course I have. And it'll be so Goddamned easy you won't believe it." He gave me a hard look. "Now, don't you be giving me any lip, Em, about not wanting to do it. You did all them other things with me and showed me you got the guts in you, and we got to stick to-gether, remember? I know you want to reform, but you got plenty of time to reform later on. We're gonna do this, you and Will and I, and we're gonna do it to the night after next, in Alila. I got ahold of the schedule and I've figured it out, and we can get in and out clean." There was no room for argument in his voice.

"What about Grat?" I asked miserably. I didn't bother trying to stand up to him this time; I knew there was no use.

"Grat's in Fresno, so he'll have to miss this party. We'll tell him about it later, though; make him good and jealous." Bob laughed, a careless, dark laugh, and I realized he was drunker than I'd first thought.

"Come on," Will said to us. He took his six-gun from his holster and twirled it around his finger by the trigger-guard. "We'll need to practice up, just in case we run into resis-tance." He laughed suddenly. "What a damn joke this'll be!" He swept out the screen door into the darkness.

Bob started to follow, but he stopped next to me. "Cheer

up, Em," he said jovially to me, slapping me on the back. "By tomorrow night we'll be rich as Goddamn kings. You can buy that little girl of yours something pretty." He went out the door after Will, banging the door behind him and laughing.

I sat for several minutes in that dark room, unable to form any sort of coherent thought. I felt numb again, like I had back in Indian Territory. After a few minutes I got up and went to get my gun, hearing Will and Bob already shooting in the back pasture.

THIRTEEN

"YOU ALL RIGHT, Emmett?"

Laura's soft voice broke into my thoughts, and I suddenly realized with a start that it had been a long time since I'd said anything.

We were walking along the riding trail that joined her Pa's land to Jane's brother's, something we'd started doing every Saturday afternoon when there weren't socials that night. We normally talked and joked and enjoyed each other's company; sometimes she even let me kiss her or hold her in my arms as we sat together and watched the sunset, but today I couldn't muster much of a good mood and our conversation had been almost nonexistent. Late tonight Bob and Will and I would ride into Alila, so I was having a hell of a time thinking about much else.

"I'm fine, Laura," I said finally, trying to give her a smile, but it felt tight to me, like I couldn't do it proper.

She didn't miss much. She put up a pretty hand and brushed back strands of her hair that were blowing around her face, and looked at me funny, like she knew I was lying like a rug. "Why're you so quiet, then, if you're fine?" she finally asked.

I knew, of course, that I couldn't tell her what was wrong with me, that I'd been torn up inside since the night Bob had woken me with his plan. I couldn't tell her how the bottom had about dropped out of me when I'd realized that Will, who'd taken us in and promised to help us go straight, was showing to be of the same mind about certain things as Bob. I couldn't tell her that I was more scared of being called yellow and given the cold shoulder by Bob and Will than I was of being caught, even though I hated myself for it right then. So instead I settled for telling her a part of the truth—or what I figured would be the truth, no matter what happened tonight.

"Laura, Bob's thinking about leaving here soon," I forced myself to say. I'd been dreading this moment but I had to be square with her—I'd fallen hard for her; in truth she was the first woman I'd ever really loved—but if we got away with this job we'd be hunted here now, too. We'd have to leave, and I'd have to leave her behind. And if we *didn't* get away with it, I'd end up behind bars...or shot up. Neither choice left any future for us.

"So?" she said, in that bold way she had that didn't match that lovely, delicate face of hers. "So let him go. You'll stay here, won't you?" She reached for my hand and held it between both of hers.

I bit my lip and looked away, suddenly unable to look her in the face. "If Bob wants to go, I'll have to go with him," I said.

"Why?" she asked, her voice going sharp, and I could tell she was real upset. "Why does it matter what *Bob* wants?

What about what *you* want?" She'd stopped walking by now, just stood there in the middle of the path with the hem of her dress dragging in the dust.

I let my breath out and faced her. "He's my *brother*, Laura. I gotta stick with him, no matter what."

Even as I'd said it I'd known she wouldn't understand, and I could see in her face that she didn't. Her eyes seemed to go a darker green and I realized she was holding back tears. "So that's it, then, is it? You're sayin' there ain't no chance for us at all, if Bob leaves?"

I tried to keep myself together; Lord knows I tried hard, but it didn't work. I felt all sorts of feelings coming up in me then, but the only one I could seem to get out was frustration. "You can't go with me, Laura. And if you knew why, you wouldn't even want to." I pulled my hand out of her grasp.

"How do you know?" she threw back at me. "Maybe I want off that ranch. Maybe I don't want to be stuck in this little nothing town for the rest of my life." She suddenly grabbed at my hand again, her voice changing. "Maybe you've done some things, Em. Maybe you ain't proud of them. I know you don't want to say it. But maybe I don't care about what you've done. Maybe all I care about is what you're gonna do from here on out."

I swallowed hard and stared down at her. I never had understood women-folk too well; that intuition they had spooked me sometimes, like hers was doing now. I'd never said a single word to her about anything I'd done, or anything Bob had done, or what he wanted me to do now. But she seemed to know it all anyway.

Finally my voice started working again, but I didn't seem

to have any control over what came out of it. I heard myself say, "how did you…"

She was crying now, softly. "You got all them guns on you all the time. You and your brothers never come to church. They say you showed up all of the sudden and would never say anything about why you came out here. I figured you must've done something to run away from. But it doesn't matter to me at all. I *know* you're a good man, Emmett. I know you didn't mean whatever it was you did."

I had to end this. Bob would never let me agree to take her with us, and I couldn't condemn her to a life on the run, no matter how much she said she didn't care. I knew she *would* care, if she went and did it. And I had honor in me. Mother had seen to that.

"I wouldn't be a good man if I took you with me, Laura," I said to her, hearing my voice sort of catch on itself. I took ahold of her shoulders, gently, as she kept crying. "I'd be forcing you into a life you ain't ready for, and wouldn't want. I'd only end up hurting you. So you need to forget about me. I know what I'm doing."

My voice had steadied and it sounded strangely calm. I put my hands in her hair and brought her face forward, but I only kissed her forehead, instead of her lips. "I'm sorry, Laura. I'm sorry I spent all that time with you. If I'd known how things were gonna turn out here, I wouldn't have, I swear it."

She didn't say anything; she was crying too hard. The sound hurt me like a physical thing, but there was nothing I could do about it. "Come on, I'll take you home."

She suddenly shook her head, violently, and twisted

herself out of my grasp. Then she turned and ran back the way we'd come, toward her house, her hair tumbling down over her shoulders.

I stood for a few minutes where she'd left me, and numbly I watched her go inside. Then I slowly turned for where I'd tied my horse, farther up the lane.

As I mounted up I thought again about that plan Bob and Will had hatched. It didn't scare me now like it had earlier. Maybe I'd get shot in the process. The thought didn't bother me none anymore.

FOURTEEN

WE LEFT THE house at dusk, enough guns on us for a small army. I had my two Colts and my Winchester, and Bob and Will had the same, plus both of them had guns in their shoulder-holsters and guns hidden in their boots. Bob made us all tie black neckerchiefs around our necks to pull up over our faces, and Will and Bob had on long black frock coats. Our hats were pulled down low over our foreheads.

When we got to the outskirts of Alila, we stopped behind an outcropping of big rocks so that Bob could go over the plan one more time.

We were to take the train just before it was to roll out of the depot. I would flag her down, and then Bob and Will would enter and find the express car and the safe by way of whatever company men they found inside. I was to follow them and cover the passengers, and also keep any would-be heroes from trying anything. None of us were to shoot any persons unless we had to defend ourselves; Bob expected we would have to fire some warning shots to get our point across, though. Our horses would be tied at the corner of the building so we could get to them fast once we were out.

I hadn't said a word to either one of them since we'd left, and before then I'd only spoken to them when necessary. The afternoon with Laura had made me quite sure I wouldn't ever let myself care deeply about anything again, and so I'd just done as they'd said. Strangely, neither of them had pressed me on what was making me so apathetic. Bob threw glances my way as we rode, but he left it alone. I supposed he was too busy anticipating the job to try and get to the bottom of my unpleasant disposition.

When we were in sight of the depot Bob took out his watch and checked it. I heard him mutter "almost..." under his breath to himself. He checked his horse, which was fidgeting underneath him. Will moved his jaw back and forth and kept rearranging his reins. I sat on my horse and did nothing, not even sick to my stomach like I always had been before we'd stolen horses.

At Bob's signal we rode down and circled around to the back of the depot, tying our mounts to a small tree near the building's corner. Crickets were chirping and I heard a coyote yap somewhere off in the distance. My horse swished its tail at a fly and stamped a hoof. The noise sounded loud on the packed dirt.

I pulled my Winchester out of the saddle skirt and waited while Bob and Will got themselves ready. There wasn't anyone around. Bob and Will pulled crowbars from the skirts of their saddles, where they'd jammed them in alongside their rifles.

Then we waited. Will rolled a cigarette and only took a few pulls off it before he ground it out with his boot. That small gesture and the way he'd been messing with his reins earlier were the only signs he was nervous at all; otherwise someone might've thought he was out for a leisure-ride on a cool night. Bob looked keyed-up, excited. His eyes were as wild as a spooked horse's in the dim moonlight. He kept fingering his guns.

We heard a whistle, low, in the distance, and the telltale rumbling of a train. I shifted my weight from foot to foot, listening to my spurs jingle softly, and then moseyed on toward the platform, easy-like. When the train got closer I took my hat off and hailed it, still feeling strangely calm. I think, at that moment, I was absolutely sure I wasn't going to live through that night. The idea didn't rile me up any.

As the train came to a halt, I stepped back into the shadows to raise the bandana over the bridge of my nose, while Bob and Will, already masked, sprang forward.

They burst into the first car, guns at the level, and I came up behind them.

There were only a few passengers in that front car. "Don't any of you be courageous, now!" Bob shouted, his voice deeper and gruffer than usual. He shot into the ceiling and a few of the passengers let out screams.

The engineer came rushing through the car toward us, but I leveled my rifle at him, and he stopped cold, looking like he'd seen a spook. "Stay where you are, and let them go about their business," a cold, matter-of-fact voice said. I blinked when I realized it was my voice. He stayed where he was.

Bob and Will eased past the engineer, pretty as you please, and I followed more slowly, keeping my gun on that engineer and watching those passengers. I made the engineer walk in front of me, nice and slow, into the next car, where I could keep an eye on both him and the two cars of passengers I was in between. Everyone seemed scared stiff and no one tried anything.

Another company man appeared in front of Bob and Will then; the fireman, I thought. Will cocked back the hammer on his other Colt and said, calmly, "You wanna show us the way to the express car, friend?"

The fireman looked scared, but he held his ground. Even from where I was standing I could see sweat popping out on his forehead, making tracks on his sooty skin as it ran down his face. Bob shifted his posture a little to a more threatening stance. "He ain't gonna ask you again, and neither am I. Take us to that car, now!"

The man nodded. "Easy, easy...this way." He started moving.

I kept easing the engineer forward. None of the passengers tried to get up or pulled anything. I'd lost sight of Will and Bob; they were two cars up, but I figured I should stay where I was and keep the engineer busy staring down the barrel of my rifle.

I heard a ruckus somewhere ahead, the sound of crowbars going at metal. The express messenger had most likely refused to open the car, and Will and Bob had taken the bars to it. I waited. The engineer kept his eyes down and his palms up. There was sweat shining on them.

The ruckus in the back stopped, and it got real quiet. All of the passengers were afraid to say anything; most of them seemed afraid to breathe. One or two women sniffled into their handkerchiefs.

Come on, *Bob,* I thought to myself. I was sweating, now. The strange apathy that had been on me since I'd watched Laura run off seemed to lift, and I felt a wild desire to get out of there start to climb up on me, like an animal going up a tree.

I heard a scramble from that back car, and a shot. I heard Bob curse, and the sound of crowbars on iron again.

Suddenly, one of the passengers in the back of the car I was facing got up. "Sit back down, now!" I growled. He didn't, so I shot above him, aiming for the ceiling.

He sat down, quick, amid more screams and gasps. My aim had been just a little off, and the shot had ricocheted. Before I could try to figure where it had gone, I heard more shots from the back of the car. A voice cried out, the distinctive cry of a wounded man, and I heard Bob curse again. Then more shots came.

I ordered the engineer to the floor and ran toward the express car, my boots and spurs thudding loudly. My heart started pounding with a sickening rhythm and I grew short of breath. Something had gone wrong, I could feel it.

When I got to the door of the express car, which was scarred and damaged from the crowbars, I saw the fireman slumped over on the floor, bleeding from a bullet wound in his gut. His face was gray, his eyes were closed and I could tell he was mortally wounded. Bob and Will were throwing down their crowbars in disgust. The safe was still sealed, their bags empty.

There was a roaring noise in my ears, but I could still hear the sound of boots running up the aisles of the cars we'd come from. They were after us, a man was dead, and the whole thing was going to hell.

"Come on!" Bob barked, and he ducked out the express car's back door. Will followed, and so did I, still hearing men coming.

We leapt from the train and hit the ground hard; I stumbled but was back on my feet in an instant. Bob had turned in mid-run and was firing at the car with both Colts, running backwards. The company men were firing back.

"Leave it!" I screamed at Bob, and lunged for my horse. I was up and going away from there before Bob and Will even got their horses untied, but as I maneuvered my horse over the uneven ground, I heard them coming behind me. There were still shots going off, but they were growing fainter. I slapped my reins across both sides of my horse's neck and opened him up as we got to the trail we'd used to get here. Then I veered off, going wild into the brush, heading for the mountains, where we'd agreed to head. Bob and Will were following.

We rode hard, pushing through thick shrubbery and crossing small streams. When we thought we were far enough away, we checked the horses, who were sweating and spooked good.

"There's a cave up here aways," Will said tensely, the first words any of us had spoken since we got on our horses. Bob nodded, drawing his wrist across his brow. A coyote howled somewhere close, and my horse snorted and threw his head up, almost rearing. I got him calmed quick and we went off, single file, into the woods, with Will leading the way.

Bob kept looking back over his shoulder, and I spoke up. "They ain't gonna track us tonight, Bob. They'll wait till daylight, and we'd better be elsewhere by that time."

We didn't speak again until we'd reached the caves Will knew about. They were big enough to lead the horses into aways. They didn't want to go in, but we forced them, and Will went back out and tried to scuff out some of our tracks.

"What happened back there?" I blurted out, when Will had come back inside. It was too dark for us to really see each other, but we didn't dare light a fire.

There was a silence, and then Bob spoke. "The son of a bitch wouldn't open the safe," he said. "And he wouldn't open the door before that. Whole thing took too damn long." He was angry, I knew, that his plan had failed, and that we were now empty-handed and on the run again instead of scot-free and rich.

"Who shot the fireman?" I asked, bluntly.

There was a pause. "I don't know," Bob said, finally.

"What do you mean, *you don't know?*" My voice sounded hard, even to me.

Will shifted from boot to boot; I could hear his spurs rattle. They were bigger than the ones Bob and I wore, flashier, and they made more noise. "There were all kinds of shots going off when he was hit, Em. We heard *you* fire, *we* were firing…"

Something dropped out of me then and I almost keeled over. I felt like I was gonna puke for real, this time. I'd fired that wild rifle shot. I hadn't seen where it'd gone. What if *I'd* hit the fireman?

I turned away from them for a minute, squeezing my eyes shut, hard, willing my stomach to stop its flopping. I tried to catch my breath. Maybe it hadn't been my bullet. I *had* to believe it hadn't been. Otherwise I figured I just might lose my mind for pondering on it so.

"Em? You all right?" Will moved a little closer to me in the darkness.

"I ain't sure," I said weakly.

"Don't get weak between the ears on me, now," Bob said. I heard his boots scuffing against the rocks and the horses shifting around restlessly. The coyotes started up again outside. One of my brothers reached over and put a hand on my shoulder, bracing me. I figured it was Bob. Some of my nausea passed.

"Well, that whole thing sure went to hell, didn't it?" Will asked us. His tone was light, like our situation was funny. "The Sheriff'll be out soon, I bet, and the damned railroad's got its own lawdogs. We should split up. I'll go on back to the house first. You boys come on along after awhile, but come by one of the roads. We gotta play this right—if people don't see any of us for a couple days they're gonna figure we had something to do with it."

I wondered, through all those strange uneasy feelings I was having, how Will seemed to have things all figured out, like he was some kind of experienced robber. As far as I knew he'd never taken part in anything like this before. I didn't ask him; my mind was still working on how we were gonna get out of this new mess we found ourselves tangled in.

FIFTEEN

WILL LEFT THE cave just before dawn, telling us to lay low for a few hours before we followed. When he'd gone Bob talked with me about how we'd hide out over at Will's for a day or so before we left the area. I knew he planned on us going back to Indian Territory, which I still thought was a bad idea, but when I half-heartedly pointed this out he just told me that the law would want us worse here than there, now. He seemed to have things all figured out, as usual. I was trying to keep my mind off that fireman, and also trying to plan ahead for whatever we might face. As miserable as I'd been all day, and as downtrodden as I felt now, I'd thought on it a little more and realized that I wanted to live, and I wanted to live free. The idea of capture was seeming pretty grim to me by now.

Will and Jane's home had a small attic, and Bob had fixed it up for hiding out in before we'd left on this little disaster. There was a small door he'd rigged to lead up into it, and he'd hauled an old feather-tick up there, in case we had to stay still and quiet. Will, he told me, would hang the big etching from the front room over the door to hide it if anyone came snooping around the house. They'd thought, it seemed, of everything.

Toward the afternoon, Bob thought it was safe for us to leave the cave, and we cautiously walked our mounts out of there, looking around as we did so. No one was in sight; we were pretty deep into wild country. We walked the horses over to a nearby stream and let them drink, then got on and started for Will's, keeping to the trees awhile.

Long about the time we got close, Loughlin McDonald, a neighbor of Will's who we were friendly with, came trotting up the road behind us, hailing us to stop. Bob threw a glance at me, like he was warning me, and put a hand near his hip.

"Bob, it's *Loughlin*, for God's sake," I hissed, under my breath.

"Everyone's an enemy right now, Em," Bob replied in a low voice. We waited, tensely, as McDonald came up to us and reined in.

"Sheriff O'Neil and another fella are coming this way; seems like they might be heading for your brother's place," he said without preamble. "I thought you boys might want to know. They didn't look like they was just out on a pleasure ride." He gave us a pointed look, then reined his horse away and went off toward his ranch. My heart sank—we were suspected already, it seemed. I looked at Bob, and we both kicked our horses into a run, heading for Will's. We veered off the road and went the back way, cutting across ranch land so we wouldn't call as much attention to ourselves.

"What are you doing?" I cried to Bob after we'd gotten into the barn. He was quickly untacking his horse. "We ain't got time, Bob!"

"We can't leave the rigs on, Em," Bob shot back. "If they search the barn they'll see the tack still on the horses and know someone just came back here. Get your saddle off, quick!"

He was right. Grimly I began yanking the cinch loose on my saddle.

"They're lathered," I pointed out as I pulled the saddle blanket off. There was a darker rectangle of sweat on my horse's back where it'd been. "It's clear they've been running aways."

Bob shook his head and dumped his saddle on a stall partition. "Will can say he's been plowing with them. Get a move on, Em!"

I put my saddle away and hastily threw my bridle onto a nail as we went out the door. We ran across the yard, scattering the chickens that were pecking there, then burst in through the back door.

Will was in the lean-to and he looked strangely amused by the whole affair; his eyes were twinkling and there was a funny little grin on his face. "I heard," he said, when he saw Bob about to speak. "One of the McDonald boys came up and told me they were coming. You'd best make yourself scarce. I'll hold 'em if when they come. I don't dare go up with you. O'Neil knows me too well and he'll get suspicious if I ain't around."

We didn't waste any more time. We scrambled up into the attic, and I heard Will hang the heavy gesso frame over the door. Then I heard his boots recede up the hall toward the front room.

Bob backed away from the door and laid out across the bed on his stomach, facing the door. He took out one of his revolvers and held it in his hand at the ready. I followed suit and we laid there, silent, ready to shoot anyone who came through that door.

We heard nothing at all for a good long while. Then we heard Jane rattling around in the kitchen as she cooked. Will must've swung one of the children up in the air; I heard a child give a squeal and a shriek of laughter.

A little later I heard the inevitable knock at the front door, and the sound of two strange men's voices.

"Come on in, Ed," I heard Will say loudly. The floorboards creaked.

"This is Bill Smith. He's a detective for the Southern Pacific," the Sheriff said.

"Mr. Dalton, I won't mince words, here," Smith said. "There was an attempt on the Alila train last night. A man got shot up and killed. Word is your brothers might be involved."

"Well now, that don't seem right to me, Bill, but I got quite a few brothers, for a fact. You want to let me know which ones you're meanin'?" Will was talking very loudly, I noticed. He always spoke in a booming voice but this was almost theatrical. I looked at Bob and winced.

"All of you Daltons are suspects, quite frankly," Smith said. His tone was less than friendly. "I'm looking for Bob and Emmett and Gratton right now, though."

"My brother Gratton's in Fresno," Will said firmly. "You won't find him anywhere near these parts. And Bob and Emmett left the state day before yesterday."

I heard boots shift on the floorboards. "You sure about that, Dalton?" That was O'Neil's voice, and he didn't sound convinced.

"Look around, if you'd like," Will said. "You won't find them here."

I heard them come across the front room and begin pacing the house. My heart seemed to stop for a minute when I heard them come right up below the door. They paused, then I heard them go into the bedrooms. I thanked God we hadn't left any of our belongings laying about.

They walked back into the front room, and I heard O'Neil speak. "Well, Will, I suppose they're not here. But I'm not so sure they won't be showin' up sometime soon."

I heard Will laugh, a big, rolling laugh, and then he said, "They won't be, Ed. And how about you and Smith here stay for supper?"

If I didn't have a bottom to my body, I believe my heart would've fallen right out onto the bed. I shot another panicked look at Bob. He met my eyes, clearly aggravated, too, but didn't say anything; we didn't dare speak. As we were finding out, sound carried well in this house.

Irritation flooded me as I lay there, my palm growing sweaty around the handle of my gun. Will, ever the jokester, would think this whole situation hilarious, no matter that he'd taken part in the holdup.

"Well, I think we'll just take you up on that, if you're sure it's no trouble," O'Neil said. I bit down, hard, on the inside of my cheek. Bob was gritting his teeth.

For what must've been over an hour, we lay there like that, our guns still at the ready, listening to the faint clinking of silverware against plates. Will and O'Neil talked politics. Heat from the cookstove and the coal heater rose up into the attic and made sweat come out on our brows. I didn't want to even move my arm to wipe it away for fear I'd make a noise; pretty soon it started running down into my eyes. I heard Jane clearing dishes below, and prayed that they'd leave soon, even though I knew they probably would smoke some cigars down before they went on their way.

A little while later I heard Will get out his guitar, and I resisted the growing urge to shoot something. I bit my cheek again, so hard I drew blood this time. Another guitar started; O'Neil must've been playing the other one Will owned. I'd often heard talk around the socials about what a good guitar player the Sheriff was, and I had visions of them playing together all night. I looked over at Bob and he rolled his eyes.

As they played, they sang or talked. I heard the sound of pacing boots the whole time, going up and down the hall and the front room. Finally O'Neil stopped playing and said, "Smith, why don't you sit down, man? You're gonna wear a damn hole in the floor."

"We should be out tracking those fellows, not sitting here making music," Smith shot at him. "I'm not entirely convinced they're really gone, as you say." He must've been talking to Will, now.

"Why, Mr. Smith, I've got no reason to lie to you," Will said in a wounded voice. "Even though they're my brothers, you can be assured I'd tell you if I knew that they'd done something they shouldn't. I've got a lot invested in this community, you know." He was talking good and loud, again.

I shook my head to myself and fought the urge to laugh. Despite our discomfort and the seriousness of the situation we were in, the events taking place were so absurd they were almost funny. *You Goddamned devil, Will,* I thought.

Glancing over at Bob, I could tell right away that he didn't share my amusement. His eyes were narrowed and his face was flushed red, he was so mad. The knuckles of his hand were white as he clutched his gun. I didn't envy Will when Bob got out of the attic.

My urge to laugh grew and I stuffed my fist into my mouth to hold it back. My middle shook and I felt my eyes start to water.

"Knock it off, Em!" Bob hissed at me in a whisper so soft I could barely hear it. I squeezed my eyes shut and turned my face away from him, fighting to do as he said.

I finally managed to get ahold of myself, right as I heard Will say, even more loudly, "it's late and you fellows have come a long way. Why don't you bunk down here for the night?"

"God damn you, Will!" Bob swore, still whispering.

"He must have a reason," I whispered back, speaking for the first time since we'd come up there.

"Reason, my ass," Bob replied. The fingernails of his free hand dug into the surface of the feather-tick. "He's treating this whole thing like a damn joke!"

I heard Smith's boots start pacing again, and I smacked Bob's arm to get his attention. When he looked at me I put a finger to my lips. He shut up, but he looked grim.

O'Neil and Smith must've accepted, cause I heard the brass bedsteads in our room rattle with their weight, and pretty soon they were snoring loud enough to wake the dead. I thought I heard Will laugh softly as he went into the big bedroom with Jane.

Neither Bob nor I slept a wink that night.

SIXTEEN

WHEN HE WAS sure the lawmen had been gone long enough that next morning, Will moved the etching and slowly opened the door, calling out to us. "You can come out, now."

We got clumsily off the feather-tick and put away our guns, then squeezed through the trap door. Bob glared at Will the second he was out of there and for a minute I thought he might try to fight him. "What in the *hell* did you think you were *doing* last night?" he exploded. "Did you think that was *funny*, trapping us up there?"

Will held up his palms and backed off a little ways. Bob was much taller than he was and when he was mad like this he was as strong as an ox. "Easy, now, Bob, just put your horns away, hear? I knew what I was doing. Keeping them over like that lowered their guard some. I had to be sure they were satisfied you weren't here and weren't gonna ride in; otherwise they might've had men on the house all night and all day today. But I went out and took a look this morning when I did the barn chores; there ain't anyone around. I checked the whole property, too, pretending to ride the crop fields."

Bob calmed down some, but I could tell he was still good and mad. He stalked away from us and went out to the privy. I was so thirsty my tongue felt like cotton, so I headed for the kitchen. Will went with me and I threw him a sideways glance. "You got a good laugh out of it, though, didn't you?" I smiled at him; I couldn't help it.

He grinned back. "I sure did."

I shook my head and laughed under my breath. "You're a damned devil, Will, you know that?" I reached for the dipper in the water bucket and took a long drink.

Jane was looking at me in concern. "Emmett, you've got circles under your eyes. I'll bet you didn't get a bit of sleep last night, did you?" She threw a disapproving glance at Will.

I shook my head. "I surely didn't, not with that racket those two were making. I never heard anyone snore so loud!"

Will laughed, then sobered as Bob came back inside, calm now. He got himself some water, then looked at me. "I reckon it's time to go, Em."

"Cut out through them hills in back, Bob," Will said. "There's caves and places to lose your tracks for a good twenty miles or so."

Jane had prepared some provisions for us, and we took them and kissed her cheek in turn. I'd miss her; she'd been kind to us, and had put up with a lot.

"You boys be careful, now. And you're always welcome with us," she said. We didn't say goodbye to the children; Bob was afraid one of them might accidentally say something to somebody. There wasn't a doubt in our minds that there'd be a posse out after us, and the less the children knew, the better.

Bob and Will went outside to get the horses ready, but I paused for a minute, turning back to Jane. "Jane, if you see Laura Stevens…" I cleared my throat a little and looked down at the toe of one of my boots. I'd scuffed it up good when I'd stumbled coming off the train. "She won't likely want to hear anything about me, but if she does…tell her I'm sorry." I didn't wait for an answer, just turned and headed for the barn.

Will had my horse almost tacked, and I thanked him and finished up. He'd filled our canteens from the pump out back. After a few seconds watching us, he reached into his coat pocket and pulled out two boxes of bullets, handing one to each of us. "You plannin' on heading back home?" he asked gravely.

"More than likely," Bob replied, putting the bullets into one of his saddlebags. "I ain't gonna let a few head of stolen horses keep me from going where I want to."

"Well, I know I don't need to tell you this, but watch your-selves." He seemed unable to say anything else. Instead he just followed us silently as we led the horses out of the barn and mounted up. I turned in my saddle and leaned down to grasp his hand, real quick. Bob did the same. Then we took off, none of us ever having been real good at goodbyes.

As we were cantering away I looked back at him, once. His face was a little pale and he looked troubled; perhaps he had some inkling as to what would transpire for him over this whole affair. I turned back to follow Bob as we pushed on, heading off the ranch and into wild country, leaving our life there for good. Laura Stevens' lovely face appeared in my mind then, but I shook myself out of thinking about her, for it wouldn't do me a damn bit of good.

There was a posse out after us; we were sure of that, though we never saw anyone. We rode harder than we ever had, both of us plagued by a nagging feeling that we were being watched at every turn. For several days we didn't even stop to camp, instead just eating out of our saddlebags and letting the horses graze here and there. We braced ourselves with whiskey.

Bob talked to me a lot, as we went. He told me how the failure at Alila weighed on him, and how it had been sloppy on his and Will's part. He hated sloppiness; that part of it bothered him almost more than the fact that we hadn't gotten any return on our investment, so to speak. He was especially angry about the fireman getting shot; he considered that an unnecessary turn of events.

I was still upset over that, too; there'd been no reason for the man to die and I still had the nagging, nauseating fear that I might have been the one that had fired that fatal shot. I never confessed that fear to anyone, though, and it festered within me like a wound. I wondered if I'd ever be able to stop thinking about it.

I set it aside, some, when Bob told me he figured we'd have to try another railroad, whenever we got to where we were going. He said he wanted more men with us this time, so nothing would get botched.

"Who do you have in mind, Bob?" I asked him. I was so tired from being on the trail so long, and heartsick at leaving Laura behind, that the fight had gone out of me as far as our latest pastime was concerned. I didn't try to talk him out of it. He wanted to correct our mistakes, and I knew I'd have to go.

"Newcomb, Pierce and Broadwell," he said breezily. "Those boys are always up for a lark. We'll look them up. I know a fella by the name of Charlie Bryant that'll be willing, too."

I didn't answer, just hoped that maybe something would happen that would turn Bob's mind off of it somehow, though I knew it wasn't likely.

We came to a little town on the California border, and we finally braved going into a store there for provisions. Both of us had good beards going by that time; we'd been clean-shaven for most of our time at Will's so we figured the whiskers were disguises enough. No one bothered us or looked at us funny. Bob got a paper, too, and he looked at it later when we camped. That's how we found out that not only Will, but Grat, too, had been arrested on suspicion of the Alila job. They would be put on trial later in the year.

"Grat wasn't anywhere near that train!" I said, pounding my fist against the ground in frustration. "There must be witnesses to put him in Fresno!"

"There will be," Bob said calmly. "He'll get off, Em, don't worry."

But I couldn't help worrying. The paper referred to us as "the Notorious Dalton Brothers." We were getting a reputation, it seemed, and I wasn't sure I liked that. Bob, however, seemed to thrive on it, and that day was the first time I realized that my brother craved notoriety. I hadn't seen it until that moment.

"Just you wait, Em, until we get those boys with us and get back to country we know well," he said. "Once we get started, we'll be bigger than the James Gang." There was a gleam in his eyes as he took the paper from me and crumpled it into a ball, then tossed it into the fire and watched it burn.

"Bob," I said carefully, "look at what happened to Jesse James—murdered in front of his own wife and children. Look at what happened to our cousins."

Bob looked at me square, his eyes boring into mine. "That ain't gonna happen to *us*, Em. If we plan things right, pick and choose our jobs, we'll come out on the winning side and richer than you can imagine. And so long as we have the right men to ride with us, no one'll get the bulge on us. Trust me. I got it all figured out. Everything I want in this life, I'm gonna get out if it, and I ain't gonna let anything get in my way."

There was something about the way he said it that left no room for doubt, as though just by saying the words it would all come to pass exactly the way he wanted. I had never shared Bob's cockiness, his bravado or his capacity for violence, but there was something in me that found it impossible to doubt him when he spoke like that. Something in me believed him, even though it was against my better judgement; something in me wanted to follow him even though I knew it was wrong. The paper he had just burned seemed to prove the point I had pondered so long ago, camping by that lonely cemetery the night before we'd gone into Newton. It looked to me like they'd arrested Grat for a crime he'd had no part in, simply because his last name was Dalton. It seemed they had a score to settle with us.

Well, I thought grimly, we had our own score to settle now, with the law we'd once upheld, and I would help settle it. I had nothing to lose now, nothing to hold onto except my brothers. Bob had always guided me, both when we were children and over the past two years. I'd always trusted him before. I had to keep on trusting him.

SEVENTEEN

"TIME TO GO, boys. Gather your parts, get your guns and let's be off."

Bob's voice, raised in volume and cool in tone, woke me from the doze I'd been in, and I sat up from my bedroll in the corner, wincing at the soreness in my back from sleeping on the hard dirt floor of the dugout near some abandoned ranch-land we'd been calling home the last few weeks. All around me, the others were getting to their feet and collecting their guns as Bob watched from over near the door, cradling his Winchester like a child, one leg bent jauntily at the knee, the spur on that boot gleaming in the dim light from the lantern.

Bitter Creek Newcomb slung his gun belt around his waist and cinched it, sliding his six-guns into the holsters, throwing a carefree, excited grin at me like that of a kid about to go downstairs on Christmas morning. On the other side of him, Charlie Bryant shook himself awake and reached for his rifle, then put on his hat, pulling it down low over his brow.

We'd been back in Indian Territory for over two months now, laying low and gathering men for our cause. Bob had finally picked a job for us, our first since Alila. We were to take the Santa Fe train at Wharton, and this time, Bob had said, there would be no mistakes.

I eyed Bryant as he sauntered over to Bob. Often called "Blackfaced Charlie" due to a powder burn on his cheek, Bryant was a former cowboy like myself and Bitter Creek. I'd seen for myself that he was a good shot and daring almost to the point of insanity, but something about him gave me pause. He didn't have much to brag about in the way of brains, which Bob liked, for it made Bryant less likely to cross him, in his mind. He was also trigger-happy. I was afraid these traits would make him more likely to botch things up, but Bob, as always, was the boss, and when I'd brought forth my concerns he'd just told me we'd see how things went.

I pulled my watch out of my vest and peered at it as I got myself together. The dugout was always so dark I could never tell what time it was by the light. I saw that it was nearing the supper hour. We were to ride to a concealed spot about ten miles out from the station, and then just before the train pulled in we'd head out and begin.

As usual, Bob went over things with us for a final time when he was sure we were all awake and ready to go. Bryant would stay with the horses which we would hitch at the stock-yards. Bob, Newcomb and myself would take the engine and get them to move the train up the track to the stockyards. Once there we'd have them uncouple the engine and open the express car, take the haul and get back to the horses.

It was a warm night out, for May. The air was unusually still and the stars were coming out bright in the clear sky. We rode slowly but with purpose to the little outcropping of rocks Bob had scouted out, and waited, Bob checking his watch every so often. Bitter Creek sat on a boulder, drumming his fingers against his knee. Bryant smoked and paced. I stroked my horse's neck absently, listening to the familiar sounds of night—the crickets, night birds, and the rustling of animals on the hunt in the tall grass.

Bob's watch snapped shut again and he spoke, tensely. "Let's get a move on."

We hitched the horses and left Charlie with them, who stood smoking his cigarette at the fence. I watched the end of it glow in the darkness, then followed Bob and Bitter Creek, our spurs jingling softly in a rhythm as we walked back to Wharton.

Silently we crouched in the shadows of the decrepit-looking depot, well-concealed by the darkness, our bandanas up around our faces. My heart was racing so fast I was sure they could hear it, but neither of them looked in my direction.

The train was coming now, right on schedule. I could hear its faint whistle and the rumble of its wheels. Somewhere off in the distance a couple of wolves let out long howls in response to the whistle.

"Here she comes," Bitter Creek remarked, an eager note to his soft voice. He pulled out one of his revolvers, and Bob did the same. As the train roared to a stop before us, I pulled out my own Colt.

We made for the engine, and heard the conductor give the signal to move out. We sprang then, leaping up into the engine's cab.

"Evenin', boys!" Bob called out as we entered, his gun leveled. The engineer and the fireman turned toward us, their faces going pale, their hands rising to the ceiling. "Wonder if you could do us a favor," Bob drawled pleasantly. "Take her on up to the stockyards, if you please. Do what you're told, now, and no one'll get hurt."

They hesitated, clearly scared out of their wits. Bob cocked the hammer back on his other revolver and raised it, making his point. "Go on, now. Get a-movin'."

They scrambled to do as he said, sweating now. Hovering in the doorway behind Bob and Bitter Creek, I glanced back and saw the conductor hovering in the doorway of the next car, his eyes wide. I faced him and raised my gun to the sky, ready to fire a warning shot. "You let them go on about their business and don't try anything heroic, now," I told him sternly. "No one'll get hurt if you don't try anything."

He nodded and stayed where he was, probably so I'd know he meant it. The train started going, easy, toward the stockyard.

When we pulled up there, Bob ordered them to uncouple the engine. He had to fire a warning shot into the floor, but they finally complied. Bob turned to Newcomb. "Get on out and cover the rest, while we deal with the express car."

Bitter Creek nodded and jumped down, disappearing into the shadows. Bob motioned to the engineer. "Let's take a walk, then," he said, his tone still pleasant but underlined with iron. The man swallowed hard; I could see his Adam's Apple bob, and slowly began to head for the door.

When we got to the express car, Bob put up a hand and knocked. The messenger stuck his head out. "What's going on?" he asked. I saw the color drain from his face as he was answered by the barrel of Bob's gun under his nose.

"Evenin'," Bob said. "Think you might have some things in there we could use. Get back, now. Don't try anything." Someone ran up along side the train and spoke to Newcomb, I recognized Charlie's voice. He'd left the horses. I shook my head and turned back to the express car.

Bob and I entered it and Bob backed the messenger up. "Go ahead and open that safe."

"I...I don't have the combination," he stammered, his hands stretched toward the ceiling.

Bob let out an exasperated sigh. "Come on, now, I don't have time for that game. Open it."

"I swear to Jesus, I don't have it," the messenger repeated. "They lock these safes in Kansas City and don't give us the combination!" He was on his knees now.

Bob took a step closer, his boots sounding loud and ominous on the floor. "It's too bad this company's got a liar working for it. Now *open...that...safe.* I ain't gonna say it again." He fired a shot into the floor as punctuation to his words. Behind me, I heard Bitter Creek fire once, twice, then a third time, keeping the conductor and passengers in line and orderly. Bryant fired once or twice, too.

The messenger looked at Bob's blazing eyes, then at our guns, and put his palms out and stood. "All right, all right, don't shoot me. Hang on." He reached out with shaking fingers and unlocked the safe. Bob held out a hand to me, and I gave him the feed sack I was carrying.

Bob cleaned out the safe, then nodded to me. We backed out of the car. "There now, that wasn't so hard, was it?" he asked the messenger. "You tell the company the Dalton Gang is much obliged." With a laugh, he ducked out of the car and onto the ground, and I followed.

Bob let out a sharp whistle, and Bitter Creek and Charlie came running. We untied the horses and jumped on, putting our spurs to them. Bitter Creek let out a whoop and Bob was laughing. "God damn, I *told* you boys it'd be easy!"

I didn't answer, just laid out flat over my stud's neck and asked him for more speed as we zigzagged among the trees. I was worried about the way Bob had announced us like that; I didn't think it was wise. But another part of me felt a strange exhilaration I couldn't explain. *We'd gotten away with it.* No one had gotten hurt, this time, and everything had gone like Bob had planned. Maybe it'd be out of his system, now, for a bit.

We raced back to the dugout, rubbed down the horses, and then went inside to divvy up. We'd taken less than we'd hoped, but still almost seventeen hundred dollars. As I took my share, Bob gave me the look he did sometimes, the one that spoke of his pride in me. I looked away and put the money into my saddlebags, which were underneath my pillow.

The usual nausea came, but it was less strong than usual.

EIGHTEEN

WE SPLIT UP for a time after the Wharton job, with New-comb and Bryant going their separate ways, both telling Bob he knew where to find them for the next job he planned. We would never see Bryant again; Bob and I would learn some-time later that on his way to visit his brother after leaving our camp, he'd become ill and gone to a doctor at Hennesey. Too sick to get out of bed, he had been captured there by deputy Marshal Ed Short. Short had gotten Charlie on a train, and a shootout had occurred when Charlie had gotten ahold of a stray gun. He'd shot Short, a fatal wound, but before the Marshal died he'd shot Charlie back, killing him.

Bob kept abreast of things with newspapers, and we had connections with ranchers in the area who kept us informed, sharing our hatred of the express companies and the railroad. Our sister Eva's in-laws kept us warned, too, and Bob had a sort of sixth sense about posses who were out after us.

I don't remember when Heck Thomas first came to our attention, but he would never leave it from then on. He was a Deputy Marshal who'd worked with Frank, and met us back in our lawing days. He had, apparently, made it his life's mission to take us down, and he almost did, a few times. Being hunted so started to wear on us. At some point Bob decided that enough was enough, and we would leave the country and give up our outlaw career for good.

———————⊸((◉))⊶———————

The idea, Bob told me, was that we would go to South America. A man could raise cattle there quite successfully, or so he'd heard.

We made our way to Missouri and sold our horses, then got on a train at Springfield. From there we went on to Memphis, and it was there our plans changed, just a little.

"We'll have to get shed of these clothes," I told Bob when we arrived in Memphis. "We'll call too much attention to ourselves, looking like cowboys."

"You're right. Come on." Bob led me to a dry-goods place, and we took turns going in. Bob went for a suit, and I donned overalls, a straw hat, and shoes, almost immediately mourning the loss of my heeled boots and jingle-bob spurs, which I was used to wearing. But I couldn't keep them; the illusion had to be complete. We kept our Colts, of course—I hid mine in my overalls, and Bob had his up under his coat.

Our intention was to go to Atlanta, then to Tampa to catch a steamer to South America. We got on the Atlanta train and took seats, and I opened up a newspaper, my eyes carefully scanning over the latest article on "the Notorious, Desperate Dalton Gang," which, I noticed, was full of inaccuracies, claiming that we were currently surrounded near

Tulsa and that Bob had been killed in a gunfight.

Bob had gone tense beside me and I looked at him out of the corner of my eye. "What's the matter?" I asked in a low voice.

"Didn't you hear the fellow when we passed by? The one with the bowler and the beard up there." He motioned with an almost imperceptible motion of his head.

"No. What did he say?"

"He said you walked like a cowpuncher, not a farmer," Bob replied, in an even lower voice.

I felt my heart sink a little, but I took a deep breath. "So maybe I switched occupations, Bob. Don't get excited."

As I said it I noticed two peace officers pacing the platform right outside our car. I elbowed Bob gently and flicked my head toward them, not moving my paper. Bob's eyes clouded a little, his jaw clenched, and I had the thought that if he'd been a dog, his hackles would have raised.

We sat there, trying to decide what to do. The policemen were definitely concentrating on us, and it was making others in the car look at us funny. I heard the sound of someone clear their throat loudly, and a young man sitting near us suddenly said, without looking in our direction, "Seems to me certain folks should see about themselves."

His message was clear. He was warning us. I glanced at Bob, and he looked toward the door. "Go into the next car. I'll follow you once you're in."

I waited a few minutes, trying to look natural, then nonchalantly folded up my paper, sticking it under my arm. Then I got up and walked into the other car. Outwardly I was calm, but my heart was going like a hunted animal's.

I turned to make sure Bob was following me, and when I turned back I ran smack against another man. As I apologized I realized that it was one of the peace officers from outside; his badge shone out at me from his vest like a beacon.

"'Scuse me, son," he said, eyeballing me from my straw hat to my shoes.

"No, excuse *me*, officer. I guess I wasn't looking where I was going." I was afraid my voice sounded funny, but he didn't act like he thought so. I swear to God above, my heart had stopped beating for a second.

He gave me a nod and continued past me, edging past Bob, who was coming along. I managed to walk on, and hopped off the car. I heard Bob do the same, and we walked silently away from the train.

By some unspoken signal we ducked into an alley, and as soon as the train began to pull out we looked at each other and burst into laughter.

"Well, I'm damned. That was too close for my liking!" Bob managed to get out, still chuckling.

I wiped the water out of my eyes and caught my breath. "What're we going to do now, then?"

Bob looked at me and grinned. "Let's go to New Orleans."

———————⋙«(◉)»⋘———————

We rented a room in a boarding house on Driett Street, and Bob decided we would rest awhile and try to enjoy ourselves a bit before we bought passage to South America. That was a relief to me; I was so tired of looking over my shoulder at every turn. We wouldn't let our guard down, of course, and we would still keep a careful eye on the newspapers, but Bob felt we were safer there and I shared the feeling.

We kept careful track of the money we each still had from the Wharton job, but Bob felt we could afford to play a little bit. We went to the saloons in the evenings and played poker or Faro, and it was nice to see a whiskey bottle again. Bob took up with a few of the saloon girls at our regular place.

One evening we'd gotten into a game, and were having a streak of good luck. The fellows we were playing with were affable and just good enough at cards to challenge us some, and we lost track of time—and both hit the whiskey a little too hard. I hadn't been drinking hardly at all over the last few months, and it went to my head faster than I'd thought it would. About that time I noticed two of the whores making eyes at us from across the room. One of them was tall and blonde, and she was eyeing Bob. I glanced at the other one and felt my heart contract a little, like a fist was closing around it. She was small and young and she looked, in my inebriated state, very much like Laura Stevens.

It wasn't her, of course. This girl wasn't quite as slender, her hair not quite as thick and lustrous as Laura's. But the resemblance was there nonetheless. She looked small and alone, standing over there, like maybe she was new at whoring. I forced myself to look away and tried my best to concentrate on the game.

It wasn't any use, for I kept looking back up at that sad little girl. I wanted to help her for some reason, more than anything else a man might want to do with a saloon girl. It wouldn't be smart of me, though. I was still too worried about keeping our profiles low. "I'm gonna get some air, Bob," I said, low, to him, and he nodded. I got up from the table and steadied myself—I'd had more to drink than I thought—and went outside onto the gallery.

The night air revived me some, even though it was muggy out, but I still felt the liquor. I hoped Bob might want to go back soon, But, to my dismay, I went back inside just in time to see him disappearing up the stairs with the blonde. He had her giggling as they went, and she was almost helping him walk.

I sighed, leaning against the wall a minute, unsure whether I should go back alone, or stay and wait for him. Knowing Bob, he'd likely take all night, then pass out from the whiskey. Before I could make up my mind the girl that looked like Laura was coming toward me, slowly, uncertainly. A garishly-dressed older woman standing watchfully nearby gave her a sharp look, and she quickened her pace, cringing as if she'd felt a whip on her back. The older woman must've been her madam, I thought, feeling even more sorry for this poor young thing.

She came up to me, her gaze focused somewhere near the top button on my vest, instead of my face. Then her lashes swept upward and she looked at me, once. Her eyes were big and they were hazel, not green like Laura's. Up close she looked a little older than I'd first thought—eighteen or nineteen, perhaps, but still young. The sleeves of her dress and her chemise were pulled down, revealing the curves of her shoulders, and her corset was laced so tight her waist was as small as a sapling. "Evening," she said, in a voice I could barely hear.

"Evening," I replied, but said nothing more, waiting.

"So...you looking for any company?" she asked boldly, but her words were quick. I guessed she didn't really want to say them. I guessed someone had told her what to say.

"Not especially," I said bluntly, but I tried to soften my words with a kind tone.

"Why not?" she asked, moving a little closer to me. She looked at me again, and I thought I saw something a little desperate in her eyes. "You got a sweetheart, or something?"

"I had one," I replied, watching the way the lamplight moved over her face.

"She ain't here, then?"

"She's in California. And I will likely not ever see her again." The words hurt as I said them.

"That's sad," she said. She moved a little closer. "You look like the type of feller a girl should hang on to, if she gets you," she said. She didn't sound like she was reciting lines now.

"Well, she wanted to. But things happened that prevented it." I leaned my head against the wall and closed my eyes; the room was swimming a little and it was getting warm.

She edged even closer, almost touching me now. "I bet I could help you forget about her."

I opened my eyes and looked down at her. "I doubt that."

"Not for good. Just for right now." She boldly put out a hand and touched my arm, quick, then dropped it.

I had no intention of taking this girl upstairs, not even at that point, but just as I was about to tell her so, the madam moved closer to us, watching the girl like a hawk. She bit her lip and ducked her head, trying to avoid the madam's eyes.

"That your...?" I asked, letting my voice trail off. I spoke quietly.

"Yes. She'll get me good if I don't get a customer to-night. I ain't been here long and she's hard on us new girls. I'm...I'm new at this and I haven't made her much money."

She could've been lying to me, but something in me knew she was telling me the truth. "What's your name?" I asked her, one eye on the madam.

"Lily," she said, looking up at me desperately.

"Well, Lily, I'll tell you what. I ain't looking for the kind of company you're thinkin.' But she don't have to know that. Let's go upstairs, and I'll pay you like usual, but you don't have to...we'll just wait a bit, and I'll leave, and she'll never know the difference."

Lily looked up at me, her eyes shining like she was gonna start crying. I put my arm around her shoulders and led her to the staircase, and we went up together, both of us imagining we could feel the madam's gaze on our backs.

Lily led me to her room, and although it was small it was neat and clean. Besides the bed with its worn blanket there was a wash-stand and a dresser with a mirror over it. That was it. A lamp was on the dresser, and she lit it and then sat down on the bed. I leaned against the wall.

We stared at each other for a few minutes, and then she gave me a wobbly little smile. "Thank you," she said. "Thank you for doing this."

I looked at her, knowing the sadness I was feeling for her was showing in my face. "Why are you doing this?" I asked her, gesturing at the room. "Ain't you got any family?"

"No. My Pa died last winter and my Momma died when I

was only eight. I've got no kinfolk in this part of the country. My older sister lives in Round Rock. She's got a husband and a baby, but I think she'd take me in. I just gotta raise up the money to get there."

"You're not from New Orleans, are you? You talk like you're from Texas."

She nodded. "I was born in Austin. I came out to New Orleans in the spring with a man I was supposed to marry. He just up and disappeared one morning, taking all of my money and my things. So I was stuck here. I didn't know what else to do."

"How old are you?" I asked her bluntly.

"Eighteen last month," she said. She was working her hands in her lap and she fell silent. I did, too, and we stayed that way for awhile. Then she spoke up. "What happened to your girl in California?"

"I had to leave," I said. "My brother and I had business elsewhere, and I couldn't take her along. You look a little like her," I blurted out, then cringed inwardly. I hadn't wanted her to know that.

She got up and came over to me. "I know you don't want me like most men want me," she said. "'Cause I can see you're different. You got morals, I can tell. But I ain't gonna let you pay me for nothing." She was very close to me now.

"We talked. We can consider it a paid conversation," I said nervously.

She shook her head and her hair swayed around her hips. "I owe you a kiss, at the least." Before I could say anything, she'd stood on tiptoe and was pressing her lips to mine.

I'd had no intention of touching her. But her lips were

soft and brought Laura's lips to my mind. I suppose it was the whiskey that made me take her head in my hands and kiss her proper, a long kiss. My heart started thudding and I felt overly warm. Sweat started coming out on me and I couldn't sort out any of my thoughts.

When she broke way she just stared at me with them huge hazel eyes, and I knew I had to leave or I'd end up doing something I'd just said I wouldn't. I reached into my pocket and pulled out some bills—far more, I suspected, than she normally charged, but enough, I hoped, to get her home to Texas. Then I reached out and sort of cupped her cheek with my palm. "Take care of yourself, Lily. Get yourself away from this place and that biddy down there." I reached for the door.

"Wait!" she cried, and I turned back, my hand still on the knob.

"You never told me your name," she said.

"William," I said quickly, using whatever name popped into my head.

"Thank you," she said, her voice catching a little in her throat. She looked like she was gonna cry again. I got myself out of there, quick, and went back downstairs.

I went out into the sweltering night air, trying to get ahold of myself, and went back to our little room on Driett Street. It was a good long time before I was able to sleep.

NINETEEN

THE MORNING CAME when Bob decided we should get our passage to South America. We were on our way to the ticket office when I realized I'd left all my money up in our room, and we had to go all the way back to get it.

"You should be more careful, Em," Bob said, acting his part as my older brother. "What if our room had got broke into?"

"It didn't, did it?" I replied tartly. I was twenty now and hated it more than ever when Bob acted like I was a child.

I got my belt with my money, and caught sight of the paper lying on the bed. I hadn't looked at it yet this morning. I picked it up and tossed it at Bob. "You seen where we are today?" I asked him curiously, hoping to divert him from his scolding.

Bob took a look at the headlines, and I saw his eyes widen. Some of the color left his face. "Emmett..." he handed me the paper and pointed out an article.

I looked, and felt my heart drop. *Notorious Train-Robber Grat Dalton Convicted,* it said. I looked up at Bob. His face looked like a mask, his eyes were full of rage. "We ain't going to South America, after all, Em," he said to me, and I knew he was right. We couldn't skip off scot-free to South America while Grat was being punished unjustly.

I took a deep breath. It looked like our vendetta was back.

We left New Orleans and returned to Indian Territory, where Bob spent a good deal scouting out hiding places, figuring the law would be on us more than ever the next time we tried a train. He wanted choices of places we could flee to, and with good reason, for Heck Thomas and his posse were still after us, relentless in their pursuit. We looked up Bitter Creek after awhile and found Charley Pierce with him; Charley told Bob that whenever he decided on the next job, he was with us, if Bob would have him. He said it all solemn-like, as if he was swearing some oath. He and Newcomb also knew where Dick Broadwell and fellow former cowhand I'd met on the old ranch named Bill Power were staying, and said they would join us, too, if Bob agreed.

"Tell 'em if they ain't yellow and are up for a good time, they can come along," Bob said almost carelessly, something brittle in his eyes. He was still furious about Grat's conviction, and he wanted revenge for it, but planning our next job would take time. We rode away from our visit with Bitter Creek and Charley, Bob telling them we'd contact them when the time came.

A few weeks later fate seemed to intervene in our lives when we walked into a lonely little saloon and found my old friend Bill Doolin there among the handful of patrons.

"Why, Bill!" I said, startled to see him after so many years. He looked exactly the same to me, with his sweeping brown moustache and his pale blue eyes, filled with their same old insatiable zest for life; his form still long and lean from life on the trail.

"Well, now! Ain't *you* a sight for sore eyes!" he said in his cheerful way, grinning at me so wide I figured it'd hurt his face if he kept on like that. He did not, I noticed, greet me by name, a sign that he'd heard tell of the infamy I was coming to know. "Come on outside, now, and tell me how you've been." He ushered us out of earshot of anyone else. "By the Lord Almighty, Emmett, you've gone and turned into a man of some fame since I last saw you!" he said once we were away from there, clapping me on the back like he was proud of me. He gave me a sly look. "Told you the law wouldn't agree with you none."

"I suppose that's the truth, when you get down to it," I said, a little uneasily. I gestured to Bob. "Bill, this is my brother Bob. Bob, this is Bill Doolin, an old friend of mine. He sorta took me under his wing when I worked at the cattle ranch. Taught me a lot and looked out for me—depending on which way you want to look at it." Bill gave me a knowing grin, sly as ever and clearly unapologetic for some of the corruption he'd started in me back then, like introducing me to red-eye whiskey in the bunkhouse my first night there.

I turned to Bob and was utterly taken aback by what I saw in his face.

I could read Bob like a book; we'd always been so close and had spent so much time with no company other than each other's, that his moods were easy for me to decipher. And I could tell, right then and there, that my brother did not like Bill Doolin.

The realization stunned me; I'd always thought of Bill as someone Bob would get along well with. They were both devils, both full of bravado and daring, and both hard-headed and stubborn as hell. Both lived for the moment at hand, and any excitement they could manage to get out of it. I stood there and puzzled on it as Bill, apparently oblivious to Bob's cold reception of him, went right on talking, telling Bob how he'd read about us, and how he was glad he'd run into the man that was being talked about as "the brains behind the Dalton Gang."

"If you need a man on your next venture, I put myself forward, Bob," Bill said bluntly. "I got relations who were pushed off land by the damn railroad companies, and still others who the banks put out of their homes. I got no love for those sons of bitches, nor the law in this God-forsaken Territory, and I'll stand with the shooter, if that's called for." He punctuated his remark by spitting a stream of tobacco juice off into the shadows.

Bob narrowed his eyes a little, but when he spoke his voice was very even. "Well, Emmett here's talked about you in the past, says you're handy with a revolver and as brave as they come, so I suppose I'll take you on as a favor to him; see how things go."

Bill smiled. "All right, then. I got a claim just south of here. Come see me when the time comes." He turned to me and grinned again. "I sure am glad to see you again, Em. I always knew you'd go on to bigger and better things once you got off that ranch." He put a friendly hand on my shoulder and went off into the night, whistling 'The Yellow Rose of Texas."

Bob stood there for a minute, watching him go, something both thoughtful and dark in his expression and his posture. I reached out and hooked an arm around his neck the way he often did to me and spoke in a light voice, trying to draw him out of his stew. "C'mon, Bob, let's go play some poker."

It was only later on that I would come to realize the reason for Bob's underlying distaste for Bill Doolin—jealousy. Not of his character or his deeds, but because for the first time, Bob had met someone who'd ever come even a little bit close to matching his role in my life.

～((●))～

Train jobs, I came to find, all had the same ingredients. The waiting in the darkness, straining one's ears to hear the telltale whistle. Picking the exact moment to enter the engine. Trying to subdue the passengers and company men so that no one got hurt, then getting into the express car and cleaning out the safe as fast as possible. Wheeling away into the night on fast horses and dividing up the spoils. In spite of that repetition, I never did get used to it. My stomach got to where it didn't feel quite as queasy as it had before, and I became efficient at doing whatever Bob wanted me to, but inside I still cringed each time, those few minutes we were actually holding the train up.

One cool September night we waited in the old familiar shadows, this time at Leliaetta, Oklahoma. Our target was the Katy train this time, and Bob was hoping for a big haul this time out, mainly because there were so many more of us than there had been at Wharton.

We were a force to be reckoned with this time, I had to admit. Besides Bob and Bitter Creek and me, we had Pierce and Broadwell, Bill Doolin, and Bob's newest addition to our rag-tag band, Bill Power. He'd worked with me on the ranch, just as Doolin and Broadwell had, and it was strange to be making ready to hold up a train with the three of them. I put it out of my mind, though, when we sprang into action, our moves rehearsed. Bob oversaw the whole job with his usual cool head, and he didn't have to bring his temper out this time. Our reputation had grown and with it Bob's notoriety as our leader. We got away clean, with a fair haul.

We met up at the dugout, where Bob divvied up the spoils. The new members of the gang laughed and talked fast with each other, still excited. Most of them had never had as much money at one time as they now held in their hands, and the sheer ease of it became the topic of the night. Bob sat near the door, his rifle laid across his knees, the lamplight shining a soft glow over the planes and hollows of his face and making his eyes gleam as he watched and listened, like a boss wolf surveying his pack. He looked smug. Invincible.

I rested in my corner, watching him watch them, trying to figure out what was going on in his head. I'd always understood him so well, but in times like these I felt clueless. I guess I'd finally started to accept that my mind didn't work the same way as his, and no matter how much I looked up to him, it likely never would.

I glanced at Doolin. He'd done well by Bob that night, never flinching, brave to the point one would've thought he was wearing a suit of steel. He'd followed Bob's orders to the letter, but I still sensed trouble. Bill wasn't the type of man to be held under another's heel, and that was bound to be bad somewhere down the line.

They got out whiskey from their saddlebags, and set to getting good and drunk, positive we were all hidden away well enough from Heck Thomas and his ever-closing posse to celebrate the good job we'd made of things. Doolin offered me a drink, but I shook my head. I realized I had somewhere else I wanted to be right now.

I got up and put my coat and hat back on, nodding to the others and heading for the door. Bob wouldn't let me through it right off. "Where're you off to, Em? The law might be out."

I looked at him, square. "I'll be careful, Bob. I need to clear my head."

Bob gave me a hard look. "You ain't just going out for some air," he said, reading me just like I usually read him. "What're you up to?"

I sighed. "I'm gonna go see Mother, Bob. Just for a bit. It's been too long and God knows she's probably worried out of her skull by now."

Bob stood up and pulled me outside so's we could talk privately, not that the gang would've heard. They were too busy concentrating on counting their money over and passing the whiskey around.

"Listen here, Em," Bob hissed at me, his voice earnest. "That ain't a good idea. The less Mother knows, the better. I don't want her involved in this, and it ain't a good time."

"Bob, you know I ain't gonna say anything," I protested. "I just want to check on her. We're all over hell, the bunch of us, and she don't have anyone around to look in on her other than the girls and Sam. I'll be careful. I ain't gonna let anyone catch me, or track me. Now let me go."

That last bit startled me, even as I said it, but I didn't take it back. I'd done my part and showed my sand, just like the last two times, and I wanted to get away from it tonight. "I'll meet up with you back here in a few days," I told him, and went to get my horse. Surprisingly, he didn't argue with me anymore, just watched as I mounted up and trotted off. When I'd gone just a little ways something made me turn and look back at him, and when I did I thought I saw him lift his hand in a wave, but it was dark and I might've been seeing things.

TWENTY

OUR HIDEOUT WAS sixty miles south of Mother's claim; it took me two days to get there. I hated to arrive in the middle of the night, but if I waited until daylight I might be spotted. I knew Bob was probably right; it wasn't the best time to pay a call such as I was planning, but I'd missed her and I felt duty-bound to see her. I'd often worried that she was lonely, with only Sam and Leona at home with her now.

I was careful; Bob had passed on some of his knowledge to me about watching for parties who might be tracking us, and I made it there safely. The little cabin was dark and the barn quiet. I rode up to the side of the house, concealing my horse in the shadow it made and tying him up to a tree there. If I went into the barn it might be heard in the house, and like as not Sam would come out with a gun, thinking it was horse-thieves. He was thirteen now and the man of the house, and I knew he had some skill with a rifle—I'd taught him myself, and he was a Dalton, after all.

I took a look around, and when I was satisfied no one was waiting to waylay me, I went to the back door and knocked, not going inside for the same reason I hadn't gone into the barn.

I waited, rubbing my hands together against the September chill and listening to the chirping of crickets. After a few minutes I heard shuffling of footsteps and saw the faint glow of a lamp coming under the door.

It opened a crack, and a voice said, "who's out there?"

"Sam?" I whispered stupidly. His voice had changed. "Sam, it's Emmett."

The door opened, and Sam stood there in his nightshirt, holding a lamp in one hand, and Pa's old Sharps rifle in the other. His eyes were big as he stared at me, clearly stunned I was there. He set the lamp down so hurriedly the kerosene sloshed in the bowl, then leaned his rifle in the corner, moving aside so I could come in. He'd shot up even taller since I'd seen him at Pa's funeral, and his wheat-blond hair had darkened. I even thought I saw a bit of stubble starting to come up above his lip.

I came in, and he hesitated, then hugged me. "Em, where did you come from?"

"Aways," I said evasively.

"Sam, what's going on out there—oh, my Lord!" That was Mother. She'd been pulling a shawl around her shoulders, but when she saw me she let it fall to the floor and ran to me, putting her arms around me. "Oh, Emmett, thank God. Thank God, you're all right." She was crying into my coat, still holding onto me as if she never wanted to let me go. I held her back and put my cheek against the top of her head. Her dark hair had grayed even more since Pa's death, and the lamplight illuminated the weariness in her face, lines earned by a lifetime of hard work and the bearing of fifteen children. But she was still Mother, still had her strength.

"I'm well, Mother, I promise," I said. "I'm sorry to come alone in the middle of the night like this—"

She shook her head and pulled away from me, wiping at her tears with shaking fingers. "Don't you apologize, you hear me? I've been worried so about all of you, never knowing what—" She stopped suddenly, like she didn't want to tell me her worries. She looked me over. "You're thin, Emmett."

I gave her a crooked smile. "I'm fine, Mother," I repeated. "I've been...moving around a lot, is all."

She shook her head again. "Don't you tell me anything. I don't want to hear it. I don't want to know anything that would cause me pain, Em. Seeing you here and knowing you're safe is enough for me."

I reached out and hugged her again, feeling my throat start to close up. I'd always thought the best parts of me had come from Mother, and her words reaffirmed it.

Leona had come out by then and she greeted me with an awkward, sisterly kiss on the cheek. She eyed the two guns and the cartridge belt around my waist like she was scared of them, but she said nothing.

I took a deep breath. "I can't stay here long, Mother. I just...needed to make sure you were well."

"I am, Emmett," she said, leading me into the front room as Sam put the rifle back over the door and Leona lit a few more lamps. "Sam and Leona are a great help to me." Her words were strong, as usual, but I sensed a sadness in her voice that hurt me. Mother had done her best with us, just as Pa had tried to, and look at what her boys put her through.

I vowed then and there that if there ever came a time that I could truly be rid of the life I'd chosen, I would do everything in my power to be the son she deserved—the son she believed I could be.

I stayed at Mother's only until just after supper the next night, knowing I didn't dare remain any longer. My sister and brother didn't ask me why I wore my guns constantly, nor did they ask me anything about the life I'd been living since I'd last seen them. Mother must've warned them against it, or else they were too scared of learning the answer, just like Mother seemed to be.

I helped with a few things that needed doing around the claim, keeping my hat pulled down low over my face and only venturing outside when I had to. Mother didn't ask me anything about Bob except if he was well, and she seemed relieved beyond belief when I told her he was. She knew, of course, what had befallen Grat and Will, but she didn't mention anything to me.

The whole time I was there I avoided looking at the photograph Mother had framed of Frank. I'd done it once, curiously, almost like I'd been looking at a stranger's picture, when I'd first arrived; seemed his face was sort of fading in my memory, since it'd been so long since he'd died. Almost as soon as I'd done it I'd looked away, for Frank's clear gaze seemed to stare at me, come to life through that picture, like he knew what I'd been doing and he didn't much approve. I never looked at it again.

At dusk I kissed them all, murmuring words of reassurance to Mother, and tacked up. I was on my way back to Bob by the time darkness fell.

TWENTY-ONE

AWHILE AFTER TAKING the Katy train we came to learn that Grat had broken out of jail in California, and despite of the law's best efforts in chasing him down and bringing him back, he'd vanished from the area. We knew he'd do his best to make his way back into our company, and so we settled down to lay low and wait.

It wasn't long before I felt restless and penned-up, like a cornered animal. We hadn't taken any trains or done anything we shouldn't have since Leliaetta, but that did nothing to deter Thomas or anyone else who was after us; there were big rewards on our heads. I started taking horseback rides by myself during the evenings or early mornings; staying close to the dugout or any of the other places we camped got me good and bored, and the little outings helped break up the monotony of laying low. Bob always stayed behind; Bitter Creek and Charley, or Power and Broadwell, would show up out of the blue and draw him into a poker game or some other pastime, leaving me on my own if I didn't care to join them.

The time Bob and I had spent in New Orleans came to my mind often, for we'd been able to let our guard down a bit down there and I'd begun to really think on how nice that had been, and how I despaired of ever being able to do that here on home turf. But I knew we couldn't leave the area; with any luck Grat was on his way to join us and we had to wait for him. It would be slow going for him, we knew, for the law would be looking for him just as they were us. During our wait we learned that Will had been acquitted at his preliminary hearing and set free; he'd had his good standing among the community in his favor, and no record besides.

One afternoon I'd gone into town for provisions; we felt I was less recognizable than Bob. I was coming back early the next morning when about a mile out from the dugout, I caught sight of a figure on horseback coming toward me at a canter, and quickly veered off into the tree line, ready to light a fire under my horse if need be. The sun was just barely starting its rise in the eastern sky and it took a minute for me to figure out who the other man was. I held my horse in, the reins taut, waiting.

After a few minutes I recognized the horse and its rider; it was Bitter Creek Newcomb. I spurred my horse and went out to meet him.

"Emmett!" he called. He reined in and sat in his saddle, waiting until I came up beside him. "Where the hell'd you go off to?" His russet eyes were snapping sparks and he looked excited.

"I went for provisions, Creek," I told him. "What's the matter with you?" My horse pranced in place beneath me, eager to run, but I held him in check. It was windy out and he was fired up over the tall grasses brushing back and forth against his legs—he kept getting spooked.

Bitter Creek gave me his famous fox-like grin. "You'll never guess who showed up just a bit ago," he said. He pushed his hat back aways, flashing that coppery hair of his, and leaned back a little in his saddle.

"Who?" I demanded, tensing up. Thoughts of Heck Thomas or other lawmen entered my mind.

"Grat."

It took just a minute for my brother's name to register with me, and when it did I felt my mouth fall open a little bit. I'd never dreamed he would've made it back so fast. "How the devil—"

Newcomb cut me off with a laugh. "He's been riding like hell to get here," he told me through his chuckles, slapping his thigh. "I swear to the Lord Almighty, you Dalton boys just keep on surprising me! I never met a more reckless or luckier bunch. I still can't believe the gutsy son of a bitch broke out of jail and got away with it."

"How'd he do it? Did he tell you anything?" I asked, still stunned, and relieved beyond belief. It had grieved me, all these months, to think of Grat stewing in his rage in jail like that, especially since he hadn't done anything to warrant being there this time out.

"Sawed through the bars of his cell and scaled down a two-story wall, if you can believe it. Someone left him a gun hidden outside the jail, if I heard correctly. He wouldn't say too much about it, which I'm fine with. He gets himself in something of a temper, when he talks about it, seems like. I don't gather he cared too much for jail life."

"He's back there with Bob now?" I asked.

"Surely is. Bob was gettin' worried about you, thought

you'd been gone too long, but when Grat showed up out of nowhere, looking like a mongrel dog, he found himself occupied. Told me to see if I could spot you anywhere around as I left. I'll see you the next time out. You'd best get back before it gets too light out, just in case."

I waved goodbye to Creek, then put my horse into a lope and got back to the dugout quick. I hurried inside, feeling gladness that Grat was all right and free mixed with that old familiar sense of foreboding that came whenever I was in his presence.

Grat was standing with Bob just inside the door, smoking a cigarette. He was dressed in an odd mix of worn clothes; I figured he must've picked things up here and there on his way back, whenever the opportunity presented itself. His hair was longer than I remembered it and he had a bushy beard grown out. There were scratches on his hands and face, almost healed up but still visible, like he'd had to take cover in some sort of sharp underbrush at some time or another during his escape. He was thinner than he had been and there were shadows under his pale blue eyes. He was dirty and bedraggled and sure looked as though he'd been riding hell bent for leather.

"Grat!" I said, and they turned to me. Grat gave me a half-smile and looked me up and down, just like he had that day when I'd shown up in Wichita.

"Hello, Em. You got a rougher edge on you since I saw you last," he commented.

Bob threw me an affectionate glance. "Em's become quite the longrider since you were with us, Grat."

"Did you see Will at all?" I asked Grat, wanting to steer

the conversation away from my part in our activities.

Grat nodded. "Briefly. He's gonna quit the place in California. It don't matter that he got off; folks around there are shooting off their mouths about Daltons and he's done with it. He'll come out to Kingfisher, file on a claim."

I came closer to them. "Are you all right, then?" I asked cautiously. There was bitterness and rage in his eyes like I'd never seen before.

He shrugged off my question. "I'm alive, ain't I? I've been better, but at least I'm out of that hole and away from those sons of bitches. But I'll tell you something, Em." His eyes narrowed and he threw his cigarette down, grinding it into the dirt floor with the heel of his boot. "That Goddamned express company and those bastard detectives that put me in that cage are gonna pay for it. I figure I owe them." There was something deadly and black in his gravely voice.

"We all do, all of us Daltons," Bob said. "We'll give them something to remember us by, if I have any say in the matter." His eyes gleamed at the thought. He put a hand on Grat's shoulder. "Let's cook up some chow, get some meat put back on you."

Bob never asked Grat if he was with us in our coming ventures; he didn't need to. The Dalton brothers, as he'd always said, stuck together, no matter what.

———— ((◦)) ————

"Something don't look right to me."

Bob's voice was so quiet I almost didn't hear his words,

and I turned to look at him, struggling to see his face well in the darkness. We were crouched here and there around the Red Rock station, our guns at the ready, masks drawn up. The train had pulled slowly in and the seven of us were tense, waiting for Bob's signal.

But he didn't give it. He was staring hard at the train, suspicion emanating from him like something I could pick up in my hands. Feeling uneasy myself now, I looked at the train.

I saw what troubled Bob. The light emanating from some of the passenger cars was unusually dim, and other cars were dark altogether. Seconds ticked by, and Bob did nothing. Steam wafted up around the train.

"Ain't you gonna give the signal sometime this *year*, Bob?" Charley hissed impatiently. "She's gonna leave before we can get ourselves situated!"

"Shut up, Charley, and stay where you are," Bob retorted forcefully. "That train ain't the one we want. Something's wrong with it."

"What the hell are you talking about?" Doolin suddenly piped up, irritation plain in his voice. "You know damn well she's got a haul bigger than anything we ever took in that express car, and if we miss our chance—"

"Go ahead, Doolin! You want that train so bad, there she is! Take her by yourself, if you want her. *I ain't going*, and neither is any man who's with me. See if I shed any damn tears when you get yourself shot up or thrown in some calaboose." Bob's voice was ice-cold and filled with something brittle and sharp, like shards of broken glass. I saw the moonlight reflect off the nickel of his revolver when he shifted positions, coming out of the shadows a bit.

"Easy, Bob," I soothed. "Put your horns away. You too, Bill. Bob's right, something's wrong with that train."

"She's too dark," Grat confirmed. I heard him shift from boot to boot behind me, his spurs jingling softly.

"There she goes," Bitter Creek commented, as the engine gave a puff and the wheels started going, slowly at first, then speeding up. We stayed where we were, Doolin too, and watched it go.

"Well, what'll we do now?" Dick asked, after a bit. We all looked over at Bob, who was staring thoughtfully after the departing train.

"We wait," Bob said firmly. "We'll take the next one, when it comes."

"What if there's no cash in the next one?" Doolin asked, clearly still angry.

Bob turned and gave Bill a deliberate stare; we could all make it out as the clouds above shifted and the moonlight shone out clearer. "Then I suppose we'll just consider it a practice run." He took a step forward, moving past me, toward Doolin. "You don't like the way I do things, Doolin, you just say so. You're free to quit, anytime." His tone was heavy with the promise of violence, contradicting his conciliatory words; I could almost feel it coming out from him. If Bill challenged him, Bob wouldn't hesitated to take him down.

"Bob," I said nervously. Everyone froze. I could see the others' eyes darting from Bob to Bill and back again, and Grat stood back, watching.

Doolin stared right back for a minute, then deliberately put his hands out, palms toward Bob. "Don't get riled up,

Dalton," he said. "I'll stand behind you. I guess you've shown you know best." Bill was my friend, I liked him, but even I thought that his words didn't sound very sincere. I got a sinking feeling in the pit of my stomach. Bob gave a slow nod, then went back to watching for the next train. The rest of us stayed quiet after that, and when the second train came, we were ready.

It was only later that we would learn that that first train had been loaded with lawmen, expecting us and ready to take us out. Bob's sixth sense had saved all of us—for now.

——⋙⟨⟨◉⟩⟩⋘——

Doolin left immediately after Bob had divided up the spoils, taking Newcomb and Pierce with him. Only Broadwell and Power stayed the night, and they were up and off early the next morning, eager to find more fun. I didn't much like the feel of things. Bob said everyone was welcome on our next job, Doolin too, but I still had the uneasy feeling that the gang was set for a change. Bill was just as stubborn as Bob and the undercurrent of tension between them had been growing steadily since the Leilaetta job; afterwards Bill and I had sat talking a good long while, and Bill had been telling Bitter Creek and Charley stories about when I'd started at Courtney's place, back when I was sixteen. Bob had clearly been bothered some by that; I hadn't known why at the time. But when I brought it up to Grat the morning after Red Rock, as we were out watering the horses and Bob was inside cooking breakfast, Grat had grunted in a knowing way.

"Bob's jealous of Bill," Grat said briskly, like it should've been obvious to me. I stared at him in amazement.

"But why? Bob's better than Bill with a gun, and braver. Hell of a lot smarter, too, when it comes down to it."

Grat closed the corral gate and turned to face me, leaning his arm on the fence-rail. "He ain't jealous of *that,* Emmett. He's sore about how Bill tries to act like he's responsible for you, for makin' you what you are. Bill took a liking to you when he worked with you, that's clear. You've said yourself he took you under his wing, so to speak. Taught you to drink whiskey. Taught you to play cards better. Things that Bob figures *he* should've done."

I stared at Grat, my brow furrowing. "But…Bob wasn't there for those things."

Grat sighed and kind of rolled his eyes, like I was suddenly short on brains and he needed to talk me through something I should've understood right off. "He *knows* that, Em. But since he always was the one to look out for you, he figures he should've taken you with him in the first place when he and I started out, instead of leaving you at home and letting you go off cowboyin'. It makes him mad when Doolin brags about you like you're something he can take credit for."

I tried to take in what Grat was saying. I was having a hard time with it, not just because I'd been too close to the whole thing to see the truth in what Grat was saying, but also because I was taken aback at the unusual perceptiveness Grat was showing me. Of all of the gang members, I never would've taken *him* to be the one that saw the cause clear of Bob and Bill's dislike of each other.

He sort of cuffed me on the shoulder, the most affectionate demonstration I could ever remember him making towards me, then went back to the hideout. I stayed where I was for a minute, just thinking on things, then followed him.

TWENTY-TWO

"DROP YOUR GUNS and throw up your hands, boys! We've got you!"

The voice that bellowed out those words was far behind me, down by the smoking car, where the officers employed to guard the train had evidently been riding. I heard gunfire begin exploding back and forth, and Bitter Creek's familiar whoop of excitement. "Send 'em to hell, boys!" he shouted.

Grat hit me on the arm, drawing my attention back to what I was supposed to be doing—covering him and Bob as they and Doolin convinced the messenger—by way of their guns—to open the express car and then the safe. I heard a man scream out in pain as Creek and Charley, Power and Broadwell returned fire, and sweat started pouring off me.

Bob paid the fight no mind. Instead he fired a few shots into the express car. "I'm gonna keep shooting until you open it!" he called almost pleasantly.

"Hold your fire! Hold your fire!" someone yelled from down by the smoking car. I didn't recognize the voice, so it wasn't one of ours. The express car door eased open and a pair of hands appeared, palms out.

"Thank you kindly," Bob said, marching us into it, backing the messenger away from the door and past the safe. "Sounds like it's gettin' a bit messy out there," he remarked to the terrified messenger, like he was making idle conversation. The messenger declined to answer.

It was hot out, even at night, and the July air seemed thick. The stock of my Winchester felt slippery with sweat and I shifted it from hand to hand, wiping my palms over my britches. We were at Adair, south of Vinita, and everyone was back with us for this job. Doolin had been overly polite to Bob the whole time, on his best behavior, but I could tell it was taking an effort for him to do so, and it was clearly taking an effort on Bob's part not to lose his temper with him. Now that Grat had enlightened me as to the reason for their feud, I was careful to be deferential to Bob and not spend too much time shooting the breeze with Bill.

"Go!" Bob snapped out a command to us, bringing me out of my reverie, and handed the sack to Grat. We piled out of the express car, Doolin coming out last, still covering the messenger. "So long!" Bob called to the messenger, a sly grin crossing his face.

Bob let out a sharp, shrill whistle that split the air, like the gunshots had been doing earlier. This was his signal to get back to the horses. We heard the sounds of running boots and chiming spurs, amidst screams from some passengers, moaning from whomever had been injured and hoarse, excited voices that must have belonged to the other guards. Bitter Creek, Charley, Bill and Dick appeared, their eyes wild above the neckerchiefs hiding their faces, and the bunch of us dove for our horses. Gunfire started again in our direction, and we fired back, wheeling our mounts away to the west.

Bob and Bitter Creek and Doolin were all laughing as we went, store buildings and homes that lined the street flying by. Suddenly we heard more shots, and we turned in our saddles and fired back. I saw people coming out onto porches, but I didn't pay them much mind; I was too busy returning fire behind me. The other boys were, too—in all directions. Doolin, Pierce and Newcomb enjoyed gunplay more than the rest of us; sometimes I thought they craved it, and when they got like this they'd shoot at near anything that moved. I saw them carelessly firing off into the buildings along the street, not even aiming for the men out after us.

"What the hell are you crazy sons of bitches *doing*?" I heard myself yell at them, hoarsely, before I even thought.

"Knock it the hell off, shithogs!" Bob screamed at them, and I cringed; I could tell he was furious, and that didn't bode well for any of us in the outfit.

I heard a moan of pain from one of the store porches; someone had been hit, and it hadn't been one of the men chasing us. My heart started thudding even more wildly than it already was. I took my reins up and whipped them back at my horse's rump, asking for more speed. It seemed like a good many folks were getting hurt this time out, and that could only mean one thing—trouble, from Bob, the law, and my conscience. My stomach turned over in its old fashion and I felt myself weave a little in the saddle. The gunfire stopped. We pushed on, getting away from there.

Not a thing was said until we'd put up our exhausted mounts and taken refuge in an abandoned claim shanty Bob knew about. We filed inside, some heads hung like naughty schoolboys caught in mischief, others sulking, defiant. Bob closed the door and readied guns within easy reach of it, just in case we'd been tracked, then turned to face the group of us, his face coloring in the lamplight.

For a second, there was silence. Then Bob exploded, his usual cool head gone, his temper completely frayed. "What in the name of almighty God do you think you stupid sons of bitches were *doing* out there?" he raged, addressing Doolin, Newcomb and Pierce, angrier than I'd ever seen him. "What the hell was going through your fool skulls?"

Pierce and Newcomb cringed, but Bill stared Bob down, his eyes narrowed. They weren't twinkling like they usually were. "Lower your voice and cool your heels, Dalton," he growled. "You think you've pulled off every Goddamned lark you've ever tried clean as a whistle and pretty as a picture? We got away, didn't we? We got the haul. So some idiots got themselves a little shot up. We didn't kill anybody."

"Did you stop to *look*, Doolin?" Bob hissed. "Every damned one of them could die, for all you know! It was careless and damned *sloppy*, and I won't have it in my outfit, understand?"

Doolin put a hand on his hip, appraising Bob coolly. "Well, son, I'm sorry you see it that way," he said, reminding Bob of his greater age. "Guess maybe we'll take our parts and be off, then. It ain't worth gettin' into a scrape over."

Bob glared at him for a moment more, then set to divvy-ing up the spoils. Doolin took his and glanced at Newcomb and Pierce. "You boys goin' with me or stayin' here?"

Newcomb hesitated. He looked at me, something like desperation in his eyes. I stared back at him levelly. I liked Creek, but I wouldn't stop him from going with Doolin. He shifted from boot to boot, then took a deep breath. "I guess I'm going with you, Bill."

Charley scuffed the rowels of his spurs in the dirt, first one, then the other, his hands shoved down into the pockets of his britches. I sensed that he wanted to stay, but if Creek was going, he would go too. I never saw Charley Pierce with-out Bitter Creek Newcomb. "Guess I'm going, too."

Bob crossed his arms over his chest. "Get a-goin', then." His words hung heavy in the air. Broadwell, Power, Grat and I knew what they meant—they were a dismissal. The three of them would not be asked—or allowed—to take part in whatever else Bob had planned for us.

Newcomb and Pierce headed out, muttering farewells to the rest of us. Doolin started to go, but he stopped when he got to me. "You take care of yourself, now, Em," he said to me, giving me a sad smile. "You ever change your mind about this, you look me up." He put a hand on my shoulder, then disappeared out into the night, his rifle tucked up under his arm. I could feel Bob's rage, even though he said nothing.

Though their infamy would continue for several more years, I would never see the three of them again.

The headlines told us what we'd only suspected: five men had been hit during our little fiasco; three during the fight outside the smoking car, and two doctors sitting together on a porch in town. One of the doctors had later died as a result of his wound. Bob crumpled the newspaper into a little ball and threw it into the corner of the room in disgust. We would be wanted for murder. The law would be out for blood, now. I felt my heart sink down into my toes. Wounding anyone was bad enough, but killing an innocent bystander was far worse—and the man had been a doctor, besides. I went outside after hearing the news, wove for a second on my feet, and then puked up my breakfast, unable to force it down this time. I knew the fatal bullet had likely been fired from the guns of either Doolin, Pierce or Newcomb; I'd seen them firing off in that direction, but I couldn't know for sure, and even if it hadn't been *me*, I'd been a part of it.

We needed to stop. Our luck was running out, seemed to me, and something told me that none of the railroad companies would stand for us taking another one of their trains. I took a deep breath, willing my stomach to stop heaving, and as I sat on my heels there in the shade of the shanty I made a promise to myself that I *would not* help in another train robbery, if Bob proposed one. I wouldn't leave the gang; I knew I had to stand by my brothers, but if they went, I'd stay behind.

"Emmett? You all right?"

Grat's voice startled me; I hadn't heard him come outside.

"No," I replied weakly, closing my eyes against another wave of nausea.

"You eat something bad?" Grat asked slowly, coming toward me. I took a few more deep gulps of air, rolling my eyes a little. Grat wouldn't understand; his conscience had never troubled him the way mine did. Grat's anger at the world and at life in general prevented him from knowing such inner torment.

"No," I replied, hoping my voice sounded stronger. "I'm fine, Grat." I steadied myself, then stood up, wiping my wrist across my mouth.

"You'd better get inside," Grat cautioned. "We're gonna move on soon. Bob doesn't want to stay here too long."

I went to the well dug near the shanty, pulled up a bucket of water and splashed some over my hot face, rinsed out my mouth, then went inside.

TWENTY-THREE

BOB DIDN'T SAY anything about another train job, much to my relief. But I was still uneasy, for Bob wasn't saying much of anything. For several days he was quiet, clearly grinding something down in his mind. Once in the evening of the fourth day I saw him crouching in the cleared-out area by the fire, drawing something out in the dirt and muttering to himself under his breath when he thought I wasn't watching him. It became clear to me he was planning something, but whatever it was, he chose to keep it to himself for the time being. He scuffed out whatever he'd been drawing in the dust before I could get a look at it, clearly not ready for Grat or I to see it.

We moved about the Territory, never staying in one campsite for more than a day or two. We abandoned the old claim shanty hideout since it was where we'd gone after the disaster at Adair, and we seldom went back to the dugout. We watched the papers and narrowly avoided capture several times.

Months passed, and nothing was ever said about the next job. Grat asked Bob about it, once, but Bob simply shook his head and said, "we're done with the railroad." Grat didn't ask again.

Then one evening in late September, just after we'd eaten supper, Bob cleared his throat and said, "listen here, Grat and Em."

I looked up from the knife I'd been sharpening against a rock. Bob was laying with his boots toward the fire, propped up on his elbows. Grat got out his tobacco pouch and started rolling himself a cigarette.

"I'm thinking, boys, that we need to get ourselves out of the country, pretty soon," Bob said slowly. "It's getting too hot here for my liking. I think we need to quit while we're ahead of the game."

My body flooded with relief at his words, but it was short-lived. We didn't have enough money to go to South America and start any sort of a life for ourselves down there.

"We're gonna need to get ahold of a big haul, though," Bob said, confirming my fears. "Big enough so's we never have to worry about money again."

"Not another train," Grat said wearily, exhaling smoke through his nose.

"Hell no," Bob said. "That's over with. I told you that already, remember? I'm talking about a bank."

For several seconds I froze, my knife paused in mid-scrape, my mind racing. I knew, of course, that men such as ourselves robbed banks; Jesse and Frank James had become famous for it, as had our cousins and others. I'd just never thought of *us* actually doing it. The idea sent a cold streak through my blood. "Bob…" I said.

"Emmett, just listen to me for a damn minute," Bob said firmly. "You *know* we got to get out of here. You know it's gonna take money to do that. We can't waste time on trains or stages or the like. We need one more job, a big one, and then we'll go. I ain't gonna get put behind bars as long as I'm breathing, and I won't let you two get put there, either. This is the only way."

I kept on scraping my knife until it was good and sharp. I said nothing, for I knew Bob had his mind made up and there'd be no changing it. Besides, if we were really gonna quit, I guessed I could handle one more job, bank or not.

"What do you have in mind, then, Bob?" Grat asked.

Something made me look up at Bob right then, and I saw a slow, smug smile come across his face. His eyes gleamed almost hungrily in the firelight. "We need to get Broadwell and Power, and I'll tell everyone together. I'll tell you boys this, though: we're gonna lower Jesse James's record with *this* escapade."

Grat and I looked at one another, both of us pondering what he meant. I felt a chill move through me at that remark, a strange sense of foreboding moving over me and making the hair on the back of my neck stand on end. When Grat passed me the whiskey bottle he'd pulled out of his saddle-bag, I took a good tug of it, hoping the warmth of the liquor would get rid of that chill.

It didn't.

On the night of October first we sat around the fire again, sheltered by the walls of a little gulch we'd found. Broadwell and Power had joined us that day, and they and Grat and I all looked at Bob and waited for him to begin his explanation of this mysterious grand scheme he'd come up with.

He tossed the remnants of his cigarette into the flames and leaned forward a little, his gaze intense. He looked at each one of us, then spoke.

"We're gonna do a bank job, this time," he said. "This'll be our last, and won't nobody forget it when we're through."

Power shifted his chaw of tobacco to his other cheek, his eyes narrowed a little bit. "What do you mean, 'last,' Bob? We're just getting started! We've only been at it, what, about—"

Bob cut him off, curtly. "You boys can do what you like," he said, "but I'm telling you that after this Em and Grat and I are done. I'm tired of that bastard Thomas breathing down my neck and hunting me out like a Goddamn game animal."

"What's your plan, then, Bob?" Dick asked, shooting Bill a glance.

Bob smiled. "There's a town in Kansas called Coffeyville," he said. "Ever heard of it?" Broadwell and Power shook their heads. I tensed and felt my mouth drop open aways, and shot a nervous look at Grat. Bob kept talking. "Em and Grat and I grew up there, for a time. I know that place like the back of my hand, and I figure we owe it to them, too, since our Pa got foreclosed on by one of them Goddamned banks. This'll settle that score, and set us above the James boys to boot. Ain't no one gonna remember *them* after we get through."

"I don't follow," Broadwell said, a puzzled look in his eyes. "Why would robbing a bank in some little nothing town in Kansas put us above the James boys, after all they did?"

Bob smiled again, and he knitted his long fingers together calmly. "Why, that's easy, Dick. Because we ain't gonna rob *a* bank. We're gonna rob *two* of them. At once."

No one said anything, nor even moved for a few seconds. I stared at Bob; at that moment I truly believed my brother had actually lost his mind. Power and Broadwell were gaping at him, too, and Grat had a look halfway between pride and fear on his face, as though he couldn't decide whether to praise Bob for his cunning or chew him out for being a damn fool.

"Bob, you can't be serious," Dick finally managed to stammer.

"I'm *dead* serious," Bob replied. "I got it all figured out, and it'll work. I know it will. Hear me out, now, boys," he said. "There's a plaza in Coffeyville where two streets come together, Walnut and Union. There's two banks right near one another there, the Condon and the First National." As he spoke, he was drawing a map out in the dirt. "We can ride in in the morning, just after they open, and hitch up here." He drew an 'X' at the corner of 8th and Walnut. "Then we'll split up. Grat will take two into the Condon, since it's bigger, and I'll take one into the First National. We get as much as we can, meet up at the horses, and then ride like hell, scot-free, outta there." He sat back on his heels a little and looked at us. "Think of it, boys! Crops've all come in by now, so the banks'll be runnin' over with cash. It's hunting season, so no one'll care if we go in with our guns. It'll be *easy.*"

I thought I heard something in the grass aways out of the gulch, and I tensed up, my fingers curling around my rifle. The others tensed, too, going for their guns and looking out where I was looking, but after a minute we saw the eyes of a coyote reflecting the flames of our fire, and it paused, staring at us, its big ears flicking back and forth for a minute before it ran off. We all relaxed, letting go of our guns. Heck Thomas was closer to us now than he'd ever been; Bob had said so just that morning. How he knew, I didn't know. But I trusted him, for I'd seen many a time how his intuition about those things was always right.

"So when're we gonna do this?" Dick asked after a bit. "Assuming I'm fool enough to go."

"I'm thinking Wednesday, middle of the week coming up," Bob replied, ignoring the last part of Dick's words. "We'll camp out the night before in the hills just above town. Then we'll waltz right in around nine." He laughed, almost to himself. "This'll top everything we've done, get us everything we want, and when we're through, you won't even believe how damned easy it was."

Whatever else he might have had, my brother Bob had a gift for being able to make a man believe something just by how he said it. There was never any uncertainty in his words, never any fear or doubt. I could see that gift of his was working its magic on Power and Broadwell. Grat, I could tell, was already on board.

I took a deep breath, figuring, as always, that I was the only one doing any worrying at all. "I ain't sure, Bob," I said slowly. "Seems like suicide, to me, when it comes down to it. You ever stop to think what might happen if we *don't* get away with it?"

Bob slowly turned his head and gave me a stare, a look that cut into me like a knife blade would. "Now, Emmett, the way I figure it is, we'd only muck it up any if one of us lost his nerve and turned yellow in the middle of the damned thing. We've all of us proved we ain't yellow, if I recall correctly." His words were slow and deliberate, and they hung heavy in the air. His tone was pleasant but we all knew what he meant, and none of us would stand for anyone, especially Bob, thinking we didn't have sand enough in us to try this thing.

"So what do you boys say, then?" he asked, finally looking away from me and at Broadwell and Power. "You in?"

Dick and Bill looked at each other, then at Bob. "We'll give her a go, Bob," Dick answered for them both.

"Grat?"

Our brother let a smile spread over his face; I thought to myself that only Grat could make that expression so consistently unpleasant. "Damn right, I'm in."

Finally, Bob looked at me. "Em?" His eyes glittered intensely in the firelight, but it wasn't with their usual warm twinkle. There was something almost warning in them, like he could read what I was thinking and he didn't much approve.

I took a deep breath. "If you and Grat are going, then I'm going, too," I said.

The look in Bob's eyes softened to one of deep affection and pride, and he gave me a little nod. "'Course you are," he said. He reached over and laid an arm across my shoulders, giving me a bracing squeeze. "And you're gonna be with me in the First National, while Grat and the others take the Condon. There's no one I'd rather have at my side, Em. I mean that."

I tried to give him a smile, glad that he had no way of seeing the uncertainty I was still feeling inside, the little ball of apprehension that had lodged itself in my gut. Bob said it would be easy, and he had to be right…didn't he?

———◦《◎》◦———

I had a dream that night as I slept by the fire, my rifle laid out at hand beside me. In the dream I was a child again, very young, barely six years old. I was running through the tall grass out behind the house I was born in, heading for some unknown destination. I could hear some of my brothers and sisters playing closer to the house, but I kept going, away from them, far out into the open space towards where the cattle were grazing.

Suddenly I heard the heavy tread of hooves, and the low bawl of an angry cow. I turned to see one of the big, half-wild bulls that belonged to Pa charging at me, horns lowered, eyes shining red. It had been grazing, but I'd wandered too close into its territory and it saw me as a threat, as small as I was. Vaguely I heard my brothers and sisters shout out in panic, and heard Mother scream out my name. I froze, unable to move, unable to cry out, and watched that big animal come at me, its nostrils flared, its broad head tossing this way and that, its big split hooves churning up chunks of grass. It was going to trample me, or gore me with its horns, and I couldn't seem to do anything to save myself.

Out of nowhere, Bob suddenly grabbed me, hauling me under my arms and half-carrying me, half-dragging me, out of the way of that bull. He pushed me away, then picked up a rock and hurled it at the animal, his aim true even then. The bull had wheeled away, tail thrown up over its back, more surprised than hurt, and run out to join the other cattle. Bob took his chance, snatching me up again and hauling me to safety, even though he himself was only eight.

"You're all right," he told me, breathing hard, once he got me to the house. "Don't be scared, Em. I won't let anything hurt you when I'm around, I promise."

And I'd believed him, trusted him. The dream was a memory, it had actually happened. I hadn't thought about that day in many, many years and I wondered why it had come into my mind now.

I woke with a start and sat up, shaking off the dream, and saw Bob sitting on a rock near the top of the gulch, his rifle laid across his lap, ready for anything as he kept watch. And I realized that as crazy and gutsy as Bob's plan sounded, I needed to trust him. He'd always looked out for me, just as he'd promised that day long ago, and I owed it to him to stand with him, even though I didn't see any wisdom in it. That sense of foreboding was still dogging me, but it wasn't as strong anymore.

———◦《◎》◦———

"Time to get a move on, boys."

Bob woke us with those words on the morning of October 5th, and the four of us rooted ourselves out of our bedrolls and gathered our parts, saddling up quick. Bob had gone over the plan again last night as we'd made camp, and we all knew it so well we could recite it in Bob's exact words. None of us had slept well; the anticipation of the job and the growing specter of Thomas and his posse had robbed us of all but the poorest rest, but our courage and our daring was running high, because Bob was emanating confidence and it was catching. If my brother had ever had any doubts in his head about what we were going to do, I never saw them.

We loaded our guns. Bob had three revolvers on him— in his vest, his gun belt and his boot, and his Winchester. Grat had his Winchester and a pair of revolvers. Dick and Bill had two guns each, and I had my two revolvers and my Winchester. We weren't worried about hiding the rifles when we got in; as Bob had pointed out, hunting season was here and no one would think it odd to see them. We shared some whiskey as a brace, Bob checked his watch, and then there was nothing left to do but head out.

Bob put a foot in his stirrup and swung on, checking his eager mount, then turned back in the saddle to face us, flashing us a devilish grin, his eyes snapping blue sparks of excitement. "Let's get ourselves into the history books, boys."

He put his spurs to his horse, we did the same, and the five of us set off for Coffeyville.

TWENTY-FOUR

WE SLOWED OUR mounts when we got to the outskirts, pulling up to a trot, then a walk. The first thing that hit me was the changed size of the place. The last time I'd been to Coffeyville, it had been small town where life moved at an easy, unhurried pace. Today it seemed to be thick with folks of all kinds, and grown up bigger than I could've thought possible in such a short amount of time. The pit of my stomach got a funny feeling and I started feeling nervous, right off. I glanced over at Bob, who was riding in between Grat and I, with Dick and Bill trailing behind. Bob's face was carefully blank, but I saw his eyes moving methodically over the townscape, narrowed and hard, taking everything in. He didn't look at me. I checked my horse a little in surprise as we headed down 8th street. The street was torn up and being worked on near the intersection we were heading for.

There was no hitching rail at the corner of 8th and Walnut anymore.

I threw another desperate glance at Bob, feeling a little panicked now. That intersection was where we were supposed to hitch the horses; it was close enough to both banks that Bob had counted on it being a good spot to tie our tickets out of there. I saw Grat's brows coming together, too, and he also shot a look at Bob, his expression plain. *Now what?*

Bob answered our glances and then neck-reined his horse to the right, nearly cutting off mine. "Follow me, boys. Keep your heads," he muttered. I could barely hear him as he passed me. He headed south on Maple, heading for a narrow, quiet little alleyway that faced the plaza where the banks were. Uneasily, we followed him. The plan had been so in-grained in our heads that having to stray from it even a little bit was giving us all pause. We followed him, trying to look natural. I began to feel that everyone we passed was sizing us up, but really, no one was—yet. It was only my imagination. We walked the horses up the alley until Bob spotted a long section of fence. He stopped his horse there and dismounted, and the rest of us did the same.

If I craned my neck a little around my horse I could see straight down the alley to where it opened at the plaza, and the big empty space in front of the Condon. Just beyond it, a little ways down Union, was the First National, where Bob and I would go. I stuffed the tow sack Bob had furnished me up into my coat.

We pulled our Winchesters out of our saddle skirts and made ready to take our walk. Out of the corner of my eye I saw Bill brushing his palms across his britches repeatedly; they must've been sweating. Dick reached up and tugged his hat down a little lower, and Grat and I did the same.

Bob didn't give us any signal this time; he just started walking, calmly, toward the plaza, and, as always, we followed him.

The crisp fall air nipped at our faces as we walked, our spurs chimed softly in unison. Our boots sent up little puffs of dust into the sunshine. I glanced at Bob's face, once, and wondered how he could look so damned calm yet radiate such excitement at the same time. I thought I saw the man sweeping the porch of his store that we were walking past glance at us suspiciously, but I forced myself to ignore him, not wanting to call any more attention to us. I tightened my grip on my Winchester, willing my lungs to move in and out, willing the fluttering in my gut to cease. I thought we'd been walking for miles and would never get there, but we'd really only been walking for a minute, and the plaza was looming ahead of us.

I was twenty-one years old. I was strong, in the prime of my being. I could handle myself; I could be what Bob believed I could be. I could protect my brother, just as he'd always protected me. All these thoughts were flying through my head right then; it would only be later that I would realize that I'd been thinking all those things so hard just so I'd convince myself of them.

Grat looked at Bob as we came out into the plaza from the alley, and Bob gave him a nod and a wink, a playful gesture that spoke of his supreme confidence our plan.

Grat looked at me next, but he seemed to look past me, his eyes flaring with the old bitterness I knew all too well, and I knew he was letting all those dark feelings he had harbored for years against anyone at all he'd ever thought had done him wrong in life boil up and brace him for what he was about to do. There were so many of them, in his mind: the men who'd murdered Frank. The marshal that had discharged him in

Indian Territory. The men who'd jailed him at Fort Smith. Those who had arrested and convicted him in California. The lawyer who'd lost his case there. Our father, who'd always seemed to have something better to do than to really buckle down and raise his boys for any great length of time, then up and died after Grat had come to know him best. Grat was angry and he was going to have his revenge against all of them, here in this last act of infamy by the Dalton Gang, and maybe when it was done, he could finally let go of it all.

He gave us a brief nod in answer, signaled Bill and Dick, and veered off into the Condon. I threw a glance over my shoulder as Bob and I kept going, and the last I saw of them right then were their backs as they stepped through the doors of the bank.

Bob and I walked, quickening our pace just a little. He brushed his fingers against my arm, once, a gesture meant to give me courage. I glanced over at him as our boots hit the gallery, and for a second I saw him in my mind as a boy again, grinning at me in that old devilish way after having convinced me to tag along on some act of mischief which I would have to get us out of by making sad eyes at Mother, who could seldom resist them, even though she tried.

Then we were at the door and he was the Bob I knew of now, the fearless leader of the Dalton Gang. He marched right in in front of me, and we raised our rifles in unison, as if we'd rehearsed it all like some theater show.

"All right, nobody move or try anything stupid," Bob said loudly, his voice seeming to thunder through the bank. "Everybody get down on the floor, now!"

The customers, three of them, went white in the face and

did as they were told, and the teller and the cashier turned gray, their hands rising toward the ceiling. Bob advanced, and I covered him, my aim steady. In my mind's eye I could see Grat, Bill and Dick in the Condon, doing the same thing we were.

"Bring out the cash, now," Bob said to the cashier. "Let's get on with things."

The cashier started bringing out money, but he was dragging his heels, and each second felt like a year to me. I knew Bob wouldn't stand for it for long, and I was right. He went up to the teller after he'd collected what the cashier brought out.

"We'd be much obliged," Bob said pleasantly but firmly, "if you'd attend to the vault." The teller didn't move. I saw sweat trickle down his temple. Bob shoved the muzzle of his rifle a little closer up under the teller's nose. "We don't have all day," Bob said, his voice hard and sharp-edged now. "Get going."

The teller nodded shakily and began backing toward the vault. Bob looked at me. "I believe you've got the sack," he said. His eyes locked onto mine, something encouraging in them. *Go on, Em,* they seemed to be saying. *I trust you to get the job done.*

He stood in the doorway that connected the bank's lobby to the back area, covering the prone customers and the bank employees. The teller opened the safe and stood back, looking away from me, at the floor. I saw him swallow hard. His hands were up again. I moved almost mechanically forward and began scooping stacks of bills into my tow sack, my heart pounding. I'd never seen so much money at once before, and hadn't counted on it being so heavy.

"Let's go," Bob suddenly said. I hoisted the sack and came over to him, keeping one eye on the teller to make sure neither he nor the cashier tried anything. But Bob motioned to them. "Come on, I said let's go."

They looked at each other, a quick, fearful glance, then slowly began coming toward us, their hands still up, the sweat coming up good on their temples now. I glanced at Bob, confused, but he wasn't looking at me. He was looking at them, and his eyes looked hard and cold, that look I'd always dreaded seeing. And then I understood; he meant them to be our hostages.

"Go. Hurry up, now. I told you we don't got all damn day," Bob said sharply. They eased past him. Then Bob pointed his Winchester at one of the men laying on the floor. "I need one more, and it looks like you're elected, bub. Come on, get to your feet, now. Hurry it up."

The man got to his feet, his hands up. Bob leveled his gun at the three of them. "Make for the door, now. Nice and easy. The rest of you," he said, raising his voice, "keep your faces on that floor, or there'll be hell to pay. I'm not kidding around."

Apparently satisfied that none of the customers were going to try anything, Bob marched the other three men toward the front door. I followed behind, my Winchester in one hand, the bulging sack in the other. My stomach started its old tricks again, but I forced myself to ignore it, as I'd learned to do over the past year. My heartbeat was going funny, though; it was too loud. It was throbbing in my ears and I was afraid Bob could hear it, but he didn't turn, just ushered the three hostages out.

My ears cleared up just in time to hear gunfire split the air—and not just from one gun. Where a second ago things had been quiet, now lead was being pumped all over the place, seemed to me, and from all directions; smoke hung black in the air already. Sweat began to pour off of me and I caught Bob's eyes once, my own wide with shock, his snapping sparks of rage, before he hurried us all back inside. Somehow, we'd been found out, and there were men out there with guns, ready to stop us. My mind flashed back to that night on the Alila train, that seemed so long ago now. *The whole thing was going to hell.* Bob hadn't counted on resistance. He hadn't counted on ordinary folks taking up arms against us.

"All right, turn around, now!" Bob bellowed, shoving the hostages toward the back of the bank. "Get going! We're going out the back door!" He snapped a command at the men still lying on the floor, now covering their heads and necks with their arms as bullets smashed through the windows, showering glass all over them. "Don't any of you move or I'll make sure you don't *ever* move again!"

With that, he made us run, and we barged out the back, the three men in front of us. I caught sight of a kid about Bob's age coming toward us, a pistol in his hand.

"Don't you be a fool and do something you'll regret!" Bob warned him, his voice sounding deeper to me than usual. The kid kept coming. Bob did not hesitate. He raised his rifle and fired, his aim precise as always. Feeling like I was trapped in a nightmare, I saw the young man drop like a buck at hunting time. Bob had hit him in the chest, and I knew he was dead.

I'd never seen Bob kill anyone before. I'd seen him threaten to, but he'd never had to do it; at least, not in my presence. Bile rose in my throat and for a minute I thought I'd vomit, right there in the middle of the chaos that had taken over Bob's simple little plan.

Gunfire was still coming, from all over. Bob reached over and grabbed me by the sleeve of my coat. "Come *on*, Em! We gotta leave! We gotta get to the horses, *now!*"

I got ahold of myself as best I could, and looked away from that poor dead soul and his pistol laying in the grass next to his hand. His eyes were closed and he looked like he was asleep. Bob abandoned the three hostages, intent on getting us out of there. One of them wheeled and ran for the building next door, the hardware store, but Bob ignored him.

We ran up Union, heading for 8th, kicking up dirt into the air to mingle with the wafting gun smoke. Before we got very far both Bob and I saw two older men standing on the gallery, looking away from us and toward the plaza, where more gunfire was roaring. I realized Bob and I weren't the only ones in trouble. As this thought entered my mind I saw those two men turn back toward us, and I recognized them. They were George Cubine and Charles Brown, the town cobblers. They'd lived here when we had, and they knew us. Cubine had a rifle in his hands. Bob lifted his, sighted, and fired, so fast I almost couldn't follow his movements. Cubine dropped.

Nausea rolled up in me again then, so strong I almost couldn't fight it this time. I *knew* these two men. *Bob* knew them. But they were armed, and those arms were against us. Bob saw Brown take up Cubine's rifle, and Bob dropped him. I faltered. Bob grabbed me, his fingers digging into my coat with a vise-like grip. "*Come on*, Emmett! We have to *move*! We can't let them kill us!"

My vision blurred a bit and I realized I had tears in my eyes. *What had we done?* All those other times—the horses, the trains—paled and faded in my conscience, for this event was to leave no room there for them any longer, it seemed.

The hostage who'd made for the hardware store came out its front door now, and he had a gun. Bob shot him and the bullet hit his face, just under his eye. He flew backwards onto the gallery.

We ran. I heard shouting, screaming and more guns. Horses were whinnying shrill cries of fright from somewhere. I heard the thud of our boots, the chime of our spurs. The heavy bag of money was starting to pain my arm, and it bumped awkwardly against my legs and my boots as we went. My Winchester lay silent and ready in my other hand, but I didn't aim it at anyone. I just kept running.

My racing mind turned to Grat and the others. Were they still in the Condon, trapped like penned animals? Had they gotten out? Had they reached the horses? I thought my heart would burst out of my chest, it was pounding so.

The gunfire seemed to be coming from somewhere else, now, and I realized as Bob and I ran for the alley that we were running right into it. But we were running too fast, too intent on the horses. I felt like I was floating somewhere above my body, watching myself and Bob run into a lion's den, but there was nothing I could do to stop it. I could see two men coming through the livery yard and another coming through the vacant lot near the horses. The third man, who had a badge glinting out from his vest, suddenly stumbled and fell dead as a bullet hit him, fired by someone I couldn't see yet. Then one of the men coming to cut us all off raised his rifle and shot at whomever had killed the lawman in the lot.

As Bob and I made it into the alley I turned my head to see whom he had fired at, and my heart sank, and my eyes flooded. Grat lay on his back in the dirt, a bullet hole in his throat, his neck at an awkward angle. I knew he was dead. The brother who'd always seemed so large and intimidating to me in life now looked small and almost slight in death. My vision seemed to blur in and out, but there was no time to grieve. The rest of us were marked for death, too. Aways down the alley lay Bill Power, facedown, his arms spread out on either side of him like he'd been crucified. He was dead, too; I could tell by the stillness of his body. The gun smoke thinned out for just a moment, and the sun glanced off the revolver laying under his hand. Dick had made it to a horse—Grat's—and he was riding away, but he was slumped over funny and I saw blood on his shirt. He'd been hit, too.

Bob was firing at anyone he could see, his eyes aflame with rage, his desire for revenge insatiable now that he'd seen Grat laying there in the dust. I ran for my horse, still lugging the money, and somehow got it tied to the pommel of my saddle. Bob was still firing, trying to keep away anyone after us. His face looked like all the color had gone out of it, but I saw no fear in it, only anger and grief.

I heard several shots then that seemed louder than all the others, several that seemed to rise above the drone of firing rifles and revolvers. At first, I didn't realize that I'd been hit by some of them. My right arm and shoulder seemed to go strangely numb and I couldn't seem to make them work. My Winchester dropped from my hand. Then another shot came and I turned behind me to see Bob stumble back as if he'd been shoved by strong hands. He went down into a sitting position, then slumped against a rock on the ground. I saw a glistening red stain on his vest.

I couldn't see anymore, through the water in my eyes, and the smoke that was stinging them. I couldn't breathe. I couldn't seem to do anything except somehow scramble up onto my horse, the money still tied there. I felt something warm and moist trickle down my right side and vaguely I realized it was my own blood; I could smell it. I felt the pain come on then, a burning hot agony that took over my whole body, made my stomach turn and the bile rise up in me again. My back and hip felt like knives had been plunged into them and were slowly twisting. I gritted my teeth and started to spur my mount out of there, but something made me turn and look back.

Bob was still slumped over where he'd fallen, but I saw him move a little and I realized that he was still alive. Every other thought left my head then save for one—getting Bob out of there. Saving him like he'd saved me all those years ago. Repaying all of the times he'd taken care of me or braced me in hard times. He was my brother and I loved him and I *would not leave him there,* no matter if I died in the process.

I managed to wheel my terrified horse around, and I rode without hesitation into the hail of bullets still raining through the air. I felt them flying past me, but none of them found their mark. I felt no fear; all I could think about was Bob. I got to him and leaned down, searching his gray face frantically for any sign that he would live.

"Bob!" I choked out, hoarsely, sobs coming up in me and squeezing off what little breath I was able to still get. "Oh, God...no...."

His eyes flickered open, somehow found mine through the haze of his pain. I saw him shudder, saw his throat bob as he swallowed. He spoke, and though his voice was weak and the guns were still going I could hear his words plainly.

"Goodbye, Em," he said. "Don't you surrender, hear? Die game."

"*Bob, no!*" I cried out in agony. I leaned farther down, reaching with my left hand for his coat, desperate to pull him up onto my horse. Then I felt something hit me in the back, hard, knocking the breath out of me and sending me down out of the saddle. Added to the pain I'd already been feeling came dozens of red-hot stings, as if I were being bitten by millions of sharp teeth. I'd been hit, I realized, with the blast of a shotgun. I hit the ground hard, biting down on my tongue as I did so, tasting the metallic bitterness of my own blood in my mouth.

I saw the bodies of Grat and Power out of the corner of my eye as I fell, but it was Bob I focused on. He had blood coming out of his nose in two thin ruby streams. He was on his stomach now, his rifle laying askew where he'd dropped it after firing one final shot. He was looking at me, and his eyes were clouded; their color faded, and the old sparkles had gone out of them. He focused his gaze on my face, looking straight into my eyes, and spoke again, weakly, over the horrible rattle in his throat. "I'm dying, Em." His voice sounded like it belonged to someone else. A strangely serene expression came over his white face, his lips twitched up in a smile, and his eyes drooped shut. I saw his whole body relax as the life left it.

"No!"

The cry wrenched itself out of me, coming around a sob and surprising me. My voice sounded weak and torn-up. I wanted to scream, I wanted to rise up and take the life of the man who'd taken his, but I was too weak to do either one. This wasn't happening. It *couldn't* be. Bob was the strong one, the bravest of us, the luckiest. He'd always gotten out of any jam he'd ever been in and come out of it with a laugh. He *couldn't* be lying here next to me on a street in Coffeyville, his life extinguished like a candle that had been casually snuffed out. I would surely wake soon, come out of this nightmare. I would find myself sitting around a campfire with my two brothers again, and Bob's eyes would shine in the firelight, and he would laugh that familiar rolling laugh that always made me smile. I would know, as always, that my brother was there to look out for me.

And then the pain rolled over me again, into every part of my body, jarring me down to my very soul. The sunshine in my eyes dimmed, like someone had blown out a lamp. A merciful nothingness came over me and I felt no more pain. The gunfire stopped, the smoke cleared over the streets littered with dead and dying horses and dead men, and there was nothing but darkness and silence.

TWENTY-FIVE

WHEN I CAME to I heard voices jabbering loudly from somewhere near me, going in and out as I faded back and forth between consciousness and nothingness. Snatches of their words came to me through my haze of pain, which was back with a vengeance.

"....I don't care if he's still alive, he won't be for long!"

"Get a damn rope! String the son of a bitch up and let's have done with it!"

"That Goddamned Dalton Gang has terrorized this country enough. He's one of their lot. He don't deserve to live after all they've done!"

They must have been, I realized, talking about me, but I felt no fear or anger at their words. I didn't blame them for wanting to lynch me, and perhaps it was for the best, anyhow. I didn't know for sure at that moment that I was the sole survivor of this mess; I hadn't learned that Dick was dead, too, but I knew that Bob and Grat were dead and I didn't see much point in me living when they didn't.

"Hold on, now, just wait a minute!" That was a different voice, much closer to me than the others. I opened my eyes with a struggle and looked in the direction it had come from, and saw the hazy form of a man crouched beside me. His watch chain was dangling just above my face and it glittered in the sunlight. My vision was still blurred by pain and tears and I couldn't see his face well. I didn't know who he was or why he was seemingly trying to defend me from the lynch mob. Dully I looked away, not caring to know any of those answers. None of it seemed important just then.

"What are you doing, Wells?" I heard someone exclaim angrily. "He's a damned outlaw and he'll swing from a tree for it!"

"Don't you think there's been enough bloodshed and murder here today, Kloehr?" my benefactor retorted, his voice hard. When he spoke again his voice was raised to a loud level, as if he were pleading with a great many people. "For God's sake, *look* at him! He's got more bullet holes in him than all those others together. He won't live long. Let him die by God's hands, instead of having his blood on all of yours!"

There was a silence as the mob apparently thought over his words. The man defending me leaned down closer and I saw him better now. He had a kind face, and his dark eyes were filled with compassion, which surprised me. "What's your name, son?" he asked me.

I stared up at him, reluctant to use my real name, partially out of habit, partially because I was sure that saying it would send the mob into a frenzy again. A name came out of my mouth, I don't even remember what it was. McLoughlin, I think. I heard others mutter in protest.

"He's a damned liar. He's a Dalton!" someone hissed.

"Calm down, Cary," the man leaning over me ordered. He looked back at me, still compassionate. "Come now, son, tell us your name. Your *real* name."

I gritted my teeth against the waves of pain that were coming on stronger and stronger as I came around more fully. "Emmett Dalton," I admitted, the fight going out of me. What did I care if they did lynch me? At least it would spare me more pain—and the horrible memory of the life fading from Bob's eyes. I waited.

"You see?" The voice was snide.

"Yes, I see," my savior said grimly. "And Dalton or not, I meant what I said. Now, who will help me move this boy out of the street and to my office, where he can face judgement for his sins with some manner of dignity?"

"He don't deserve any dignity," someone muttered, but even as that man spoke, others came forward and suddenly I felt hands on me, lifting me up and laying me out on a blanket. I cried out in pain as I was moved, praying that God would be merciful and either let me die or make me black out again, but apparently He wasn't listening to me just then. They used the blanket as a stretcher and carried me off, and I felt myself being tipped up as they carried me up a flight of stairs. I felt tears squeezing out of the corners of my eyes and trickling down the sides of my face; every step they took, every small jiggle of the blanket meant agony for me. I saw a doorway and the ceiling of a room, and then they set me out on a bed of some sort. The room spun a little and for a moment I was sure I would vomit, but I didn't. My benefactor was standing at my head and I saw him turn to the other men.

"Thank you, gentlemen. I'll attend to him, now."

I heard boots scuffing against the floor, and the sound of a door thudding shut. Then the man who'd saved me from the lynch mob looked down at me. "Emmett, I am Doctor Wells," he said. "I'm going to clean up your wounds now, and dress them. I know you're in pain, but this must be done."

"Why didn't you let them string me up? I wouldn't blame them for it," I managed to ask. My tongue felt thick, and sore from where I'd bitten it, and I thought I sounded as if I'd been drinking too much whiskey. The nausea came back in waves, receding mercifully for a few moments, then cruelly coming back again. I closed my eyes, fighting against the feeling.

"Because as I said out there to them, I don't believe any more lives should be taken by men today," he said firmly, moving busily around and collecting little glass bottles and instruments. His shirtsleeves were rolled up to his elbows. "If you are to die—and you very well may, with as many shots as you've taken—then it should be God who takes you, not angry men."

I didn't answer him; I was in too much pain. But I turned my face away from him, hot tears welling up in my eyes again, the image of Bob's dying face coming into my mind. A few minutes after he started his work I lost consciousness once again, my body giving in to its agony.

⋙●《●》●⋘

"How is he, Walter?"

I came around to the sound of a strange man's voice saying those words, and I tried to move but found the effort it took to do so too much to muster.

"He's poorly, Tom, as you might expect," Dr. Wells answered in a low voice. "I've cleaned him up and dressed him as best I could, and removed the buckshot. His right arm is useless; it's been broken by the bullet. I'm amazed he's still alive, frankly. I don't expect him to live for any great length of time, but I could be wrong. The human body has a remarkable ability to withstand things it shouldn't."

There was a pause. And then, the unknown man spoke again, his voice soft this time. "My God, he's just a kid!"

"Yes," the doctor replied. "Not much more than a boy, really. One wonders how men his age get wrapped up in these doings."

"The leader of 'em was young, too," the man named Tom said. "Not too much older'n this 'un. You let me know if he wakes. We got all the bodies of those damn bandits in the jail; he'll have to identify them for the record."

The doctor murmured his consent. I felt my stomach, already nauseated, turn over again and I managed to turn my face farther into the cool pillow.

They must've seen my movement, because I heard steps come closer to my bedside, and Dr. Wells was suddenly leaning over me. "Emmett? Can you hear me?" he asked.

I made a sort of groaning noise, nodding weakly. Dr. Wells straightened up and looked across the room. "He's awake now, Tom."

"Set him up, then. Get some pillows behind his back, or

whatever you're gonna do. I'll have John and some of the others bring them stiffs in here now, get it the hell over with. I'll send up some man to guard him, too."

"Is that really necessary, Tom? He's certainly not in any condition to go anywhere. He can't stand, much less make a run for it."

"Even so, I want that boy under guard. He'll have charges filed against him, if he lives. Ain't gonna take any chances." There were heavy steps, and the sound of the door opening and shutting.

Dr. Wells came over to me, carrying some pillows. "I'm going to have to prop you up a bit, Emmett. I don't know how much of that you heard…"

"I heard it all," I said weakly, after feebly licking my cracked lips.

"That was Sheriff Callahan," he told me. "He'll likely let a reporter in here, too, when he comes back. The *Journal's* been covering the whole…incident. They've been taking pictures of…everything. They'll probably want yours."

I knew he meant the bodies of my brothers when he said "everything." I didn't answer him, for I couldn't think of anything to say. Painfully I submitted to being helped into a partially-sitting position, my wounds throbbing, by body aching as if I'd been beaten. I was shirtless and my body was crisscrossed by bandages, my arm supported by a white sling. I heard the ticking of a clock somewhere in the room. There was a framed picture of a bunch of men on horseback on the wall next to my cot, and a lamp on the little table there. My eyes moved around the room, taking an uninterested inventory of the items and furniture for lack of anything better to do. I fought to stay awake, and fought to think of anything besides Bob and Grat. I wasn't sure if it was still October 5th; but the morning we'd rode in seemed like a year ago. Dr. Wells kept to himself, apparently sensing that I didn't wish to speak.

After a bit I heard boots on the stairs, and the door opened. A man with a badge on his vest who must've been the sheriff came inside, and, seeing that I was sitting up as best I could, motioned to someone outside. A man carrying a notebook and pencil came in; I supposed he was the reporter. A photographer followed him and quietly began setting up his camera on the other side of the room. The photographer took my picture, and I let him, looking straight into the lens, knowing everything I was feeling was showing in my face.

After that a few men carried in a blanket bearing a body inside, and, without ceremony and without any words of con-dolence to soften the experience, held it up in front of me, gripping the corpse under its arms. It was Bob.

My eyes welled, my stomach turned, and I felt my body flush first hot, then cold. I couldn't help it, I let the tears spill over my lower eyelids. His hands were bound stiffly in front of him at the wrists, as if he were still alive and needed re-straining, and his hair looked strange to me, as if it had been cut in places. His boots were gone and one of his trouser-legs had been cut away in pieces almost up to his knee. The bloodstain on his vest looked like an ink stain now. They'd wiped away the blood from his nostrils.

"Emmett Dalton, can you identify this man of your group for us?" Sheriff Callahan asked me.

I swallowed hard, trying not to bawl, and took a deep

breath. "That is my brother Bob," I said, fighting my pain and my nausea and my sorrow. The sheriff nodded to another man, who wrote that down. I tried to look away from Bob's body but found I could not. They laid him back down in the blanket and carried him out; before I could recover they were asking me questions about Bob.

I somehow collected myself and tried my best to answer. They asked me Bob's age and I told them; they seemed somewhat surprised when I said twenty-three. I admitted that Bob had been in the Adair robbery and the Alila attempt. I did not, however, implicate myself, for I knew better. I could hear Bob's voice in my head at that moment. *"Don't surrender."* I'd always followed his instructions before, and I would continue to do so.

Then they were bringing in the next. It was Grat they held up this time, bound at the wrists like Bob, his eyes closed, his hair mussed as if it too had been cut away, lock by lock. It made him look older. My eyes were drawn to the round, dark bullet hole in his throat, just below his Adam's Apple. He was so pale in death that his moustache stood out in prominence from his face. I had the strange thought that he looked somehow more peaceful in death than he ever had while living, and I prayed fervently that he'd somehow been released from all of the bitterness and torment he'd carried around with him in life.

"Emmett?" Callahan prodded.

"That's my brother, Gratton Dalton," I managed to get out, my eyes welling up again. I closed my eyes and looked away, unable to bear the image another second.

They took Grat out and asked me similar questions. I told

them Grat was thirty-one, and that he'd been at Adair with Bob.

They brought Bill in next, and I identified him by his alias, Tom Evans. I was feeling sicker by that time and the sheriff had to move closer to catch my words since I was having a hard time making my voice come out loud enough. I told him I didn't know how old Power was.

Finally, they brought in a fourth body and I knew then that Dick had not made it. They told me he'd been found dead outside of town on the side of the road. I used one of his aliases, Jake Moore, to identify him. They asked me if he'd gone by Texas Jack at any time. He had, but I lied and said I didn't know anything about it. I felt like I was saying too much, and I just wanted them all to go away and leave me to die in peace—for I felt quite certain, just then, that I was going to die.

They weren't done with me yet, though. They asked me for a statement regarding the raid and the plan that had led up to it, and I gave them a less-than-factual account of it, with truths placed here and there among the lies. I told them how Bob had said he wanted to top Jesse James. I admitted my family connection to the Youngers, which seemed to interest them a great deal, and refused to tell them where our hideouts were as I felt it might get Bitter Creek and Bill Doolin and Charley Pierce in trouble if I did. The room had started to swim again and I heard myself slurring my words. At some point in my story I lost hold of my composure, thinking about watching Bob die, and I couldn't speak any longer. The sheriff made everyone leave, then, and I thought I heard a different note in his voice, a note of compassion, but

I might have imagined it.

Finally he went away too, and let me be, and the man assigned to guard me and Dr. Wells sat quietly near as I let blackness overtake me again.

TWENTY-SIX

AN ATTORNEY NAMED Dooley came up to see me when I next awoke, late at night. He took my statement again, under oath this time. I told him the same story I'd told Callahan and his lot. I was in so much pain I could barely speak and I doubted my words were coherent. Dr. Wells gave me some morphine for the pain and told me some of my family was coming to see me. I felt shame flood me when I thought of Mother; I didn't know how I'd face her, but at the same time, I desperately wanted the unique sort of comfort only she had ever been able to give me.

The morphine put me to sleep, and when I woke, my breath caught and my chest felt like a rock had been placed upon it, for Bob sat at my bedside, his face tilted downward, his hand laying over mine.

And then my vision cleared up and my mind sharpened, and I saw that it was not Bob, but Will.

His profile was filled with sadness and his gaze was focused on my hand that lay under his. I licked my parched lips, swallowed with some difficulty, and struggled to speak. "Will?"

He started a little bit and his eyes raised to my face. He seemed surprised and relieved beyond belief that I was awake and speaking to him.

"Oh, Em," he breathed, his voice smaller than I'd ever heard it. "I'm so glad you've woken. It's good to hear your voice, son." He squeezed my fingers a little. I saw him swallow hard. "Are you in awful pain?"

I struggled to shake off the fog that the morphine had left behind. "Some," I said. "It doesn't seem quite as bad, just now." I could barely hear my own words.

Will got me some water and carefully helped me with my pillows. His face was pale and his eyes looked bloodshot, as though he hadn't slept in a long time. I asked him what day it was and he told me the 6th, which surprised me; I thought more time had gone by. We were alone in the doctor's office, with not even a guard present, which surprised me. Will told me quietly that they'd thought I was dying and so they'd given us some privacy.

He sat silent for a few minutes, and then he took a breath that sounded unsteady. "Emmett, I'm afraid I got something I need to confess to you. I know you ain't in much shape to hear it, and maybe I'm saying it more for myself, but…"

I tried to focus on him, for I was feeling very ill at the moment. He spoke again, abruptly. "It was supposed to be a *joke*, Emmett." His voice broke. "A Goddamned joke. I never meant…"

"What are you talking about, Will?" I managed to ask, my voice so weak I was afraid he couldn't hear it.

He looked at me then, his eyes reddened and puffy, tears pooling up in them. The sight shocked me, for I'd never seen

Will cry. Whatever he was about to tell me was eating at him and tearing him up inside. "That train in Alila, Em? That was my idea. *I'm* the one that turned Bob's mind to it. It was supposed to be a game, just the one time. I never thought he'd make a career out of it, and drag you and Grat along. I never thought..."

I swallowed painfully and let my face turn away from him a little. "It's not your fault, Will. Bob had it in him. You know he did, and I know he did. He would've done it anyway." My voice sounded dull. Emotionless. "There was no one could've stopped him, Will, except himself. When he got an idea in his head, he up and did it. You know that."

My eyelids were sinking as I mumbled that last bit to him. I had no more fight left in me and I gave in to delirium, knowing instinctively that I had a fever. Will kept talking to me, but I could no longer understand his words.

Will sat with me for a long time, but in my state of pain and fever he wasn't always Will. Sometimes he was Bob, looking at me with sorrow in those familiar eyes instead of warmth or laughter. Sometimes he was Grat, giving me that strange gaze of his that could look both angry and sad, at the same time. And other times he was Frank, tall and proud, holding my hand between his two big ones, the goodness in him shining out through his eyes. But no matter who my ill mind took him to be, he was always talking to me, telling me I would live, and that I would heal.

I must've believed that somewhere inside, because sometime later I opened my eyes and felt a little further from death. Will was still there, and besides him there was Ben and Eva, and Mother.

"Oh, thank you, Lord," Mother breathed, seeing me awake. "Oh, Emmett, my dear boy," she managed to get out, tears pooling in her eyes, and she came to my side and took my free hand in hers, leaning down to kiss my forehead. I choked back tears and squeezed her hand back, even though the movement hurt.

"Em," Eva got out, reaching for my fingers after Mother had pulled back. Her eyes were puffy. I couldn't speak for the sob in my throat. Ben took a deep breath, standing at the foot of the bed, and I saw him look up at the ceiling, his lips moving in a silent prayer. I didn't know what to say to them, for they knew what had happened and I felt all of our misdeeds were exposed and laid bare before them, like a raw, open wound, and there was nothing I could say to redeem myself in their eyes.

There was a question in my mind that kept coming to the fore, though, and I had to ask it. I struggled to take a deep breath. "Where...what have they done with—" I paused to choke back a sob "—Bob and Grat?"

Mother's chin was trembling but she clenched her jaw, hard, and answered me as the others threw uncomfortable glances at one another. "They've been laid to rest, Emmett, at the cemetery here. I wanted to take them home but—" she collected herself "—perhaps they're best left at peace where they are."

I turned my face away from her and squeezed my eyes shut, trying to shut out the image of Bob's tall, strong body moldering in a grave with Grat's, his long, elegant hands crossed over his breast. It was a long time before that grim vision would leave me.

They stayed with me awhile and told me that the sheriff had wanted to move me to the jail at Independence but had decided against it, and I would be taken to the Farmer's Hotel to continue my recovery. They didn't say it but I knew the sheriff had changed his mind because of the likelihood that I would be lynched. I still wasn't sure why everyone seemed so keen on stopping that. I missed Bob's presence at my side more and more with each passing hour, and with my sorrow and my pain overtaking me at times like these, and the certainty of facing the law, I saw little point in living on.

TWENTY-SEVEN

I *DID* LIVE, though. Somewhere inside of me I had the will to survive, and the will to recover, and on the eleventh they took me on my cot and carried me out of my room to take me to the jail at Independence.

Will, who had remained with me after the others had gone home, came along. Something in him had changed over the last week; I could feel it. He emanated anger now, the way Bob had used to do sometimes, and I knew he wanted revenge for Bob and Grat's deaths and my injuries. The guilt he felt over believing he'd driven us into our infamy was joined by a growing thirst for vengeance and, I feared, a desire to be known by the world as a man to be reckoned with. No one would cross *this* Dalton. I hadn't been in too much of a condition or in any position to hear much gossip, but I somehow instinctively knew that Will had made enemies since the raid, and was headed for trouble. I could tell he was thinking over something in his mind but I didn't try to learn what it was or talk him out of it—Will was like Bob in his stubbornness. Once he made his mind up about something, it could not be changed except by his own will. He had always, it seemed to me, walked a tightrope between living honestly and living dangerously, and he'd jumped off it now, landing in darkness.

When he'd assured himself that I would live, he left me with kind and encouraging words, but there was a steeliness in his eyes that struck a chill in me. Then he was gone, pursuing his own agenda, leaving me to worry over him and to wonder. I would never see him again.

There was still talk of lynching, but Sheriff Callahan protected me well, and no one tried anything. I languished in jail and slowly healed as the months passed by and my trial approached, set for January. I'd been carried into court on a chair for my preliminary hearing, at which I'd told the judge I was not ready to enter a plea or stand trial. The ordeal exhausted me and gave me an even bleaker outlook on my future. The City Attorney, a man named Fritch, had consulted with me, but I had no lawyer. They were planning to charge me with robbery, which seemed reasonable to me, and murder—which did not. I hadn't fired a shot during that day, but I was the only one left alive to hold accountable for some of those deaths and the state was out for Dalton blood. I was damned if I'd let them take mine for something I hadn't done. I would *not* plead guilty to murder. That was about the only thing I could get too riled up about in those days.

Though I tried not to, I thought often about Bob and Grat. I dreamed about them often, too; sometimes the old dream about the day Bob saved my life, sometimes dreams about the days when we rode with the gang. Once I dreamed that we'd gotten away with Coffeyville and had made it to the ship for South America, and Bob turned to me with his old devilish grin and a wink, telling me "I *told* you we'd do it, Em!" and slapping me on the back as we sailed. That was the worst dream of all, for it seemed so real, and then I woke and saw only the cold bars of my cell instead of Bob's smiling face.

And sometimes Laura Stevens would be in my dreams, in her white cotton dress with her hair swinging in that thick dark cloud to her waist, and we'd be waltzing to the fiddle in the schoolhouse in Estrella. She'd be smiling up at me, her big green eyes glowing, her cheeks flushed with rose, and I would think that surely, life could not possibly be better than it was right then.

I started doing whatever I could to stay awake at nights, once *those* dreams started.

———— ◆ ————

"Emmett Dalton, you are charged with bank robbery and two counts of murder. How do you plead?"

I was standing in the courtroom at Independence, facing the judge. I'd almost recovered from all of my wounds, and I could walk now, but with difficulty, so I was using crutches. My arm still troubled me greatly, but at the moment, none of that concerned me.

I felt every eye in that place on me as I took a breath and answered the judge. "Not guilty, Your Honor."

A murmur of disapproval went through the courtroom at that, but I ignored it. They were trying to pin the murders of George Cubine, the cobbler, and Lucius Baldwin, the boy who'd come at us with a pistol as we were leaving the bank, on me, though Bob had shot them both. *I had not murdered anybody.* I would not buckle, and I would not take the plea deals offered me, for they involved admitting to murder. As I so often did, I heard Bob's voice in my head. *Don't surrender.*

The judge glared out over the courtroom and banged his gavel, once. "Silence, please," he warned, and everyone fell silent. He looked at me again, his thick brows knitting together, his piercing dark eyes looking right at mine. "Have you the means to provide yourself with council, Mr. Dalton?"

Miserably I shook my head. I didn't have the money for a lawyer, and neither did Mother.

He nodded. "Very well. City Attorney Fritch will represent you. Your trial will begin at nine o'clock tomorrow morning in this courthouse." He banged his gavel again, and nodded to the Bailiff, who came up to my side to take me back to jail. I heaved a sigh and went with him, glancing at Fritch as I left. Dryly I thought how odd it was that Fritch, who had once filed the murder charge for Baldwin against me right after the raid, was now to be my defense attorney. At least I knew him, having received some council from him before my preliminary hearing. He'd changed his mind about me, apparently.

I went back to jail, confident that my plea had been the right one. They had nothing to pin the murders on me, and rightly so, since I hadn't committed them.

"Emmett?"

I had been sitting on my cot in my cell reading to keep my mind off the throbbing that had started in my arm, and I hadn't noticed anyone come to the door of my cell. I looked up and saw Fritch standing there, my brother Ben beside him.

I was surprised to see him. Ben had come to see me when I'd been teetering on the edge between life and death, but I hadn't expected to see him now, for he and I had never been close—he was so much older than me, and so reserved in manner that he'd never understood the love of excitement and adventure that I'd shared with Bob and Grat. He'd disapproved of them, and now disapproved of Will, too, so I didn't figure he much approved of me, either.

"Ben," I blurted out, putting my book aside.

Ben looked at Fritch, then at me. "Emmett, I'm hoping I can talk with you awhile. Are you feeling up to it?"

I stared at him in confusion, uncertain as to why he would want to see me alone, but I nodded. "Of course."

One of the guards came and let him in with me, then stood back against the far wall, close enough to watch everything that was going on but far enough away to afford us some privacy. Fritch gave Ben a look, then went away to leave us alone.

Ben came and sat next to me on the cot. "Emmett, I'm here to talk to you about your plea."

I set my jaw, knowing what was coming. "Ben, I'm *not* gonna plead guilty to Goddamned murder!" I growled, feeling anger boil up in me. "I didn't kill those two men—I didn't kill *anybody*. I didn't even get a single shot off that day." I turned my back to him a minute. "*Bob* shot Cubine and Baldwin. I *saw* it. I was *there*. Why would you want me to admit to doing something I didn't do?" I blinked a couple of times, quickly; my eyes were stinging suspiciously.

"Emmett, I don't want you to admit to something you didn't do. I don't want you to stand up and say that you took another man's life. But if you consider pleading guilty to second-degree murder, you'll make out better. They won't prosecute you for the other man's death, or the bank robbery."

"Pleading guilty is the same as standing up and saying I did it, in my book," I retorted. I put my good hand against the bars and leaned on them a minute, weary of standing. I was so tired, and so downtrodden, that I couldn't seem to see any hope in anything except that maybe I would be acquitted. How could they convict me when they had no proof?

"Emmett, you must listen to reason," Ben insisted. He never called me 'Em,' as the others did. He always used my full name, and he always spoke formally. It was another thing that made me feel far away from him, even when I was standing right next to him. I thought of Bob and fought to control myself. Ben kept talking. "Emmett, the people of Kansas are out for blood when it comes to the Dalton Gang." I heard the distaste in his voice when he said those last two words, but I said nothing, just let him keep going. "They'll have difficulty finding a jury that's not feeling the same way. Chances are if you go on trial you'll be convicted. If you plead guilty now you won't have to face a jury, and you'll get a lighter sentence. I know Mr. Fritch has explained this to you."

"He has. But I've always said no," I replied, still not looking at him.

Ben put his hand on my good shoulder. "Emmett, think about Mother. She's just about at her wit's end, thinking about you going in front of a jury. Don't make her sit through a trial."

Tears rose up in me and threatened to choke me at that. He was trying to make me feel guilty, and it was working, but I had to admit to myself that he was not the first one to put that idea into my head. I'd often agonized over what Bob and Grat and I had put Mother through. But surely she wouldn't want me to admit to murder when I was innocent, would she? "Don't do this to me, Ben," I choked out. "I already feel sick over everything. Don't..." I couldn't finish my sentence. Instead I just leaned my forehead against the cold bars of the cell, weariness overtaking my whole body. Mother's face came to my mind then, instead of Bob's, for once, but now her image tormented me almost as much as his.

Ben's fingers squeezed my shoulder, like Bob's used to do when he was trying to brace me and give me courage. "Emmett, I'm just asking you to consider it."

I struggled to control myself. "I told them I'd plead guilty to manslaughter," I reminded him, "even though I didn't kill anyone. I'd give in to that if they'd let me. But they wouldn't accept it."

"No," Ben agreed. "Mr. Fritch and I talked about that. The state will be satisfied by nothing less than second-degree murder."

I stayed quiet for a few moments. Then I pulled my shoulder out of his grasp. "I keep thinking," I remarked, "about how odd it is that I'm the one who survived it." I bit my lip. "Me, who never shot a man nor was willing to kill one. I was always just going along, Ben. I never planned any of it. I always thought that if any of us were going to get shot up and killed during one of Bob's schemes, it would be me before anyone else." I heard bitterness in my voice right then, but it was not directed at Bob, or Grat, or anyone but myself. I'd had so many chances to walk away, to stand up and refuse to go with them. But every time the ties of brotherhood, my love for Bob and what I felt I owed to him, had clouded my judgement. It was strange, how long ago it all seemed.

I heard Ben take a deep breath. "I suppose it's not for us to know why God spared you, Emmett. But maybe He did because He saw a chance at redemption in you." He put his hand on my shoulder again, and this time the gesture felt comforting to me, like it always had when Bob did it. "You must take this chance. You're so young. Even though you'll spend some time in prison, you'll still have time to make a life for yourself when you get out."

I thought on that for a minute, and he stayed silent. Then he spoke again, and his words surprised me. "Bob never thought about what was around the next corner, Emmett. He lived for whatever moment he was in right then. Consequences never entered his mind, just like I believe they never enter Will's. But you've always been different."

I turned toward him a little and he smiled. "Do you remember when you were little, and you and Bob ate that candy Mother had been saving for Christmas after you found it while she was off at the neighbor's? Lelia was supposed to be watching you, but Bob got her all distracted while you climbed up on a chair and got it out."

I allowed myself a weak smile at the memory, an incident

I hadn't thought of in years.

"Mother came home and Lelia told her she was sure Will and Grat had taken it. Mother believed her and punished them. You could've gotten away with it, pretty as you please, but late that night you went to Mother and confessed, and you cried because she'd punished Will and Grat for nothing. Bob was madder than anything at you for telling, too, but you couldn't stand seeing anyone else get in trouble for something you'd done." He chuckled softly. "How old were you then, anyway? Seven?"

"Littler than that, I think," I replied softly. "It was before everyone started leaving home."

He sobered. "What I'm getting at, Emmett," he said softly, "is that you've got a conscience in you. You may do wrong, but you know what's right."

He looked at me, good and long, then squeezed my shoulder again and motioned to the guard to let him out.

I stayed where he'd left me for a good long while, thinking things over, and pondering the fact that I'd forgotten all about that time with the stolen candy, while Ben had remembered it.

TWENTY-EIGHT

I LAID AWAKE for a long time that night, thinking, and praying on what to do. Praying felt funny to me, like I hadn't really done it in awhile. Maybe I'd forgotten how to do it right, because God didn't give me an answer.

But when I woke at dawn the morning my trial was to begin, I'd made up my mind anyway. I called to the guard, who came over to me, and said, calmly, "I need to see Mr. Fritch, please."

Sometime later I stood in the courtroom again, Fritch beside me. Judge McCue glared down at me from his bench and knitted his bony fingers together next to his gavel.

"Mr. Dalton, I was expecting to begin your trial today but your council has informed me that you've had a change of heart. I understand that you have agreed to a plea suggested by Mr. Fritch."

I nodded shortly.

Judge McCue picked up a piece of paper laying before him and read it over. "You have agreed to plead guilty to the second-degree murder of George Cubine, and no trial will be held," he stated. A murmur went through the room again, louder than the one yesterday.

"Yes, Your Honor," I said, my voice devoid of all emotion.

He put the paper down and glared at me again, not bothering to even attempt to conceal his disgust for me, and for what I represented to him. "Very well. Then I shall sentence you immediately." He raised his voice, so that all could hear him, and said, "it is the judgement of this court that you be sentenced to confinement in the State Penitentiary at Lansing for the balance of your natural life." He picked up the gavel and banged it. It sounded like a gunshot.

I felt my body grow weak and my heart start to pound with a sickening rhythm. My eyes stung and hot tears welled up in them as I realized the full extent of what he'd just said. *Life in prison.* I was twenty-one, and I would die behind bars, for a murder I hadn't committed.

I didn't care that I was weeping openly; it was all I could do to remain standing. I felt like I did the day of the raid, when all the breath had gotten knocked out of me when I'd hit the ground. I wished, as I heard McCue's words repeat themselves over and over again in my mind like some horrible refrain, that I had died there in the dirt beside Bob. Why had I been spared, if this was my fate? Ben had been wrong— I'd have no chance at redemption now. I looked through the blur of my tears past Fritch, who looked taken aback by the sentence, and picked Ben out of the crowd of people gathered to witness my fate being handed down. Ben's face was white and he looked stunned. Clearly I was not the only person shocked by the harshness of the sentence.

"Have you any words you'd like to speak, Mr. Dalton?" Judge McCue asked sharply, and I looked away from Ben.

"Just that I believe this to be an unfair sentence, for I did not commit the murders I've been accused of, and believed I would have had a chance to prove myself a good citizen with this plea, if you had been more lenient," I replied brokenly, knowing my anger was simmering in my voice. I couldn't say anything else; I felt like something was slowly squeezing my throat closed.

Judge McCue was not moved by my words. He banged his gavel again and motioned to Sheriff Callahan to take me away. Like rubbish, I thought. Nothing worth salvaging.

I didn't remember going back to the jail. All of the sudden they were leading me out of my cell and shackling me at the wrist to the jail guard, a man named Smith. Marshal Griffey and Sheriff Callahan then took me out of there and took me to the depot, where I would take a train to Lansing—the place I believed I would never leave again until they carried me out in a pine box. A thought flashed through my mind as I stepped onto the platform at the depot. *Damn you, Bob! You said it would be* easy! *You said we'd get away with it! And now you're in a damned coffin and I'm going to die in prison.*

That surprised me, for I had felt only sorrow and regret when I'd thought of Bob in the months since the raid. I'd never thought of being angry with him, or blaming him any for what had happened. The thought made me feel disloyal and low. Being angry at Bob wouldn't help me any. Bob couldn't bear blame anymore—only I could.

Ben was at the depot to see me off and I saw actual tears in his eyes as he stepped forward to say his goodbyes. I lost my composure then, letting my own tears flow freely, for it was the only release I knew now.

I fumbled in my pocket for the little tie-pin I'd managed to hold onto, one I'd won in one of the poker games in Santa Rosa with Bob, before the cheaters had entered the picture. It was gold and had a tiny nugget on it from some mine strike in Nevada, or so the former owner had said. I put it in his hand. "Take this to Mother, Ben, and give her my love. Tell her I'm sorry." I couldn't speak any longer and let them lead me into the train. The last sight I had of Ben was him standing there on the platform with my stick-pin in his hand, his face a study in sorrow, his long coat flapping around him in the wind.

———◦«◊»◦———

When I arrived at Lansing, I was brought before the Deputy Warden, John Higgins.

He surprised me, bringing me out of my misery a little bit. He had a good, honest face and he was one of the few people associated with law and order that didn't look at me with contempt the moment they learned my last name.

I was sitting in a chair in front of his big desk, my wrists shackled, as they usually were these days. He leaned over the desk a little toward me, his hands clasped together on top of the desk. "Emmett, I'm always sorry to see a man come to this place, especially one so young as you are. I can see in your face that you have a conscience, and I can see you feel poorly about what you've done to end up here. All I can advise you to do is learn to make the best of things now. Remember that you can always ask to see me about anything that you feel the need to. Your word will be taken if you come to me first."

I nodded at him, still too miserable to speak, and was led out of his office to bathe and change into prison clothes. And then I was taken to the Godforsaken little five by nine foot cell, with its tiny window, that I would now call home for the rest of my days.

I curled up on the hard bed with my back to the door after they'd shut it, its clang echoing in my ears the way the gunfire had in the alley in Coffeyville.

I lay there and tried to remember what it felt like to be free. To feel the motion of a horse beneath me as it went where I told it to go. To feel the wind in my face as I rode, or hear the music of the fiddle band as I danced with Laura at the socials in Estrella. To go where I pleased, to do as I wished. I found that I was already having trouble remembering it all, and my hard time had barely begun. I tried again to make sense of how my life had come to this. How I could possibly have gone from cowboy to lawman to outlaw in those four short years. How I could have ended up here, penned into this cold, uncomfortable cell while two of my brothers' bodies decayed in a common grave and a third was off charging into infamy right along with us. I couldn't figure any of it out. All I knew is that in spite of everything that had happened, I missed Bob so badly I ached, and would've given anything to hear his carefree laughter again.

TWENTY-NINE

"DALTON! MAIL FOR you."

I looked up from the table I was leaning over, watching one of the inmates I was supervising carefully cut out the fabric for a vest. One of the guards was coming toward me with a few letters. I motioned to the other prisoner to keep on at his work and I took the two letters, scanning them over. One was from Mother, who wrote me faithfully, the other marked only "L.W." I wasn't certain who that was, but I'd open them both in my cell when my shift was over.

It was June of 1894 and I'd been working in the prison tailor shop since the day after my booking the previous year, spared the dreaded coal mines because of the injury to my arm. I'd learned the trade well—so well, in fact, that because of the talent I'd shown for it and the good behavior I'd become known for around the prison, I'd been made the shop's supervisor, instructing the other inmates and keeping them on task as efficiently as I could.

A change had come over me in the weeks following my arrival there, and it was due partially to the words of Deputy Warden Higgins, partially to those of Ben, that afternoon in my cell in Independence—and partially to Bob.

I'd sunk so low into my misery that I barely ate or slept, and when the moment finally came to disappear into my depression and give up, I'd suddenly seen a vision, clear as day in my mind, of Bob on horseback. He was checking his mount and edging it over closer to me, his blue eyes narrowed challengingly, a hard look on his face as he glared down out of the saddle at me. "What's the matter, Em?" he'd asked me cuttingly. "You too yellow to keep on living? Are you gonna lie there and wallow in all that damned misery you got in your gut, or are you gonna get up and face it like I know you can?"

I'd felt angry then, and determined to prove him wrong, just like I always had whenever he'd ever insinuated I didn't have the sand for something, even though I knew it was only in my mind. I'd started thinking about Ben and what he'd said to me, about how he knew I had a conscience, and how he knew I could make something better out of my life. I heard the Warden's words, too: *you must learn to make the best of things.*

And somehow, after thinking about all these things, I realized that all of them were right, Bob and Ben and Higgins. Maybe I couldn't get out of prison, but I *could* learn a trade and work hard at it, and I could do my best to show everyone that I was a good man, despite being a former member of the Dalton Gang.

I shook off the memory and continued my shift until its end, and then when I went to my cell I sat down on my hard bed and took out the letters. I took out the one from the unknown sender first, curious as to whom it was from.

I opened it and skipped to the signature, and my breath caught almost painfully in my chest. It was signed, 'Laura.' My shock made me sit there motionless for several seconds. When I finally shook it off a bit I held the letter up with fingers that trembled a little, and began to read:

Dear Emmett,

I suppose I should open this letter by telling you that I had no intention of writing it at first, and I have waited a long while to do so. But I felt I must; for you have been on my mind for the last four years, even though I have gone on most satisfactorily with my life since I last saw you. I have married and I have a child now, and by rights I should have resisted the urge to contact you and forgotten about it, but I could not help myself, for, Emmett, you are an impossible man to forget.

When I read newspapers after you left and came across your name, I always felt the pain of missing you, but as time went on I also came to understand why it was that you broke things off with me that day in California. At first I did not believe the papers; while I guessed that you'd done something to run from I hadn't taken you for a man who would ride with a band of outlaws so notorious and feared as your brothers were. And then came that October day in Kansas, the day that would forever take away any chance I ever had of being with you again. While I was thankful that you had survived I was full of sorrow to learn of your sentence and imprisonment, and I have thought of you often and hoped you are holding up all right. I want you to know that I bear you no ill will; as hard as our parting was I am thankful every day that you acted the gentleman and spared me from a life you knew I was not prepared for—you were right. I know that it hurt you deeply to do so.

I want you to know that I still believe what I said to you that day, Emmett, that you are a good man, and a moral one, and I pray that you will somehow be granted a chance to prove it to the rest of the country. I will never forget the days we spent togeth-er, and part of me will always wish things could have turned out differently. I wish you the best in whatever life gives you in the future, and despite all that has happened, I will be forever grateful to have known you—the true gentleman of the Dalton boys.

Affectionately Yours,
Laura Stevens Wallace

I sat holding that letter for a long time after I'd finished it, still scarcely able to believe that she had actually written to me. I had thought her lost to me forever, and in a way, she was, since she'd married and moved on with her life. But at least I knew now that I'd made a friend of that young woman I'd loved for a few happy months. She still thought I was a good man, and that warmed me inside better than anything else could have. Laura believed I could redeem myself, just as Ben and Mother did, and knowing it brought a smile to my face, and a little peace to my heart.

———✦———

The warmth that Laura's letter had caused in me did not last long, for just a week later I got another letter from Mother—this one telling me that Will was dead.

I felt like someone had put a fist into my stomach when I read those words and for several minutes I tried to get ahold of myself well enough so's I could read the rest of the letter. When I finally did, I learned that Will had been murdered, shot to death in front of Gracie by two U.S. Deputy Marshals intent on bringing him to justice for a number of bank, stage and train robberies that had been attributed to him. They'd said Will, who by this time was known as the "notorious and deadly outlaw Bill Dalton," had had a revolver in his hand and had resisted arrest by them, so they said they'd been forced to shoot him down. I had lost another brother.

Tears blurred my vision as I came to grips with Will's sad end, and the horrible thought of him dying in front of poor little Gracie. My intuition about him had been right when he'd left me at Independence after the raid. Fun-loving, always-joking Will, my affable brother who'd once made a good name for himself in politics, had apparently gone on to form an outlaw gang just as Bob had—with none other than Bill Doolin, Bitter Creek Newcomb, and Charley Pierce as members, among others. They had begun under the guise of wanting revenge for the murders of Bob and Grat and the injuries to me—but knowing Will as I had, I knew that the fame Bob and Grat had come to know had motivated him, too. My stomach felt queasy. Would there be no end to this? Would others I had known now rise up in Will's name, using him as a model for more crime, just as he'd seemed to use Bob and Grat and me? Was this what was to come from the blood my brothers and I had spilled that day in Coffeyville?

I put the letter away and stretched out on my bed, hoping sleep would claim me before I could think too hard about the those questions; I was afraid of the answers my mind would come up with.

THIRTY

WEEKS, THEN MONTHS, then years began to roll by, like a slow-moving train. I worked hard and dutifully in the tailor shop. I ate without complaint the food set before me, and took what exercise I could when allowed into the yard. I read many books, and took a particular liking to Shakespeare's works, which I'd not been exposed to much before coming to Lansing, and Thomas Carlyle's book on heroes and hero-worship, which made me think of Bob. My arm ached, sometimes so badly that I couldn't work or sleep at night, but it was my cross to bear for what I'd taken part in, and so I tried my best to get by and to live with the agony it caused me.

I was careful to behave as Mother had raised me to, not as I had during my years with Bob and Grat. I made an effort to speak properly instead of reverting to the common cowboy lingo I'd always used before. My manners were impeccable, my attitude one of a model prisoner, and I became well-liked by guards and other inmates alike. I began to cling to a faint but growing hope that perhaps, someday, I could obtain a pardon if I could impress enough people with my conduct.

Such a thing was not unheard of, and I began to write letters to anyone I thought might be willing to put in a good word for me. Mother worked ceaselessly toward that goal, as well, and every time I thought of her helping me I felt a rush of gratitude that I had her on my side, and that she had not written me off the way so many others had seemed to. I'd already been turned down a few times, but I refused to give up. As I aged I started to see just how big a part my youth had played in my willingness to follow Bob and Grat, and I was more certain with each passing year that I could completely overcome my old lifestyle…if only someone would give me the chance.

The world I'd known was changing while I languished in my cell. I read newspapers and learned of progress pushing its way faster and faster across the country, replacing the way Bob and Grat and I had lived, and our parents before us. The cowboy was disappearing all of these advances closed in on the open range. Men traveled less and less by horseback and more by train, or, as time went on, by automobile. I was both fascinated and a little frightened by all of these changes I read about, trying to imagine them all, and often I felt that if I did receive a pardon, I might not be able to find a place for myself in all of this progress. There might not be room for me in it.

One by one the men I'd known were picked off in the name of the law—wild, stubborn Bill Doolin, killed by a shotgun blast from one of Heck Thomas's deputies that peppered his body with holes; devil-may-care Bitter Creek Newcomb and easygoing Charley Pierce, ambushed and murdered by men seeking the rewards on their heads. Bitter

Creek and Charley had always been together whenever I'd known them; I found it only fitting that they'd died together, too. And then came the time when there were no more of them or their kind left—except me.

I was always, it seemed, destined to be the last one left, and the one left behind.

———— ❖ ————

I woke one morning in early February with bone-jarring pain shooting up my right arm. Cold weather always made it worse, but lately the old injury had been causing me so much grief that I hadn't been able to work in the tailor shop. I'd tried, but the pain had proved too great, and there was talk of taking me out of the shop. The prospect had saddened me at first; I liked my work and had made many friends there, but on the other hand I knew I could not bear the agony that my duties caused much longer.

I lay on my bed and squeezed my eyes shut, breathing slowly and deeply, trying to overcome the pain. At times like these I automatically imagined myself back in the alley, feeling the sting of the bullets again, seeing Bob's white face, and hearing his final words: *Don't surrender.*

Strangely, I'd come to take comfort in those words over the years. I *hadn't* surrendered. I hadn't given in to the horrible burden of being the only survivor of that day. I hadn't given in to despair, and I hadn't given in to pain. I hadn't given into it then, and I wouldn't give into it today.

I gritted my teeth and forced myself to sit up, wash up

and dress. I had a chance today to make a change that could move me closer to my goal, and I refused to let the old injury get in my way.

It was 1907, and I had been in prison for fourteen long years. My good conduct was well-noted and I still hoped that I would somehow earn my freedom. If all went as planned, today would be a step in that direction.

There was a shipping clerk position available at the prison, one that allowed the inmate entrusted with it to leave prison walls—without a guard. The prison mail clerk, Charles Ernst, had told me of it. He was a friend of mine and had told me he would stand up for me if I were to ask the Warden for it. I'd been doubtful at first—I was in for life, after all, and most lifers didn't get such privileges—but the more I'd thought about it, the more determined I'd become to obtain it. Perhaps my good record would count for something in the Warden's eyes. I had to try, for any freedom at all, even a mere taste of it, was a thing worth fighting for.

Warden Haskell looked up from his desk when I entered his office. "Good Morning, Emmett," he greeted me pleasantly as I sat down. "What can I do for you?"

"Well, sir, I've been told there's an outside shipping clerk position available, and I've come to put myself forward for it," I said, choosing not to mince words; I'd found the Warden to be a direct man who appreciated the same quality in others. I waited, ready to bring forth all of the arguments as to why I should be given the position, but to my surprise, Haskell merely raised one eyebrow at me.

"Will you run off if I give it to you, Emmett?"

"No, sir," I said, being completely sincere. I would not

risk any chance of a pardon by being so stupid as to attempt an escape.

"Then you may have it." He pushed back his chair and came around the desk, leaning against the front of it and looking down at me in my chair. "I wouldn't normally give such a position to a man who's been sentenced to life, you know," he told me seriously, "in fact, you're the first. But you've impressed me with your conduct, Emmett. I believe you've shown great strength of character during the years you've been here, and I'd like to reward that."

I took a deep breath. "I appreciate it very much, Mr. Haskell. I want to assure you that I'll do my best to justify your trust in me. You won't have any reason to regret giving me the position."

He gave me an approving smile. "I'm sure I won't." He paused. "The world outside has changed a great deal since you were sentenced, Emmett, but keep your wits about you, and you'll be fine."

The first thing I noticed, when I stepped outside of Lansing, was the sky. I'd forgotten how big it was, for in my cell it was reduced to a tiny square, and even in the yard it felt closed-in by the wire fences, making me feel a little like a penned-in steer. I couldn't move for a second; all I could do was stare up into its blue expanse and breathe in my fill of fresh air. *Thank you, Lord,* I thought. If I never got the pardon I so desperately fought for, at least I had been given this.

I went dutifully to the depot with my papers from the Warden, retrieving the packages I'd been sent for, forcing myself not to dawdle along the way, though it was difficult not to be overwhelmed by all of the changes I'd read about in the papers and was now seeing with my own eyes. Every extra bit of care I took could help bring me closer to my ultimate goal, and so I went right back to my hell on earth, determined to prove myself worthy of the Warden's trust. Each day I went outside the high stone walls, I always went straight back.

I'd written Mother of my new position, but it had been difficult. My arm seemed to grow worse and worse with each passing day, and tasks like writing caused me agony. Each morning I woke in greater and greater pain, until finally one morning in June I woke with a high fever, and someone standing over my bed.

"Emmett? Can you hear me?"

I struggled to open my eyes. Bob's voice above me was insistent, and had a note of worry in it. He spoke to someone else. "He's got a fever. He's burning up."

"Let's get him a doctor, then." That was Grat's voice, slow and rusty as always. I tried to move, tried to open my eyes to see them and to ask them how they could possibly be in my cell with me when I'd seen them both die, but I found I could do neither. I felt my body grow damp with sweat and a new fear with through me—was I dead, too? Was that why I was hearing them like this?

"Bob…" I managed to get out, but I could barely hear my own voice. "Help me…"

"Get the doctor in here. Hurry it up!"

"What's wrong with him? He's been fine."

"It's his arm. That old wound in it, from Coffeyville. It ain't never healed right."

Bob and Grat's voices faded in and out, droning slowly, then jabbering faster and faster. I turned my face away, wanting to die, if I wasn't already. I imagined the lynch mob was coming for me again and I hoped they hurried, so they would put me out of my misery.

I heard another voice above me, now, and felt hands on my arm. "Turn him over so I can take a look." I didn't recognize this voice—or did I? Was it Dr. Wells? "He can't continue like this; the pain must be unbearable. He needs an operation, or he'll end up losing that arm."

"He's never complained, that I've heard," Bob said.

"He ain't the type," Grat replied. "He bears things. Takes them like a man."

Their voices faded again, for good this time. I felt something cold and wet against my arm, then the prick of a needle, and then everything blurred into a merciful nothingness.

———◦(◦)◦———

I woke in the prison infirmary, my mind in a fog, throbbing pain in my arm. My fever had broken and I realized that the voices I'd heard had not been those of Bob and Grat and Dr. Wells, but of two guards who had found me in my feeble state, and Dr. Kanaval, one of the physicians at the prison hospital.

Dr. Kanaval was dressing my arm as I came around, and

he had worry lines on his forehead as he saw that I was waking. "How are you feeling, Emmett?" he asked me.

"Poorly," I managed to croak. My lips were cracked and my throat felt dry as sandpaper. The doctor got me some water, which helped, but I still felt as though I wanted to die. It was as if no time at all had passed and I was back in Coffeyville in the doctor's office above the alley where the gang had met its end.

"Emmett, your arm must be attended to," he told me seriously, "or you may loose it—or your life. You need to have the bone scraped, or else you may develop necrosis, or poisoning of the blood. That can only be done in a larger hospital, perhaps the one in Topeka." My heart sank at his words. He kept speaking. "You must write to Governor Hoch, and impress upon your family and friends to do the same. I'll do all I can, but until you have that operation, you're not likely to leave the hospital here."

I stayed in the hospital for weeks. I couldn't raise my hand to my mouth, and my body burned with fever on and off. On days when I felt more coherent I wrote letters to anyone I thought could help bring my plight to the governor's attention, though it was agony to do so. I despaired of anything being done. Was this why I had survived that day, so I could die here in prison?

Finally, just when I thought all of my pleas had fallen on deaf ears, my prayers were answered, for Governor Hoch granted me four months' parole for my surgery and recovery.

THIRTY-ONE

DR. KANAVAL WAS dressing my arm again, and it hurt, as always, but I smiled through the pain, paying it no mind.

I'd been smiling all day today, for at three this afternoon, I would be on my way to Topeka, and Mother would meet me there, to be with me when I went into the hospital.

There was a reporter there from the *Kansas City Star* as the doctor worked; they'd been following my story over the years, as had the *Coffeyville Journal,* and my parole, it seemed, was a big story. I told him I was grateful to the governor for allowing me this chance at recovery, and related that I planned to spend my parole quietly.

I felt a nervous flutter in my stomach as I boarded the Santa Fe train bound for Topeka. This operation would be a big one, and would likely determine the quality of my life from here on out—or whether I would even continue to live. If I did, I had hopes that the governor might turn my parole into a pardon.

I watched the countryside roll by as the train went on, once again marveling at the new lay of the land. I had a vision of myself years ago, galloping my horse over open plains, traversing wild lands untouched by the hand of man. Most of those were gone now, just like the men who'd once ridden them.

It made me sad to think about it.

———— ⚙ ————

"Are you ready, Emmett?"

Dr. Outland leaned over me as I lay on the operating table at Bethesda Hospital in Topeka on June 10th. He had a bottle of ether in his hand.

I took a deep breath. "Yes, I am."

He looked over at his assistants. "Then let's begin, please."

He held a cloth soaked with ether over my mouth, and my mind seemed to drift in and out. I felt light, like I was floating, and I saw a sky filled with stars above me. Then my eyelids sank shut.

After a few minutes, I had the oddest sensation that I was standing across the room, watching as they operated on me. I saw them cut my shoulder open, and my upper arm.

"Don't that beat all, though?"

I jumped and turned, and Bob was standing next to me, leaning against the wall with his boot propped up, rolling the rowel of one spur back and forth along the baseboard as he stood there. "It's amazing what doctors can do, don't you think, Em?"

I stared at him. He looked completely normal, just as he had before the raid, and he was wearing the same clothes as he'd had on that day. The gold watch chain across his vest swayed to and fro with his movements, catching the harsh light that shone down over the operating table. He was watching the doctors work.

"What are you doing here, Bob?" I asked stupidly, my voice sounding slow.

He looked over at me, then, his eyes filling with the warm, affectionate gaze he'd always saved just for me. "Why, I'm always with you, Em. You just don't realize it, most of the time."

"You died, though," I blurted out. "You and Grat and the rest. Left me alone, after all that."

He nodded. "Things didn't work out like I wanted them, to, for a fact, Em. But there's a reason for that, I guess." He pointed to the ceiling. "All part of the man upstairs' plan, I reckon. Ain't for us to know why."

"Am I going to die, Bob? Is that why you're here?"

"No, Em. You ain't gonna die," he said firmly. "It ain't your time. You were meant to go on, to live your life. And you will. You'll live for me, and for Grat. You'll do fine."

I believed him, just as I always had, whenever he'd said something in that tone of voice. He smiled at me, and then he was gone. I blinked. "Bob? Bob, come back!" The room seemed to blur in and out, and I couldn't anything anymore, just a vast whiteness. I felt like I was floating again, and then I felt nothing at all.

When I opened my eyes again it took an effort, for my eyelids felt like lead. My whole body was sore and my tongue felt thick and heavy. I turned my head a little and saw Mother sitting at my bedside. She had my hand in hers and her head was bowed a little, as if she were praying. Sunlight from the window illuminated her hair, which had gone pure white. She wasn't looking at me and so she didn't know I was awake.

I struggled to speak. "Mother?" I managed to ask, awkwardly, unable, it seemed, to make my tongue work as it should.

She raised her head, quickly, and her eyes filled immediately with tears of relief. "Emmett," she said, and it sounded like, "thank you!"

I tried to speak again but found I couldn't, but she didn't seem to mind. She put her other hand up and stroked my hair off of my forehead, as if I were a child again. "I'm so glad you're awake, Em," she said, a trembling smile coming over her face. "I thought that anesthetic would never wear off." She plumped my pillow for me as I struggled to sit up a little. "You've been out a good long while. They told me you were mumbling a lot when they brought you out of the operating room. I wasn't allowed in with you until just awhile ago." She stroked my hair again, and her touch was comforting as always. "The doctors think everything went well with the operation."

"Good," I managed to get out. I was coming around a little better now and I remembered hallucinating that Bob was there while I was under anesthesia. The words he'd said to me, about me living for him and Grat, made me smile a little, even though I knew my mind had made him up.

"What are you thinking, Em, that's made you smile so?" Mother asked me softly.

I turned to her and smiled again, a sad smile this time. "I was just thinking about something Bob said to me, once," I told her softly, able to speak better now.

She sighed a little, sadness in her eyes. "You still miss him very much, I know," she said.

"I always will, Mother, in spite of everything that happened."

She blinked back tears and kept stroking my hair. "I've grown to think of Bob and Gratton like candle-flames," she said. "Burning so bright while they were here until they up and burned out. They had so much restlessness in them. Maybe they got it from your Pa. I suppose we'll never know."

"I suppose not."

Mother went back to the hotel to rest after a bit, and I submitted to having my bandages changed without complaint, though it hurt like hell, and I was a little embarrassed by the female nurses. When one of them sat me up I twisted my neck to look at the incisions in my arm and I felt a little dizzy, seeing the long rows of black stitches, so I decided to refrain from doing that again, at least for awhile. Dr. Outland came in to see me and told me he hoped that I would eventually regain full use of my arm. Outside of hearing that I'd been granted a pardon, that was the best news I could've asked for.

When they'd all left me alone I stared out the window, looking at the sky and thinking about all I'd gone through in the last fifteen years. If I thought hard enough I could remember the days with the gang, though they seemed like a lifetime ago.

I remembered the crackle of flames as we all sat around the campfire, the warmth of whiskey sliding down my throat after Grat handed me the bottle. I heard Bob's great laugh, saw the gleam in his eyes as he came up with a new plan. I saw Bitter Creek's eyes sparkling in the starlight as we crouched around the depot, waiting for a train to take. I felt my horse galloping along under me, carrying me off into the night afterward, the others around me. I heard crickets and coyotes as I slept out under the stars. It was strange to think of it all being gone, and me still being here, trying to carry on.

THIRTY-TWO

ON NOVEMBER 2ND, 1907, I sat in the little room outside the private office of Governor Hoch. Ben sat beside me,
a calming presence, as always.

The Governor had called for me to see him late that
afternoon, and hope had blossomed within me like a plant
coming to flower. Many had spoken of the possibility of the
governor granting me a pardon once my parole had expired,
but I dared not to hope too hard, for fear of disappointment.
I'd been fully prepared to return to prison life at Lansing. I
couldn't, however, think of any other reason why he might
have called me to his office and so my mind was running
wild with possibilities as we sat and waited, the governor's
wife sitting quietly on the other side of the room and two
reporters milling about, ready to record whatever happened.

Ben caught my eye and smiled reassuringly. "Stay calm,
Emmett. The governor will be out soon, I'm sure."

I took a deep breath, trying to calm my racing heart,
and pressed my hands flat against my thighs, trying to stop
their trembling. The clock on the wall ticked incessantly.
Mrs. Hoch turned a page of the book she was reading. The

reporters scratched their pencils against their pads of paper. And I stared at the door of the governor's office, willing it with all my might to open.

Finally, it did. Governor Hoch strode out, extending a hand to me. I stood and shook it, hoping my palms weren't too sweaty.

"Hello, Emmett," he said warmly to me.

"Hello, Governor," I got out. I gestured to Ben. "This is my older brother, Governor, Ben Dalton."

The governor shook Ben's hand and greeted him kindly, then turned to me. "Well, Emmett," he said, "I've given a great deal of thought to your case. I've spoken to a great many people regarding your conduct, and all of them have said the same thing—that you are an exemplary prisoner, and I've seen that your conduct while paroled has been the same. I believe you are a good man, Emmett."

I felt a lump in my throat, and for some reason I heard Laura's voice in my head just then, a memory from so long ago: *I know you're a good man, Emmett. I know you didn't mean whatever it was that you did.*

The governor was still talking. "I must, you realize, stand between mercy and good government. But I do not believe the government will suffer any if you go free."

I swallowed hard, a roaring in my ears. Ben seemed to know what was coming, for he was more emotional than I'd ever seen him, even that time at the depot when I was being shipped off to Lansing. I heard him take a breath that shuddered, as if he were fighting back tears, and when I glanced over at him in a daze I saw that he was.

"Because of that belief, Emmett, and my belief that you

have repented for your crimes and will be a good citizen, I will extend to you this pardon." Hoch held out a hand to his secretary, and was given a document bearing his official seal. He handed it to me. "It's a pleasure for me to do this, because I feel that the confidence I'm placing in you is not misplaced."

The paper trembled in my hand and I felt my eyes well up; I couldn't help it. *I was free.* I swallowed hard again and tried to speak. "Governor," I said shakily, "I don't know how I can properly express my thanks—I don't know that there are words enough. But I can tell you that I thank you from my very heart and soul, and I will tell you with certainty that you won't ever have cause to regret this. I mean to be a good an honest citizen, and I shall, I promise." I meant every single word of it.

The governor smiled at me. "I am sure you will, Emmett."

I looked down at the paper in my hand again, still scarcely able to believe that it was real, that I would never again spend a night on a hard mattress in a cell, would never again have to look at the sky through a tiny square window. That I would never again have to ask permission of another man before I did even the simplest of things. The iron bars were gone forever, and I was no longer an animal in a cage. *I was free.* It took me a minute to take it all in. Then I pulled myself together and looked at Governor Hoch once more. "Governor, if you don't mind, I'll ask to be excused. I want to go to the telegraph office and tell Mother."

Governor Hoch nodded at me, put a hand on my good shoulder, then turned back to his office. In a daze, Ben and I left the room, heading outside for the telegraph office. I spoke to some reporters, thanking the governor once more, but I had no recollection of exactly what I said. I was too busy anticipating Mother's joy.

I sent her the telegram, then made a long-distance call to Lansing. It was late there, and a runner answered the telephone.

"Tell them I am free," I said, grinning so wide my face hurt. The runner shouted the news, and I heard, over the line, the faint sound of cheering from the cell blocks. Warmth spread through me at that sound at it was a moment before I could hang up the telephone.

When we went outside I stopped for a minute, breathing in the crisp air and staring up at the stars above me, and I thought of Bob and Grat, those brothers I still ached for, even after all that had happened, after all that following them had led me to.

"I'll live for you, I promise," I whispered. "I won't sur-render, Bob."

"Emmett?"" Ben called, and I looked away from the sky, focusing on his face. He was standing down the sidewalk aways, looking back at me in confusion. "You coming?"

I grinned at him. "Yes, Ben. I'm coming."

EPILOGUE

YOUNG MR. WHITNEY didn't say anything for several minutes after I stopped talking. It took me a minute to realize that his pad of paper was as blank as it had been when I'd started speaking. He was staring at me in fascination, and he seemed to rouse himself with a little start when he realized I'd stopped speaking.

"You didn't write anything," I said, raising an eyebrow at him.

He nodded, tapping the top of his pencil against the pad. "No, I didn't. I thought I wanted to write your story, Mr. Dalton, but now that I've heard you tell it, I think *you* should."

I laughed shortly. "What, *me*, write an article?"

"No. You should write a book."

I laughed again and shook my head. "I never thought about doing something like that," I admitted. "I always thought everyone just wanted to hear about the raid, and nothing else."

He shook his head, and there was an earnest expression in his eyes. I could tell he was serious. "You tell it better than I ever could," he said. "I'm honored that you let me hear it."

I looked at his notebook. "What will you write, then? Don't you need a story?"

"I'll write about your return to Coffeyville," he said. "What else are you going to do here, now that you've come back?"

I sobered. There *was* something else I needed to do here, before I could go on with my new life of freedom. "I need to go to the cemetery," I said quietly. "You'll understand if I need to do that alone."

He nodded. "Of course." He cleared his throat. "There's a piece of pipe there, from the alley," he said quickly. "That's how they marked it." He stuck his hand out, tucking his notebook under his arm and putting his pencil behind his ear. "I appreciate you speaking with me, Mr. Dalton, and I wish you the best of luck in your new life."

I shook his hand. "Thank you, Jim."

He gave me a grin and headed off, leaving me with my own thoughts once more. I got up from the bench we'd been sitting on, put my hands into my pockets and started walking, making my way toward Elmwood Cemetery.

It was quiet there, when I reached it, and I was grateful that there weren't any other visitors, and that folks were finally giving me a little space. I went inside the gates and moved among the crumbling old stones. I paused at Frank's grave, which was marked with a tall monument. But I didn't linger there. I headed for the lonely, twisted piece of pipe I could see sticking out of the ground a little ways away.

When I reached it I stood for a long time, just looking down at the grass there. My eyes filled with tears and the pipe blurred. I felt a huge lump in my throat and I swallowed around it, choking back sobs, thinking of Bob and Grat, who lay in this grave together. I thought again of Bob's words, that day I'd imagined him next to me in the operating room: *I'm always with you, Em. You just don't realize it, most of the time.*

"I made it, Bob and Grat," I said shakily. "I'm going to try to go on with my life, now. I have to put all we did together behind me, but I won't forget the two of you, or Frank, or Will. And we'll all be together again, someday." I choked on my words and fell silent, staring at that hunk of pipe and thinking that someday, when I could afford it, I would have a marker placed here. They deserved more than just a piece of pipe from the alley they'd died in to mark their final resting place. They'd been more than just outlaws who'd failed at a bank robbery. They were my brothers, and I'd loved them both.

"I'll live for all of you. And it'll be a *good* life."

I lingered there a little while longer, then took a deep breath and walked away. I could leave this place now, perhaps find a little peace with all that had happened. I'd been given a second chance, after all, and I had to take it, had to show the world I deserved it.

As I went out of the cemetery gates I looked toward the west, once, seeing the sun beginning its descent. I'd stayed in Coffeyville longer than I thought. I imagined, just for a moment, myself on horseback, in my youth again, Bob and Grat on either side of me as we rode into the coming night together, carefree and careless, young men grabbing life with both fists, getting all we could out of it. The thought made me smile.

AFTERWARD

Emmett Dalton went on to start several businesses after his release from prison, and in late 1908 married Julia Johnson Lewis in Bartlesville, Oklahoma. He would eventually write two books on his days with the Dalton Gang, *Beyond the Law* in 1918 and *When the Daltons Rode* in 1931. In 1931 he and Julia returned to Coffeyville, and Emmett had a headstone placed upon the common grave shared by Bob, Grat, and Bill Power. He participated as an advisor on and appeared in several films about the Daltons, and often lectured on the perils of criminal activity, encouraging young people to live crime-free lives. He also became an advocate for prison reform. He died in 1937 as a respected, peaceful citizen, having outlived a great many of his fellow "wild west outlaws."